NO LONGER PROPERTY OF
SEATTLE PUBLIC LIBRARY

Pride, Prejudice & Poison

Pride, Prejudice & Poison

A Jane Austen Society Mystery

ELIZABETH BLAKE

CROOKED
LANE

NEW YORK

This is a work of fiction. All of the names, characters, organizations, places and events portrayed in this novel are either products of the author's imagination or are used fictitiously. Any resemblance to real or actual events, locales, or persons, living or dead, is entirely coincidental.

Copyright © 2019 by Carole Buggé

All rights reserved.

Published in the United States by Crooked Lane Books, an imprint of The Quick Brown Fox & Company LLC.

Crooked Lane Books and its logo are trademarks of The Quick Brown Fox & Company LLC.

Library of Congress Catalog-in-Publication data available upon request.

ISBN (hardcover): 978-1-68331-574-2
ISBN (ePub): 978-1-68331-575-9
ISBN (ePDF): 978-1-68331-576-6

Cover illustration by Ben Perini
Book design by Jennifer Canzone

Printed in the United States.

www.crookedlanebooks.com

Crooked Lane Books
34 West 27th St., 10th Floor
New York, NY 10001

First Edition: August 2019

10 9 8 7 6 5 4 3 2 1

For Rachel Fallon, a true friend indeed

Chapter One

⁓

"'It is a truth universally acknowledged, that a single woman in possession of a good fortune, must be in want of a husband,'" whispered Farnsworth Appleby.

"Shh!" said Erin Coleridge, stifling a laugh. She and her friend Farnsworth were sitting in the back row of All Souls' drafty church basement late on a chilly Sunday morning in October, waiting for the meeting of the Events Committee of the Northern Branch of the Jane Austen Society. The church service had ended twenty minutes earlier, and Erin could hear the last of the parishioners upstairs shuffling out of All Souls.

Most of the half dozen or so committee members had arrived— the only one missing was local schoolmaster Jonathan Alder, whose absence had occasioned Farnsworth's remark. Romantically dashing, with ruddy cheeks, creamy skin, and a mass of dark curls, his recent arrival in town had excited much speculation. Several members of the society had taken to calling him Mr. Bingley behind his back. He was too friendly and eager to please to be a natural Mr. Darcy, but *Bingley* suited him perfectly.

He made the most of his charms by flirting just enough with the damsels of Kirkbymoorside to keep their hearts fluttering a little faster when he was near. Farnsworth enjoyed baiting Erin about him, and though certainly not immune to his charms, Erin treated him with detached courtesy in public, just to spite her friend.

"I don't see why you're being so coy about it," Farnsworth said. "He is eligible, and you—"

"I certainly don't have a fortune," Erin whispered back, "and I'm *not* in want of a husband."

"Well, you have a bookstore," her friend sniffed, sipping tea from the thermos she always carried.

Farnsworth Appleby was the town's Tragic Widow. Technically, she was an abandoned wife, since her husband had absconded with their savings along with the George and Dragon's Irish barmaid. But divine justice was swift and brutal—he had been run over by a Dublin lorry shortly afterward, and Farnsworth had been able to recover the money, if not her dignity.

From that day on, she'd taken in stray cats and had been referred to universally as "poor Farnsworth." Erin liked her and found her eccentricities charming. She also made the best cup of coffee in the village, maybe in all North Yorkshire. Erin knew her Tragic Widow pose was simply an act to put off people she didn't like. In reality, Farnsworth had healthy self-esteem and a wicked wit.

Farnsworth sipped delicately at her tea. "A bookstore may not be a fortune, but—"

"I think you fancy him yourself."

Farnsworth laughed, but color rose to her plump cheeks. "Don't be absurd!"

"Here he comes—behave yourself," said Erin as Jonathan Alder entered the room with ladies of varying ages and body types. All eyes turned toward him, and a blush crept across his already rosy face.

"I'm frightfully sorry," he said. His accent was rather posh, decidedly not North Yorkshire. "I got held up at school, and—"

"Please don't waste more of our time than you already have with a lengthy explanation," declared Sylvia Pemberthy from her chair in the front row as Jonathan took his place at the podium. The current society president, she was a stickler for punctuality, and no doubt jealous of Jonathan's popularity. He had been unanimously elected Events Committee chairman, whereas her own position as society president was tenuous. As usual, Sylvia wore a ridiculous hat, a nest of peacock feathers poking from the brim like tiny swords.

It was well known Sylvia liked things to run smoothly—a vain hope, given the recent folderol in the society's Northern Branch. What had begun as a disagreement over protocol had spiraled into a vicious orgy of recrimination and backbiting, splitting into two camps, each representing a different philosophy of how the group should be run.

"Lady de Bourgh has spoken," Farnsworth whispered. Erin gave her a poke in the ribs. Sylvia Pemberthy was one of the wealthiest people in Kirkbymoorside, the picturesque village nestled along the southern border of the North York Moors National Park—and lately, one of the most unpopular. Farnsworth had a point—Sylvia's imperious nature was reminiscent of Lady Catherine de Bourgh, so perhaps she was not the best person to smooth ruffled feathers.

As the society had splintered into factions, the atmosphere had become more fraught with each meeting. Old rivalries were coming to a head at a time when decisions needed to be made about the branch's future. Erin noticed the conspicuous absence of Sylvia's husband Jerome, an aloof history teacher at University of York. Rumors had been swirling for weeks that theirs was a troubled marriage.

"Now then," Sylvia said, the pompous peacock feathers on her hat bouncing up and down as she spoke, "if everyone would just settle down, we could begin."

"You'd think she was running this meeting," Farnsworth whispered to Erin, who gave her friend a poke.

"Shh!"

Sylvia's ascent to power was as contentious as her reign had become. She had a knack for making enemies, but Erin thought anyone in her position would have drawn fire from the membership. As branch president, Sylvia represented the Old Guard—conservative, mostly moneyed members who liked to dot their *i*'s and cross their *t*'s. The so-called Modernists felt the Old Guard were hopelessly mired in rules and protocol, but it was deeper than that. It was a matter of world view—the Old Guard were the same people who had voted for Brexit. Feelings around the British exit from the European Union were high, and what had begun as a local squall had turned into a typhoon.

"You have to start a bloody petition round here just to go to the loo," Farnsworth muttered, shifting her heavy body in the narrow metal folding chair.

"Quiet, please," Sylvia hissed. "If the chairperson could get organized, we could get this meeting started," she said, coldly eyeing Jonathan Alder as he pulled some notes from a battered leather briefcase.

"He's only a few minutes late," Erin pointed out.

Sylvia exploded. "That's it! I will not stand for insubordination in the society! And you can either attend meetings *on time* or not at all!" she added, glaring at Jonathan.

"Have you ever listened to yourself?" said Farnsworth. "You sound like a bloody harridan."

"You should talk," Sylvia snapped. "Everyone in town knows you're utterly pathetic!"

Erin's forehead burned with anger at Sylvia's treatment of her friend. She opened her mouth to give Sylvia a piece of her mind but was interrupted by Prudence Pettibone.

"'Those who do not complain are never pitied,'" Prudence proclaimed in her nasal voice. The lugubrious society treasurer, Prudence was known for interjecting Jane Austen quotes into the conversation whenever possible—often at the least opportune moment.

Sylvia wheeled around to face her. "I'll thank *you* to keep your thoughts to yourself!" she sputtered, sending droplets of saliva into the air, some of which landed on Pru's face.

Prudence Pettibone was a small, ungainly woman—with her dull brown hair and rumpled, ill-fitting clothing, she could pass for a vagrant. Erin winced at seeing her suffer the indignity of being pelted by Sylvia's flying spittle.

"You can't just treat people like—" Erin began, but was preempted by the Very Honorable Reverend Motley, a portly, unctuous man and All Souls' longtime minister. Having entered the room moments before, he interrupted Erin midsentence.

"'It isn't what we say or think that defines us, but what we do,'" he opined in his plummy, sententious voice, locking his thumbs together in front of his black cassock. He wore it long, in the manner of the lead actor in the popular television series *Father Brown*, with a row of shiny brass buttons down the front. Erin found it pretentious, and an obvious attempt to camouflage his substantial girth.

Not even Sylvia dared take him on—the society met in All Souls' capacious community hall solely through his beneficence, and challenging Father Motley would risk their losing a convenient—and free—meeting place.

"Of course," he continued, casting his beady eyes around the room, "those of you who attended this morning's service found it a bit easier to be on time, eh?"

Farnsworth rolled her eyes, and Erin gave her another poke in the ribs.

Sylvia straightened her hat and gave a little cough. "Well said, Reverend. Well said indeed."

"I don't see what one's religious faith has to do with punctuality," Farnsworth declared.

Small beads of sweat broke out on the reverend's forehead. "I merely suggested that had one chanced to come to the morning service, punctuality would not be an issue."

"It was perfectly clear what you meant," said Sylvia, glaring daggers at Farnsworth. "*Some* people take issue with *everything*."

Erin sighed and looked at her watch—it was past noon, and the meeting hadn't properly started yet.

Making his way to the podium, Jonathan Alder gave a decorous cough. "Right," he said. "Shall we discuss the question of raising membership dues?"

Owen Hardacker snorted. "I say do away wi'em altogether." Lean and stern, with a face like the weathered side of a barn, Owen was a wealthy farmer and owner of the largest sheep herd in the district and could trace his family back to before William the Conqueror. In spite of his money, Owen's sympathies were strictly working class. As a leader of the Modernists, he stubbornly maintained his thick Yorkshire accent, perhaps as a way of separating himself from Old Guard people like Sylvia. Erin liked Owen, with his hardscrabble manners and brusque ways, whereas people like Sylvia were a reminder of why she had left Oxfordshire.

"We can't just eliminate dues altogether," said Kurt Becker, the local baker. His store, Fresh and Hot, was popular, but he was not. With his rigid posture and Prussian accent, Kurt Becker had always struck Erin as a clichéd German right out of a war movie. His square jaw and straight blond hair only added to the image, as did his wife Suzanne, with her tightly wound personality and whippet-thin body. Erin wondered where Suzanne was. It was Sunday, so their bakery was closed.

"Ye would take her point o' view," Owen Hardacker muttered.

Becker bristled. "What is that supposed to mean?"

"Could we *please* get back to business?" Sylvia snapped.

"No, I demand to know what you meant by that!" Kurt Becker

insisted, rising from his chair. He looked as if he wanted to slug Owen Hardacker.

"Settle down, please!" Jonathan pleaded, but it was clear he had lost control of the meeting before it had even started.

Hardacker leapt from his chair. "No bloody Kraut is goin' t'tell me what t'do!"

"Please," Jonathan implored. "If we could just—"

Kurt Becker rose from his chair. "I do not appreciate being insulted!"

"'One man's style must not be the rule of another's,'" said Reverend Motley, inclining his head to peer at the baker. "There's no need to be childish."

Becker threw him a glance of pure malevolence. "I am not the one being childish," he said tightly, and strode from the room without looking back.

Sylvia turned to Owen Hardacker. "Well," she said with a sneer, "I hope you're happy."

"Get stuffed," Hardacker said, shoving his battered tweed cap onto his head. "This society is goin' t'hell in a handbasket!" he declared, and stalked out of the room.

Erin looked at Jonathan, whose face bore an expression of shocked amazement.

"The general meeting is in two days," Erin said. "Why don't we discuss it then, when everyone has cooled down a bit?"

"Good idea!" Farnsworth agreed heartily.

"I second the motion," Prudence Pettibone chirped.

In the end, even the reverend agreed that things had gotten too heated, and the meeting was disbanded. As Erin got into her car, she wondered what Jane Austen herself would have thought of such indecorous behavior. She could not know then that there was far worse to come.

Chapter Two

❧

Erin Coleridge shivered as she stepped outside the door of her used bookstore, the Readers Quarry, to take down the OPEN sign. After the brouhaha of the meeting, she had spent the rest of the quiet Sunday afternoon in her shop. Only two people had stopped by, but she had made quite a few online sales, which was how she made most of her money. Twilight was fast approaching—night fell earlier now that they had slipped into October. It was only two weeks until the annual Halloween fete and bonfire, after which visits from tourists slowed to a trickle. But during the fete, the town's population could swell from three thousand to over five thousand as people from all over Yorkshire and beyond were drawn to the weekend-long celebration beginning with an enormous bonfire in the town square.

Erin lugged the heavy wooden sign into the stone cottage serving as her store and living quarters, propping it up behind the thick oak door, which she locked and double-bolted. There was little crime in Kirkbymoorside, but Erin had learned caution from her cleric father, if not from her rather wilder mother, whose sense of abandon and joie de vivre she admired but had never quite managed to emulate. Crime was one of Erin's hobbies—she had an extensive forensic library—so she was keenly aware of what could happen to a woman living alone, even in a safe little market town like Kirkbymoorside.

Passing through the store into the rear of the first floor, Erin entered her small but well-appointed kitchen, with its gleaming copper kettles and colorful omelet pans. A creature of quieter comforts, surrounded by well-worn and deeply cherished used books, Erin was rarely ecstatic like her mother, but largely content. Her father was enjoying the robust health of the virtuous, though her mother was dead and buried, taken in her midforties by a quickly ravaging cancer fed by the fire of her forceful personality. It seemed to Erin that vivid people often died young, leaving more timid souls in their wake. Her mother had blazed and burned, like a thirsty star.

Erin had bought the historic cottage upon her arrival in town two years ago. Like so many villages in the north of England, Kirkbymoorside wore its heritage with pride and a touch of defensiveness, as if ready to respond to any challenge to its authenticity—though it was hard to imagine anyone could miss the history seeping from its weathered stone buildings and narrow, winding streets. It was this sense of the past that had drawn her to the town when the loss of her mother had left her with a desperate need to flee Oxford.

Though the radiators were turned up full, a chill wind blew in through the cracks in the ancient masonry, and Erin shivered as she examined the freezer to find something for dinner. She kept a good store of entrées from the local Sainsbury's for nights like this, when she didn't feel like cooking.

Pulling a package of chicken tikka masala and basmati rice from the freezer, Erin left it on the shelf and put on a CD of the French composer Josquin des Prez. Though many of her friends were in the iPod world, Erin found it all too fussy and couldn't be bothered. Like her father, she had a tendency to stick to the tried and true.

She shivered with pleasure as the lush harmonies filled the room, the vocal lines twisting around one another like meandering streams. Erin had recently fallen in love with early music, especially vocal music of the Renaissance. Farnsworth had been urging her to join the choir at All Souls, and she was seriously considering it.

She had spent half the day on the phone, comforting, cajoling, and soothing injured pride, reassuring everyone that it would be all right. First Prudence had called, then Pru's best friend, Hetty Miller.

"How does she get off treating people like that?" Hetty had said. "Prudence told me the way Sylvia spoke to her!"

"She wasn't very nice to Farnsworth either," Erin pointed out. "And it was definitely a mistake to take on Owen Hardacker."

"The cheek of her! Thinks she's so high and mighty. Well, let me tell you, she's no better than she ought to be!"

Hetty was full of stock phrases, this latest one coming from her devotion to the popular television series *Downton Abbey*. The implication, of course, was that Sylvia was promiscuous, a topic Erin had no wish to delve into. She'd finally had to hustle Hetty off the phone so she could wait on her sole customers, a charming octogenarian couple from Perth looking for a book on the area's Viking past.

Swathed in the mysterious, layered vocals of Josquin's music, Erin popped the chicken tikka masala into the microwave. The phone rang as she pressed REHEAT. She let it ring four times before picking up, resolving to unplug the phone afterward.

"Hello?" she said, turning down the music.

"Erin. What. On. Earth. Was. She. Thinking."

"Hello, Farnsworth."

"The woman is out of control, Erin. Totally mad. Get down from there, Wickham!" Farnsworth commanded. Her cats were all named after characters in Jane Austen novels, and Wickham was an especially naughty tabby who enjoyed testing the limits of gravity. "Someone's got to stop her, Erin."

"Many have tried; all have failed."

"And poor Prudence—Sylvia actually *spit* on her."

"Those two have never gotten along."

"It's common knowledge Pru had her eye on the presidency and Sylvia just swept it out from under nose."

Erin sighed as she pulled her tikka masala from the microwave, wondering when she would get a chance to eat it.

"And how could she treat Jonathan like that?" Farnsworth continued. "Good of you to defend him, pet," she added slyly.

"Anyone would have done it."

"Ah, but you're the one who did."

"I'll tell you what, Farnsworth. If I decide to pursue a romance with Jonathan, I'll send you a text message. Oh, never mind—you don't have a mobile phone." Erin liked to tease her friend, calling her the only person in Yorkshire without a mobile.

"By that time half the village will know anyway. You know how gossip travels round here, pet."

Erin gazed longingly at her chicken tikka masala, the sauce becoming gelatinous as it cooled.

"I was surprised to see Owen go after Kurt Becker like that," Farnsworth continued.

"I never took Owen for a bigot. I wonder what's going on in his life to make him behave like that."

"Now that you mention it, he does seem quite stressed out lately."

"And why wasn't Carolyn there?" Erin said, reaching for a bag of crisps on a high shelf. "She's keener on the society than he is. I always thought he joined because of her." Pulling the bag open, she stuffed a couple into her mouth, biting down with a satisfying crunch.

"What are you eating?" said Farnsworth.

"Crisps," Erin mumbled through a full mouth.

"I thought you were trying to cut down on them."

"I keep them in a high cupboard."

"Apparently it's not working. What flavor are they?"

"Cheese and onion."

"I like prawn cocktail."

"I have those too."

Farnsworth sighed. "Why must crisps be so delicious and celery so vile?"

Erin laughed. "I like celery."

"Then apparently you enjoy chewing on tree bark. Because that's exactly what it's like. And that's obviously why you're so thin and I am not."

"You're just right. Zaftig, I think they call it."

"When you start nattering nonsense like that, it's time to ring off."

"See you at the meeting tomorrow."

"I'm telling you, Erin, heads are going to roll!"

"I can hardly wait."

Erin finished the crisps greedily—her stomach was contracting with hunger pangs. She ate her chicken tikka at the round kitchen table with the blue-and-white cloth she had brought back from the Quimper region of France last year.

Erin Coleridge was the kind of person people turned to for comfort. They flocked to her bookstore not only to browse her eclectic collection and enjoy her excellent tea and pastries but also to feel better about themselves. That was her gift, her father always said, making people feel better.

She didn't mind—she liked feeling useful—but before trudging up the narrow stairs to her bedroom, Erin unplugged the landline and turned off her mobile phone. She'd had enough of the rehashing and recrimination that had followed the contentious meeting—and she knew there was more ugliness ahead.

After a long, sinfully luxurious bath in her lion-pawed tub, she snuggled deep into the double bed with the brass frame and down comforter, clutching an annotated copy of *Pride and Prejudice*. Some questions had come up at previous meetings, and though by no means the leading Austen scholar in the society, she was keen to look up some of the answers. Outside, an owl hooted softly as she dug eagerly into the pages, and soon she was lost in the past, swallowed up in a world of carriages, waistcoats, and silver tea services as a light rain pattered against the windowpanes.

Chapter Three

❧

Prudence Pettibone was in a bad mood. The source of her malcontent was not the dolorous drooping of her prized *Dracula simia* orchid, or the unexplained chip on her Royal Doulton teapot—she was convinced that was the work of Hannah, her clumsy oaf of a maid. Nor was it the unrelenting string of dull, rainy days hanging over the village of Kirkbymoorside with the grim stubbornness of the Yorkshire countryside and its people. Prudence rather liked wet days, as they were an excuse to sit inside with a cup of tea and a book—preferably something by Jane Austen, about Jane Austen, or inspired by Jane Austen.

The source of her irritation wore absurd feathered hats and floral print dresses more suitable for upholstery than haberdashery, had been recently elected president of the Northern Branch of the Jane Austen Society, and went by the name of Sylvia Pemberthy, née Westcraven. It pleased Prudence to think of Sylvia's maiden name, because the first Westcravens were peat farmers, and she liked to picture Sylvia's ancestors bending over soggy fields of sod. In spite of her posh airs and affectations, Sylvia sprang from lowly harvesters of dirt, a fact that delighted Prudence to no end. Sylvia's presence in her consciousness was like a slow leak in a bathroom faucet, wearing away the enamel of her patience with its insistent *drip drip drip*.

The first thing Prudence did after supper that night was pick up the phone and call Hetty Miller, her closest ally in the society. After half an hour on the phone with Hetty, Prudence was relieved to find she wasn't the only one who couldn't abide Sylvia—according to Hetty, she had plenty of enemies within the ranks.

"She just ignored you when you tried to get a word in edgewise?" said Hetty. "Who does she think she is? And what on earth was she thinking, picking on Jonathan like that? The last thing she should be doing is alienating someone like him."

"Exactly!" Prudence agreed. "Such bad manners."

Jonathan Alder was one of the few single men in the society, and the reason for the regular attendance of more than a few female members. It was Prudence who had convinced him to accept the post of chairman of the Events Committee, and now Sylvia was about to chase him away with her ridiculous nattering.

"No wonder Owen and Kurt went at it," said Hetty, "with her setting the tone like that. She won't last long as president at this rate."

Prudence could hear the sound of running water and clattering pans in the background. Hetty was probably making tea, and that made her want some, to stave off the creeping chill of the October night. She padded into the kitchen and switched on the light, cold and bright on the tile counters. She hated the new energy-saving light bulbs her husband had talked her into buying, which brought out the thick blue veins in her hands.

She opened the tea cupboard warily—as usual at this time of year, there was an infestation of field mice, as they crept inside in search of a warm place to ride out the winter. She had been nagging Winton to pick up some poison at the store, but the poor darling was so tenderhearted she supposed she would have to do it herself.

She smiled when she saw the plate of homemade brownies on the counter, with a note from Winton. THOUGHT YOU MIGHT BE PECKISH WHEN YOU GOT IN. XOXO WINTON. He was such a dear, always looking after her.

"How can she get away with such behavior?" said Hetty.

"It's shockingly uncivil, if you ask me," Prudence replied, cradling the phone on her shoulder as she held the teapot underneath the faucet. Of course she owned a mobile phone like everyone else nowadays, but there were precious few cell towers this close to the moors. Reception was spotty in the village, and most people still relied on their landlines.

She chose a decent if undistinguished Darjeeling, warming the pot before pouring in the boiling water.

"Thinks she's high and mighty," Hetty said.

"A regular Lady de Bourgh," Prudence agreed.

"And she's doing us such a great favor by holding the meeting here."

Most general meetings were held in the city of York, thirty miles away, but as newly elected president, Sylvia had persuaded the members to meet in Kirkbymoorside, where she and her husband had recently relocated, presumably to live a quieter life than in the bustling university town.

"Lord it over us, she does," Hetty continued. "But she's no better than she ought to be, if you ask me." Hetty was rather common and had a vulgar way of speaking, which made Prudence feel better about herself by comparison.

Tea tray in hand, Prudence tiptoed back to the living room with its low-beamed ceilings and rough-hewn stone walls. The house was one of the oldest in the village—possibly in all of Yorkshire—and her husband was inordinately proud of its historical significance. Legend had it that Robert the Bruce had once stayed there while fleeing English soldiers. Like many Yorkshiremen, Winton was no great fan of the British Crown and loved to regale people with the Scottish rebel's exploits. He had already gone up to bed—a creature of habit, he was rarely awake the other side of ten PM. The air rippled with the sound of his gentle snoring from the upstairs bedroom as she settled herself in the tattered green armchair before the fire, the phone handset cradled on her shoulder.

"She's just plain selfish, if you ask me," Hetty said.

"'Selfishness must always be forgiven you know, because there is no hope of a cure,'" Prudence replied. She prided herself on her arsenal of Austen quotes, distributing them liberally like conversational jewels whenever possible.

Sadly, it fell on deaf ears. Though she and Hetty had joined the society together, Prudence sometimes wondered if her friend actually read Jane Austen—or anything else, for that matter. Hetty Miller did not possess the town's most bracing intellect.

"What do you suppose Sylvia is on about?" asked Hetty. "Could she possibly view Jonathan as a threat to her power?"

"Mind you, he is very popular," Pru replied. In truth, Jonathan Alder was the subject of more than a few feminine fantasies within the society. But he remained steadfastly unattached, causing Prudence to wonder if perhaps women were not his cup of tea. She hoped that was not the case. Of course, she knew that even without the loyal Winton by her side, she was hardly a natural love object for Jonathan, but she enjoyed the frisson of her fantasies, which she liked to think were the product of her exceptional imagination.

". . . I think she's preparing herself for a coup," Hetty was saying, and Prudence realized she hadn't been listening.

"Mm," she murmured, stirring her tea.

"What do *you* think?" Hetty asked, and Prudence felt like a naughty child caught out by the teacher for not paying attention. But Winton always said, *When in doubt, agree.*

"You could be right," she said.

"That would explain her extreme behavior," Hetty rattled on, oblivious to Pru's attention lapse.

"She was so mean to poor Farnsworth, I was afraid she was going to burst into tears."

"Poor Farnsworth," Hetty sighed.

"Sylvia is vain, and 'vanity working on a weak head, produces every sort of mischief,'" said Pru, proud of herself for so deftly squeezing an Austen quote into the conversion.

"Well, that's plain as the nose on your face."

Prudence wondered if that was a dig at her own rather pronounced proboscis, inherited, alas, from her father.

"What have you heard?" she asked, taking a sip of tea, hot and strong and sweet, just the way she liked it.

"Surely you've heard the rumors swirling about?"

"Of course," she lied, feeling left out once again. After all, she was the club treasurer and secretary, and a member of the Events Committee. Why did Hetty always seemed to know more than she did? She took a deep breath. "Who wants her position, do you think?"

"Some people say you do."

This quite took her breath away. Winton had said more than once she would be a better president than Sylvia, and he'd been bitterly disappointed when she was not chosen in the last election. She had to admit the idea made her skin tingle, but she tried to console herself with the knowledge that the society was a den of vipers and anyone in power was vulnerable to the fangs of its more toxic members.

"That's ridiculous," she said. "How could anyone think I—"

"I'm only repeating what I've heard, mind you," Hetty interrupted. "Don't bite my head off."

"Who said it?"

Hetty sighed, and Prudence could feel one of her headaches coming on, a tightening above her right temple.

"I've said too much already," Hetty replied.

"Very well," Prudence answered huffily. Hetty was her best friend in the society, and if she couldn't rely on her, there were indeed stormy waters ahead. "I'm tired," she said. "It's time I went off to bed."

"Don't be cross," Hetty whimpered, but Prudence cut her off.

"Good night," she concluded firmly, and hung up the phone.

Leaning back in the armchair, Prudence gazed at the ship's clock over the mantel, its polished brass reflecting the yellow glow of firelight, the long, graceful hands almost touching as if in prayer. It was nearly eleven. Winton loved that clock, polishing the case until it shone, winding it carefully every night before bed. Comforted by ritual and regularity, he had lived their entire married life contentedly within the triangle of their house, All Souls, and the George and Dragon.

She wondered idly if she would outlive him, and thought longingly of Hetty's infinitely more glamorous life. The first thing Hetty had done after ditching her last husband was book a cruise to the Canary Islands, celebrating her divorce by dating men young enough that waiters assumed she was their mother (though if they made the mistake of saying so, they saw it reflected in their tip). Divorce was not an option for Prudence Pettibone—but death, well, that was another matter.

Shaking off her guilt at such uncharitable thoughts, Prudence rubbed her right temple. She had hoped to wring some comfort out of talking with Hetty, but now she was in a worse mood than before. She hated the backbiting politics of the society yet didn't want to capitulate by quitting. She would just have to cultivate a thicker skin. Tomorrow was the monthly general meeting, and she would have to be prepared for the inevitable infighting and squabbling. Sighing, she stood up and stretched, thinking of a quote from a letter Jane Austen had written to her sister Cassandra: "I do not want people to be very agreeable, as it saves me the trouble of liking them a great deal."

In that case, she thought, there would be very little trouble taken at the next meeting of the Jane Austen Society.

Chapter Four

～

"Order! Please come to *order!*"

Sylvia Pemberthy, née Westcraven, swung her gavel in an arc like a blacksmith's hammer, bringing it down sharply on the burnished surface of the lectern. Heads swiveled toward her, eyes opened in shocked indignation at her temerity in treating society members like squabbling schoolchildren.

Erin suspected Sylvia regretted her decision to accept the position of president three months ago. She had put her name forward because of what she saw as the disintegration of orderly behavior among the members, but it had only grown worse under her tenure.

"Could we please get down to business?" she said, affecting a stern air that wasn't entirely convincing. "Now then," she said, turning to the society's treasurer, Prudence Pettibone. "I believe you have a report for us?"

Prudence stood and cleared her throat officiously, and Erin saw her husband Winton squeeze her hand. He spoke little, but he certainly seemed devoted to his wife, gazing at her with adoration.

"Our fund for the eighteenth-century fancy dress ball is as follows: four hundred pound fifty," Prudence read from the neatly penned black ledger. She had a voice like a potato peeler, nasal and cutting. "Our total cash reserve . . ."

Erin surveyed the crowded room. The meeting hall of All Souls was bursting at the seams with people, some of whom she had never seen before. She wondered if they were breaking any fire laws, stuffing so many into the room. In addition to occupying the usual rows of metal folding chairs, people leaned along the walls or slouched in corners, some of them glowering at Sylvia. Unrest was palpable in the air, with people shifting in their chairs and muttering as Prudence droned on in the background.

". . . the question of raising membership dues was discussed . . ."

Erin took a deep breath of musty air, smelling of stale coffee, yellowing hymnals, and week-old croissants, served up to the parishioners following Sunday's service. Word was that several people were "gunning for Sylvia," so she studied each face to see which ones bore the clearest signs of malice. Last night's spat involving Jonathan Alder had been unpleasant, and she noticed he was not present. Could Sylvia have chased him away forever? She felt a sharp pang of disappointment at the thought.

Farnsworth was seated in the front row, wrapped in a shawl sprouting cat hairs and looking up at Sylvia with distaste. Kurt Becker sat with his wife, Suzanne, who was tightly zipped into a leather ensemble and looked like a German dominatrix. Her blonde hair was carefully curled and coiffed, as though she were on a fashion runway instead of in a church basement. Erin noticed that Sylvia avoided making eye contact with Kurt.

". . . so the committee decided not to raise membership dues for the time being," Prudence was saying. Then, with an officious little cough, she added, "That concludes my report," and plopped down next to her husband, who squeezed her hand.

"Right. Any questions?" said Sylvia.

Erin watched Prudence exchange a little smile with her crony Hetty Miller. No one understood what the two saw in each other. Prudence was a classic dowdy British matron, all cardigans and thick wool skirts, while Hetty Miller was the kind of woman who endeavored to hold back the tide of age by sheer willpower and force of personality. Erin had heard she was north of sixty, but with her dyed red hair (carefully curled, with just the right touch of honey highlights), slim figure, and elegant clothes, she portrayed a much younger woman.

"Now then," Sylvia said, training her eyes on one face after another. Erin wondered if she had learned that technique in her public speaking class at the community college. "The main order of business tonight is a vote on whether to approve the new rules of conduct."

"It's like the bloody Stasi," someone murmured. Sylvia's eyes darted across the crowd, landing on Owen Hardacker. Sylvia and Owen's wife, Carolyn, were quite friendly, often sitting together at village fetes, so his overt animosity toward Sylvia was somewhat puzzling. Owen sat with his long, sinewy arms crossed, wearing his signature red-and-green Harris Tweed cap, his square jaw set, a hard look in his small blue eyes. The crowd tittered nervously. There was a spate of general muttering, and a few people murmured their agreement with Owen.

Erin stood and turned to face the audience. "Shame on you," she said. "Is it asking too much to behave like civilized people, for Christ's sake?"

Sylvia twitched at the reference to Jesus—some of the society members were, if not exactly devout, faithful churchgoers on Sundays. A good many attended All Souls weekly, if only for the free coffee and pastries. And the church did have an excellent organist; Sylvia and Farnsworth both sang in the choir.

But Erin's words had the desired effect: heads were lowered, chastened expressions assumed, and the general aura of belligerence dissipated a little. Sylvia bestowed a grateful smile upon Erin, who gave a little nod and sat back down.

"Now then," Sylvia said, "if we could just take a vote on the question of the proposed regulations? All in favor?"

A few hands were raised hesitantly, but for the most part remained motionless in laps, hidden behind backs, or folded across chests.

Sylvia sighed. "And the nays?"

Hands shot into the air so quickly Erin had the uncomfortable sensation of being at a Nazi rally.

"Very well," Sylvia said, "the nays have it." She rapped the gavel smartly on the lectern. Erin inhaled the scent of lemon cake and ginger spice bread coming from the kitchen in the rear of the hall, where members of the tea committee were busy boiling kettles and setting out steaming pots of Yorkshire tea. The society had a committee for everything. "I think it's time for our break. Any objections?"

She was met with sighs of relief and, for the first time in the evening, a few smiles. One thing you could count on, Erin thought—people liked their tea.

On her way to the serving table, Erin saw Owen Hardacker approach Sylvia, a contrite look on his lean, sunburned face. In addition to his signature tweed hat, he wore Wellies. He liked to project his image as a farmer, even though he was the wealthiest man in town.

"Sorry fer harsh words," he told Sylvia in his thick Yorkshire accent. "I've nowt against you personal, like; it's just we're all fed up with goings-on."

"I understand," she said, though Erin thought she still looked put out.

"Carolyn'd throw fit if she heard me, seein' as how she and you are mates an' all."

"Where is she tonight?" Sylvia asked, scanning the crowd.

"She were feeling poorly an' decided not t'come out."

"Give her my best," Sylvia said by way of closing the conversation, walking quickly toward the tea table. Erin looked at the long line and sighed—she was parched and desperately wanted tea. Given the unexpectedly large turnout, she feared the refreshment committee hadn't prepared enough for everyone.

Erin spied Suzanne Becker approaching Sylvia through the crowd, weaving unsteadily on stilettos that looked like they could cut through concrete. She looked tipsy, though maybe it was just the four-inch heels. Erin saw Sylvia duck behind a column near the back of the room, then slide behind the people serving tea to get in line on the other side. The din of conversation crescendoed as Erin joined the line, waiting her turn. Farnsworth worked alongside the others on the committee, and Erin thought about volunteering to join in, but they seemed to have things in hand.

After collecting her tea, she was joined by Prudence Pettibone, who had detached herself from her husband, who was serving tea. Hetty Miller made her way over to them, perched on heels even higher than Suzanne Becker's.

"That was sporting of you to go to Sylvia's rescue," Prudence said to Erin between bites of shortbread.

"Someone had to," Erin replied modestly.

Hetty shrugged, her copper curls bobbing. "I agree. The crowd was getting out of hand."

"I've never seen so many people at a meeting," Pru said, scanning the room.

"They can smell blood," Hetty remarked, a smile on her lacquered lips. "Speaking of which, looks like Suzanne Becker's stalking Sylvia again."

Prudence turned around to see the tall blonde pushing through the crowd. "She looks wobbly—I wonder if she's drunk."

"Could just be low blood sugar from all that dieting," Hetty remarked.

"Why does she hate Sylvia so much?" Prudence asked.

Hetty stared at her. "Seriously—you don't know?"

"If I knew, I wouldn't have asked, obviously," Pru said crossly.

Hetty wiped a smudge of lipstick from the lip of her teacup. "Everyone knows Sylvia and Kurt Becker are having an affair."

Erin nodded. "It appears Suzanne knows, too."

Hetty lowered her voice. "Look at those ridiculous shoes. She could break an ankle."

Erin thought she detected a note of envy. Hetty loved to wear unreasonably high heels, but being at least twenty years younger, Suzanne Becker looked better in them.

"I'm past worrying about vanity," Pru declared, which Hetty responded to by clicking her tongue.

"No woman is ever past vanity. My aunt's last visitor on her deathbed was her hairdresser. Died in full makeup, wearing her best jewelry, bless her soul."

"What *is* that horrid perfume you're wearing?" Prudence asked Hetty.

"I'll have you know it's Lily's Lilies, and it's *very* expensive."

"It smells like bathroom deodorizer."

"Is that Jonathan Alder over there?" Erin said, looking over her shoulder. Everyone turned to look, but just then a scream came from the other side of the room. All heads turned toward Suzanne Becker as she staggered into the room from the side door that led to an alley.

"Help! Somebody please help!"

Kurt Becker was the first to reach her, grasping an arm to steady her.

"What is it?"

His wife made a sound somewhere between a sob and a scream. "It's Sylvia—she's dead!"

Chapter Five

～

"What's a girl got to do round here for a cup of tea?"

Erin Coleridge looked up from the poem she was writing to see Polly Marlowe astride her red bicycle, arms folded, head cocked to one side. Her hair, the color and texture of straw, was pulled into a single short braid. Erin smiled. She was always glad to see Polly, with or without her little brother, who usually tagged along wherever she went.

Erin closed her notebook. It was Tuesday afternoon, less than twenty-four hours since Sylvia had met her terrible end, yet time felt strangely stretched out, as though it had all happened weeks ago. It was an unusually warm, sunny day for October, and she was seated at the iron patio table on the small deck in front of her store, shielded from the sun under a blue-and-white folding umbrella.

"Where's your sidekick?" she asked.

Polly brushed a strand of sandy hair from her freckled face. Nearly ten years old, she was thin and pale, with a translucent complexion, and could have been Erin's younger sister or daughter. "James Chester got a penalty for fighting in school yesterday. Father made him stay home."

Erin smiled as she tucked her notebook under her arm. Everyone called Polly's brother James Chester, because his father's name was also James.

"Pity," Erin said. "But more tea cakes for you."

Polly's eyes brightened as she followed Erin into the shop. "You have tea cakes?"

"Just bought them. Good timing on your part."

"What're you writing?" Polly asked as Erin tucked her note-book into the mahogany rolltop desk by the front door.

"Just jotting down a few things in my head." Her writing was a secret she shared with no one. Descended from a cousin of the Romantic poet Samuel Taylor Coleridge, Erin didn't want people to think she was putting on fancy airs. Yorkshire was full of plain-spoken people with their own form of eloquence, and as an inter-loper, she didn't want to be seen as stuck-up. In fact, the opposite was true—she was drawn to this land and its people and felt more at home here than among her posh public school friends or her classmates at Cambridge. That she had graduated with a first in comparative literature was something she admitted only when pressed.

"What's it to be?" she asked as they waited for the water to boil. "Vanilla cream or raspberry?"

Polly frowned and bit her lip.

"A bit of both, then," said Erin, putting two of each on a blue willow plate as the electric kettle started its long crescendo culmi-nating in a piercing whistle. As she poured the water into a match-ing teapot, there was a rap on the front door.

"It's open!" she called, handing the plate to Polly, who followed her through the shelves of books to the front of the store, balancing the plate as carefully as if the cakes had been made of spun gold instead of flour and sugar.

Standing in the front of the shop was Jonathan Alder, fetch-ingly rumpled in a tan raincoat and black Wellies. Irritated by how every female in Kirkbymoorside swooned over him, Erin did her best to resist his charms, though it was impossible to ignore the fresh sheen of his skin and the way his dark lashes brought out the blue in his eyes.

"Hello, Jonathan."

He gave a sheepish lopsided smile, which only made him more attractive. "I'm afraid I'm interrupting."

"Not at all. I forgot to put out the Open sign—my mistake." As stated on her website, her store was technically open Thursday through Sunday, but she often opened it on a whim. She made most of her money through online sales of rare books but enjoyed interacting with customers in the shop.

"You're just in time for tea!" Polly declared, holding up the plate of cakes.

"Here, let me help," he said, reaching for the tea tray. His hand brushed against Erin's, and she felt a shiver of electricity and nearly dropped the tray. Relinquishing it reluctantly, she followed him and Polly out to the patio.

"We've plenty of tea cakes," Polly said, "since James Chester isn't here."

"I thought he tagged along after you everywhere," Jonathan said, helping her set the table.

"Penalty for fighting in school," Polly replied, not entirely successful at masking her glee.

"Oh dear," Jonathan said with mock seriousness. "I'm sure *you* would never incur such a penalty."

Polly blushed and giggled. "Not bloody likely."

"Language, Polly," Erin said. The girl had no mother, and somehow Erin had slipped into that role without intending to.

Polly thrust her chin out defiantly. "My dad lets me swear all I like."

"I very much doubt that," said Jonathan, and Polly giggled again.

"You're right. He'd bloody kill me if he heard me."

Erin couldn't help laughing, as did Jonathan. She took her seat with a resigned sigh, knowing that if anyone saw them, tongues would wag in frenzied speculation.

"Your brother had better behave himself so he doesn't miss the fete later this month," Jonathan said to Polly.

"Gosh, that's almost here?" Erin said. Life up here was slower, yet time seemed to fly by faster, an odd contradiction.

"In two weeks," said Polly, licking icing off her fingers.

"All my kids can hardly wait—they're talking about it already," said Jonathan.

"Polly, would you fetch another cup and saucer?" Erin asked.

"Please don't bother," Jonathan said.

"It's no trouble," said Erin.

"Back in a jiff!" Polly said, ducking into the shop.

"This is a remarkably charming place you have here, Ms. Coleridge," he said, gracing her with another of his lopsided smiles.

"Why, thank you, Mr. Alder," she replied, wondering how aware he was of his own charms.

"No less charming than the proprietress herself," he added, and she felt the warmth rise to her cheeks.

"Kind of you to say so," she murmured, busying herself stirring the pot.

"I hear there are a couple of detectives poking their noses into things."

"I should think there are. Though good luck in sorting it out. There are more suspects than you can shake a stick at."

"Do you know who they've talked to?"

"Not me, I can tell you that."

"Me neither," he said, as Polly reappeared with a cup and saucer.

"So do you have any theories?" Jonathan said, lowering his voice.

"Several, as a matter of fact."

"What are you whispering about?" said Polly, plopping down next to him.

"Elbows off the table," Erin said, and the girl folded her thin arms in a defiant gesture.

"So, what were you *whispering* about?" she repeated.

Erin and Jonathan exchanged a look.

"It's about Mrs. Pemberthy, isn't it? My dad was at that meeting. He got back really late."

"How late?" said Erin.

"The clock said one fifteen AM. I woke up when he came in."

Jonathan shifted in his chair and caught Erin's eye. "Maybe we should change the subject."

Polly snorted. "What's the matter—you think I'm too young to talk about it?"

"Yes," Erin said firmly. "Now eat your cakes before the crows get them."

"Crows don't like cake," Polly said, but her eyes darted to the thick branches of the chestnut tree.

"Crows *love* cake," Jonathan said, "especially tea cake."

Polly giggled and swung her legs underneath the chair. Jonathan's easy way with the child was another source of irritation for Erin, who set her lips as she poured three cups of tea, the rising steam evaporating into thin wisps in the October air. *If he's so great with kids, why doesn't he have a tidy little wife and a couple of his own?* Clearly there was something wrong with him—she didn't know what, but she would find out. Perhaps he was less like Mr. Bingley and more like the charming but feckless Mr. Wickham in *Pride and Prejudice*—a little too good to be true.

"I'm sorry I don't know more about the investigation," she said insincerely. "I'm afraid your visit is wasted."

"Not at all," Jonathan said, smiling. "How could such excellent tea cakes be a waste of time?"

Polly continued swinging her legs underneath her chair. She took another bite of cake, her mouth smeared with white frosting, and smiled at Jonathan.

Were his eyes really cornflower blue? *Good lord, that's simply too much*, Erin thought, feeling very cross.

Before he could continue, she heard a cheerful shout and turned to see Prudence Pettibone and Hetty Miller, Kirkbymoorside's very own odd couple. Resplendent in a creamy peach Chanel suit with black pearls, Hetty looked as if she was about to step onto a yacht. Prudence clomped along next to her in plastic clogs, a dun-colored woolen skirt, and a matted gray shawl. Her wardrobe seemed to have been plucked from the clearance bin at one of the local charity shops. Of course, Erin was no one to judge—she was wearing yoga pants under a loose gray linen top, no makeup, her strawberry-blonde hair piled on top of her head.

"Hello, Erin!" Hetty sang out as the two women left the sidewalk to cross the slip of lawn in front of the cottage. Erin worried Hetty's shoes weren't up to the task, but she wobbled gamely toward them, even as one high heel sank into a mole hole.

Jonathan sprang to her aid, gallantly offering his arm, which Hetty accepted with much tittering and blushing, teetering her way to the patio long after Prudence had plopped onto the nearest chair. Prudence shook her head as her friend lowered herself onto a chair in a cloud of lily-of-the-valley perfume, dusting the grass from her Diors.

"Always an adventure with Hetty," she said, eyeing the plate of tea cakes.

"One must suffer for beauty," Hetty said, sniffling a little. "Fashion is a cruel taskmaster."

"It's hard to imagine anyone in this village who is more of a fashion icon than you," said Jonathan.

"Why, thank you," Hetty replied, lowering her eyes.

"'Dress is at all times a frivolous distinction, and excessive solicitude about it often destroys its own aim,'" Prudence declared.

Hetty snorted. "Oh, Prudence, must you *always* be showing off?"

Jonathan leaned back in his chair. "As far as I'm concerned, Hetty is an artist of fashion, and 'an artist cannot do anything slovenly.'"

Hetty clapped her hands and wagged a finger at Prudence. "There—that will teach you to use Austen quotes against me!"

Clenching her jaw, Prudence turned to Jonathan. "What is that quote from, pray tell?"

"From one of her letters, I think."

"Polly, run and get two more cups, would you?" said Erin.

"Oh, please don't bother," Prudence said sullenly.

"Let me help," said Jonathan, following Polly into the cottage. Erin wondered why he was laying it on so thick. Who was he trying to impress? Surely not her, with her baggy yoga pants and black-rimmed glasses—and (though she felt guilty for thinking it) Hetty was old enough to be his mother.

When he was out of sight, Hetty nudged her elbow. "Lucky you! What've you done to deserve a visit from Mr. Bingley?"

"Honestly, I've no idea why he's come—he seems to have no interest in shopping for books."

"Maybe he's shopping for something else," Hetty said, winking broadly, like a bad vaudeville actress.

Prudence rolled her eyes. "Good heavens, Hetty, can't you think of anything besides men?"

"Nothing else is as much fun," Hetty replied.

Erin had to admire Hetty's insistence on being just who she was. People might call her obsessed with men—as they did frequently, behind her back—but Erin saw a comforting consistency to her personality. You could always count on Hetty to be Hetty. As Farnsworth had once said, her waters might not run deep, but they were always running.

"Here we are," said Jonathan, emerging from the cottage with teacups, followed by Polly carrying extra plates.

"It's a tea party!" Polly proclaimed gaily, arranging the plates on the table.

Erin suddenly longed for all these people to be gone, to be alone on her patio with her poetry. She had thought owning a bookstore would temper her reclusive side, but it only seemed to enhance it. At the moment she wished for nothing more than a bath and a good book. She was feeling very drawn toward Jonathan, but something told her it wasn't a good idea.

"Shall I be mother?" Hetty said, picking up the pot and beginning to pour tea into everyone's cups.

"Why not?" Erin replied, with a look at Prudence, who was obviously dying to launch into conversation.

"So," Pru said eagerly. "Who do you think could have done it?"

"I've no idea," Erin replied, handing her a steaming cup of tea.

"What have you heard?"

"Nothing, really."

"But everyone confides in you—surely you've been inundated with visitors?"

Erin stirred her tea. "You're the first."

Hetty took a dainty bite from a vanilla cream cake. "You read a lot of true crime, Erin—who do you think did it?"

"I have my suspicions."

Jonathan glanced toward Polly, who seemed more interested in the tea cakes than the conversation. "Do you think we should be discussing this in front of—"

"I'm terribly mature for my age," said Polly. "Everyone says so."

"No doubt," said Jonathan, "but as a schoolmaster, I don't think—"

"Don't mind me," Polly said through a mouthful of cake. "Pretend I'm not here."

"Look," said Hetty, "if we can just figure out who Sylvia was having an affair with—" She broke off in response to Jonathan's warning look.

"I really don't think it's appropriate," he began, but Polly just laughed.

"Seriously, have you had a look at what's on the telly these days? Hashtag get real, folks."

Prudence frowned. "Hashtag what?"

"It's an online reference," said Erin. "Twitter, Facebook, that kind of thing."

"I knew that," Hetty said unconvincingly.

"Or Instagram or Snapchat," Polly added, slurping down some tea. "Hashtags are everywhere."

"What's a hashtag?" said Prudence.

"It involves Internet links and metadata," said Erin. "Do you really want to know more?"

Prudence wrinkled her nose. "Good lord, no."

Hetty looked at Jonathan. "Do you know what all this means?"

Jonathan laughed. "I'm so used to my students understanding it better than I do that I don't worry about it much. But I still don't think this is appropriate conversation in front of—"

"The *child*?" said Polly.

"Well, you *are* only ten."

"Fine," she replied, stuffing another piece of cake into her mouth. "I told my father I'd help him in the garden anyway." She brushed the crumbs from her lap. "When I'm gone, then you can gossip your heads off," she said, heading toward her bike.

"I do have some theories," Erin said casually.

Hetty leaned forward. "Pray, do tell!"

Jonathan rose from his chair. "Wait—I'll come with you," he told the retreating Polly.

She turned around and rolled her eyes. "Afraid someone will try to poison me?"

"I expect he's just had enough tongue wagging for one day," Prudence remarked.

"Actually, I've got some work at school to catch up on," he said.

"I'm on my bike, you know," said Polly.

"No worries—I'll jog alongside. The exercise will do me good. The tea was brilliant, thanks," he said to Erin. "A pleasure, ladies."

"The pleasure was all ours," Hetty replied with a smile no doubt meant to be flirtatious, but her teeth were smeared with lipstick and the effect was unfortunate.

When he and Polly had gone, Hetty sighed mightily. "What a superb Mr. Bingley he would be. If I were only ten years younger."

Prudence snorted. "More like twenty-five years."

Hetty jutted out her lower lip. "There's no need to be horrid. I'm proud of the way I look—even at *my* age."

"'Vanity and pride are different things, though the words are often used synonymously.' What you are is vain."

"At least I have something to be vain about," Hetty snapped.

"Another Austen quote?" asked Erin.

Prudence nodded. "*Pride and Prejudice.*"

"He seemed to be in a hurry to leave," Erin remarked.

"Well, of course he was," Hetty replied with a smug smile. "He and Sylvia had an affair."

Prudence frowned. "But I thought she and Kurt were—?"

"Yes, they are now, but I'm talking about this past summer."

"How do you know?" asked Erin.

"I saw them at the village fete," said Hetty. "They were behind the barn and didn't think anyone was watching."

Prudence narrowed her eyes. "What were *you* doing behind the barn?"

Hetty crossed her arms. "None of your business."

"Speaking of older women," said Prudence. "She's at least ten years his senior, I should think."

"Maybe that's why they had the row that night—it was a lover's quarrel," Hetty suggested.

"If it's true, Sylvia certainly gets around," Erin said, surprised to find herself disappointed. So Jonathan wasn't to be trusted, and she could dismiss the possibility that he was interested in her—which of course he wasn't anyway. But could he have had something to do with Sylvia's murder? "What exactly did you see?" she asked Hetty.

"They were whispering, you know, like lovers do. And when they saw me, they looked utterly guilty."

"But you didn't actually *see* them kissing," said Prudence.

"No, but—"

"Innocent until proven guilty—which will be rather difficult, since one of them is dead," Prudence added, looking pleased to have punctured a hole in her friend's theory.

Prudence was right—there could be a perfectly innocent explanation for Jonathan and Sylvia's meeting. If she could get him alone, Erin thought, she could worm it out of him somehow.

"Well," she said, peering at the empty pot, "more tea, anyone?"

Hetty looked longingly at the remaining cakes, but Prudence stood up decisively. "I think we've taken quite enough of your time. Thank you for the tea. Come along, Hetty."

"Thank you for the tea," Hetty said, like a child being forced to obey.

Erin was amused that even though Hetty was the flashier of the two, Prudence was, as her father would say, the alpha female.

"Do let us know if you hear anything," Prudence said, following her friend across the lawn, Hetty swaying on her ridiculous shoes as she navigated the uneven ground.

Taking her poetry manuscript from the desk, Erin worked for another hour or so, oblivious to the passage of time until the pages became harder to see. Looking up from her work, she was surprised to see the sun had set. Folding the notebook, she leaned back and let the evening settle over her, dusk deepening into twilight as a chill crept across the fields. Dew prickled her skin as she listened to the brittle rattle of cicadas slide into the gentle purr of crickets.

She cleared away the tea things and went inside, switching on the light over the antique gas stove in the kitchen, savoring the gleam of its red enamel surface. The stove had come with the cottage, one of the things that sold her on the property. She liked the narrow slip of land she owned, and the stream behind the house with the little footbridge leading to a public ordinance path that eventually came out on the village green. As she puttered about in the kitchen, she thought of a favorite Austen quote: "There is nothing like staying at home for real comfort."

Erin switched on the television in the kitchen nook while she prepared dinner. A picture of Sylvia flashed on the screen. She was smiling, half turned to the camera, as if caught by the photographer in an unrehearsed moment. How uncharacteristic of Sylvia—she liked to be in control at all times and would no doubt hate that a candid shot of her was on television. But Erin didn't really believe in the afterlife and didn't think Sylvia was watching the investigation of her death.

". . . so far no potential suspects have emerged," the square-jawed news anchor was saying as the camera pulled back to reveal the news desk. "Our news team caught up with Reverend Horace Motley, pastor of All Souls Church, where Mrs. Pemberthy was found poisoned."

The monitor showed a video of a sweaty Pastor Motley standing next to a reporter holding a microphone, both of them squinting into the sun.

"It's terrible, just terrible," the reverend said, clearly nervous in the presence of the camera. "We're all just devastated. Everyone loved Sylvia."

Not everyone, obviously, Erin thought as she chopped a carrot for the salad.

"Were you and the victim close?"

"I—well, not especially, I suppose, but—I mean, she sang in the choir every Sunday."

Erin put the knife down and stared at the screen. Why was the reverend so flustered? He was used to preaching in front of an audience every Sunday, so why did the presence of a television camera put him off his game?

The shot switched back to the news anchor, who gazed at the camera with as much gravitas as he could muster. "Anyone with information is encouraged to call the police hotline." A number appeared on the screen, and Erin had an impulse to jot it down. But then, what did she know? She'd been there when it happened, yet felt as much in the dark as everyone else.

Everyone, of course, except the killer.

The ringing of her landline broke through the drone of the news report, and Erin muted the television before snatching the phone from its receiver.

"Erin, they think *I* did it." Farnsworth's voice was shaky, panicked.

"What?" Erin said, perching on the arm of the sofa.

"They were here today. They interviewed me, and when I admitted I served Sylvia her tea, they—"

"Why on earth would you tell them that?"

"What was I going to do, lie about it? I'm sure other people saw me."

"Never volunteer information to the police!"

"They *asked* me point blank, for God's sake!" Farnsworth's voice trembled, as if she was about to cry.

"Steady on—calm down."

"What am I going to do?"

"Leave it to me."

"Oh, Erin, I—"

"I'll sort it out—I promise."

"But what can you do?"

"Get to the bottom of things, obviously. Now get some sleep, and I'll talk to you tomorrow."

"Oh, thank you—God bless you, Erin."

"I thought you were an atheist," Erin said, to lighten the mood.

"And so I am. But if there were a God, he should bloody well bless you."

Erin smiled. "Good night, Farnsworth." Putting down the phone, she wondered if she had just made a promise she would be unable to keep.

Chapter Six

～

Wednesday morning dawned bright and insistent, and Detective Inspector Peter Hemming felt quite cross as he threw off his blankets. He sat on the edge of the bed peering out of the window in his room at the George and Dragon. There was something about sunshine that depressed him, a beckoning to action, a command for accomplishment that tapped into what his mother had called his "drive to overachieve."

"'Drive to overachieve'—what does that even mean?" he muttered as he shuffled to the bathroom to shave, sloughing off images of last night's dreams as he rummaged through his toilet kit. He was not a morning person. Predictably, of course, his new partner Sergeant Rashid Jarral was, as evidenced by a cheerful knock on the bedroom door. Hemming stuck his head out of the bathroom.

"What?" he growled, doing his best to sound intimidating.

But Jarral was impervious to discouragement. "I was wondering if you'd like to go down to breakfast, sir?" he sang from the other side of the closed door. Hemming imagined him standing in the hallway, face shining, hair combed and glistening, eyes bright with the call of adventure. He vaguely remembered feeling that way at the beginning of a case, but it was so long ago it felt like someone else's memory. He sighed and stretched, like a tired old dog who just wanted to lie by the fire.

"I'll meet you down there," he called to Jarral.

"Shall I order for you, sir? I believe they have kippers."

"No thank you," he said, shuddering. The idea of smoked fish for breakfast always struck him as barbaric.

"Right—see you down there," Rashid said cheerfully, retreating, the ancient floorboards creaking under his heavy tread.

"Not very light on his feet, our sergeant," Hemming murmured as he extracted the razor from his toilet kit, and immediately he felt chastened by his uncharitable attitude. After all, it wasn't Sergeant Jarral's fault he was feeling his age, or lack of enthusiasm, or whatever it was. This was always the worst part of a case, the very beginning— once he got stuck in it, he would perk up. He always managed to get caught up in solving the puzzle; when that happened, he might be rewarded with the energy of a teenager. He frowned as he swept the razor over his chin. Why was everyone so damn jolly in the morning?

He and Jarral had received the call Monday evening and, after driving up from York, had been up most of the night talking with the crime scene techs and comparing notes with the local chief constable, Hamish McCrary. Tuesday brought more of the same, as well as witness interviews, including a drive back to York, as some of the society members had come up from the city for the meeting. After ending up at the George and Dragon for a late meal and a very welcome drink, Hemming had not slept well, tormented by images of the victim and theories about her killer. This was not uncommon at the beginning of a case, but it was damned inconvenient.

Downstairs in the pub, Hemming spied Sergeant Jarral in a cozy corner booth, tucking into a plate of kippers, eggs, and black pudding. The sight made his stomach lurch—he hated black pudding.

"Hope you don't mind I started," Jarral said through a mouthful of food.

"No. It looks . . . hearty."

"I love a good English breakfast." The sergeant sighed happily, spearing a fried mushroom with his fork.

The attractive barmaid from the previous evening approached. Her hair was in a ponytail, the strip of blue hair clasped in a tight braid. Scrubbed and devoid of makeup, her face looked even younger in the pale morning light. Hemming figured she was the innkeepers' daughter—she had her mother's rounded cheeks and her father's dark eyebrows.

"What'll it be, luv?" she said in a thick Yorkshire accent.

"Just coffee, thanks."

Sergeant Jamal frowned. "What you eat wouldn't keep a bird alive." He bestowed his brightest smile on the waitress, flashing his row of broad white teeth. "He'll have two eggs, over easy, with toast and Marmite."

Hemming shook his head. "No Marmite—jam."

"Gooseberry or red currant?"

"Gooseberry, please."

She smiled at Hemming. "Good job ye've him to look after ya, luv." Hemming watched her hips as she walked away, tightly encased in black denim jeans.

"It's for your own good, mate," Jamal said, spearing a sausage with his fork. "You'll thank me three hours from now."

Hemming stared at the sausage. "Is that—I mean, are you—"

Jarral smiled. "You haven't seen me throwing down my prayer rug five times a day, have you?"

"No, I just thought—I mean, I'm embarrassed to admit it, but I don't know that much about the—er, customs."

"My parents have an enlightened view, and I never really bought into the idea of Allah. Some of my family is observant; others aren't."

He was about to respond when the phone rang—a call from HQ in York. He answered after the first ring. It was DCI Witherspoon, a prickly but fair boss.

"Lab report's back," the chief said, not wasting any time.

"It's Witherspoon," Hemming mouthed to Jarral, who nodded, happily chewing on eggs and sausage. "Any prints on the cup, sir?" he said into the phone.

"None other than the victim's."

"That's not surprising—the servers wore gloves. According to witnesses, it was Mrs. Pemberthy's idea. More hygienic and all that."

"Ironic, isn't it, sir?" Jarral whispered. "Makes it harder to find her killer."

Hemming waved him off and spoke into the phone. "What about the toxicology report, sir?"

"Arsenic," said the chief. "Enough to kill a horse."

"My money's on rat poison," said a woman's voice behind him. He looked up to see a slim young woman with reddish-blonde hair and thick black eyeglasses standing just over his right shoulder. He stared at her. She smiled. "You must be the detectives everyone's talking about?"

"And you are—?" he said, frowning.

"Erin Coleridge. I own the local bookstore."

"Well, Ms. Coleridge," he began, but the chief's voice over the phone cut him off.

"Hemming, are you there?"

"Sorry, sir—I'm here."

"I was just saying that based on trace elements, the coroner thinks it was rat poison."

"And the rest of the tea, in the samovar and the other cups?"

"Completely free of toxins."

"They tested the tea in the tin as well?"

"Yes. Whoever poisoned Sylvia Pemberthy seems to have targeted her alone."

"Thank you for the report, sir."

"Keep me updated, will you?"

"Of course, sir," he said, hanging up. He turned to the young woman. "Now then, Ms. Coleridge, as much as I appreciate your desire to help—"

"I was right, wasn't I?" she said with a smile he found on the smug side. If she weren't so strangely attractive, Hemming would have set her straight. But something about the sparkle in the pale eyes behind the thick glasses disarmed him. "Farnsworth Appleby is innocent, you know," she added.

"Why—"

"She had no motive, and isn't capable of something like that."

"Well, I certainly—"

"The victim's husband, Jerome Pemberthy, is a much better candidate."

"But he—"

"He wasn't at the meeting—allegedly," she said. "But I wouldn't be so sure of that."

"We will certainly—"

"If you've any need of forensic research material, advice, or local gossip, I'm just down Swanson Lane," she said, handing him a card. The font was cursive, distinctive without being fussy:

Readers Quarry
Books, Old and New
Hours: 10–5 Thursday–Sunday
Or by Appointment

Below that was a phone number and a link to a website, ReadersQuarry.com.

He looked at Sergeant Jarral, who was staring at her openmouthed.

"Might want to close it before something flies in, Sergeant," he murmured, and Jarral shut his mouth, a startled expression on his handsome face.

"Thank you, Miss Coleridge," Hemming said. "We'll certainly keep your offer in mind."

"'What is right to be done cannot be done too soon.'" She turned to leave, then swiveled gracefully at the waist to look back at them. Hemming tried not to look at her hips, clad in tight black stretch pants.

"I'm guessing the poison was meant for Sylvia," she said, with a little Mona Lisa smile.

He couldn't help rising to the bait. "How the deuce would you—"

"Bye for now," she said, loping across the wide wooden floor beams to the exit.

When she had gone, Jarral leaned forward. "Bit of a looker, sir, I'd say."

Hemming grunted. He didn't appreciate her pushiness, and yet . . .

"But too cheeky for her own good, though, don't you think?" Jarral added.

The detective stroked his chin, still smarting from the abrasive aftershave.

"I wonder what her game is," he said thoughtfully, looking out the window facing the street, where a young boy was being pulled along by an eager golden retriever straining at the leash. The dog nearly yanked the boy off his feet as he scurried to keep up. *It's either push or pull*, Hemming thought. He felt like the boy, being pulled along by a case with too many suspects and not enough clues. Perfect equilibrium in life was so hard to achieve, and so fleeting.

Jarral pushed back his plate, which looked as if it had been licked clean.

"That went down a treat," he said as the waitress returned with Hemming's breakfast.

"Mind—it's hot," she said, sliding the steaming plate in front of him. "I gave you a sausage—homemade t'day. Thought y'might need it."

"Very kind of you."

"If you don' want it, I'm sure he'll eat it," she added with a nod at Jarral.

Hemming smiled. "Not a chance."

"But I'm a growing lad," the sergeant protested.

"Keep eating like that and you'll grow all right," Hemming replied.

Jarral rolled his eyes at the waitress. "See what I put up with?"

"He's the boss. Enjoy," she said, laying a hand briefly on Hemming's shoulder before walking away, shoulders and hips swaying just enough to keep him watching until she disappeared into the kitchen.

"She likes you," Jarral remarked, sounding disappointed and a little surprised; clearly he was used to female admiration.

"Never mind. I'm sure the next one will have better taste."

The sergeant's olive cheeks reddened, and he took such a large gulp of tea he nearly choked. Tucking into fried eggs and thick, bubbly sausage, Peter Hemming decided he was hungry after all.

Chapter Seven

❧

"Cheer up, Sergeant—we only have another hundred or so witnesses to interview," Detective Hemming remarked as Jarral closed the passenger side door gingerly, afraid something might fall off if he slammed it. Hemming's old Citroën was, to put it kindly, "distressed"; put bluntly, it was a wreck. Or so it appeared to Jarral, who liked things shiny and modern and new. He didn't understand the English obsession with old things—his family's exodus from Lahore had been a struggle for reinvention, a letting go of the past that had evolved into a dislike of anything representing archaic values.

As the oldest son, Rashid Jarral had absorbed his parents' obsession with progress and modernity. He always had the latest-model smartphone, the hottest apps; his Twitter account had more followers than his teenage cousins'.

He looked at the society membership list. Hemming was exaggerating, but it did contain a lot of names. "Apparently there were a few nonmembers present as well—come to watch the fireworks, I expect," Jarral remarked.

"They got more than they bargained for," Hemming said as they passed flocks of sheep and the occasional stone cottage. The sun was playing hide-and-seek behind a line of fluffy nimbus clouds, gray underneath, suggesting the possibility of rain. "Who's next on the list?"

"Erin Coleridge, Twenty-Two Swanson Lane," he said, entering the address on Google Maps.

"Ah, yes, our would-be sleuth," said Hemming. "Let's see what she has to say."

"Turn just up here at the sign, sir," he said, pointing to a wooden sign with BOOKSTORE in large block letters, followed by an arrow pointing down the lane.

They swung onto Swanson Lane, past a crumbling brick wall once belonging to an old estate, now long gone, only the remains of the wall still left. The old car rattled over potholes in the narrow dirt road, which came to a dead end in a quarter mile or so. At the end of the lane sat a solitary stone cottage; as they pulled closer, Jarral saw a wooden sign on the front lawn.

Readers Quarry
Books, Old and New
Hours: 10–5 Thursday–Sunday
Or by Appointment

"Here it is," he said, tucking his phone into his coat pocket. Detective Hemming wasn't as much a fan of technology as he was. Even though Hemming relied on the sergeant's use of GPS, Jarral had the feeling he would be much happier studying a road map spread out on the hood of his car.

"Right," Hemming said, turning off the engine. "Let's see what Erin Coleridge has to say for herself, shall we?"

"Yes, sir," Rashid answered, unfolding his body from the cramped Citroën. The cigar-shaped car rode very low to the ground, and it was awkward to pull himself out of the seat. It was very different from his own late-model SUV, which was much better suited to his long legs.

He followed Hemming up the little brick path to the cottage, past a cheerful flower garden to one side and a patio on the other.

A silver wind chime hanging from the eaves tinkled gently in the breeze. The mood was so peaceful and serene, Jarral had trouble imagining a murderer could live within these walls.

Their knock on the heavy oak door was met with a cheerful "Just a minute!"—followed by light, quick steps descending a staircase. The door was opened by the same striking young woman they had met at breakfast. She was a study in pastels, with light-blue eyes, white skin, and blonde-red hair, emphasized by her black turtleneck sweater and olive-green tights. Her skin was pale as swan feathers, with a downy sheen that made Rashid's own olive skin, which he was normally proud of, seem coarse by comparison. The same eyeglasses with thick black frames accentuated the lightness of her eyes, with their blonde lashes.

"Hello again," she said in a friendly, unaffected manner. "Please come in."

After introductions, she led them through a one-room bookstore into a tidy and well-appointed living room, and Rashid couldn't help thinking that if she was the killer, she was doing a good job of throwing them off the scent. The room was furnished in warm earth tones, terra-cotta walls with tasteful landscape paintings. He didn't have the eye to know if they were originals or reproductions, but they added to the general atmosphere of refined taste.

A richly patterned green Persian carpet dominated the center of the room, with a comfortable sofa at one end and a caramel-brown leather chair with matching footstool facing it, worn at the armrests. Books lined the walls on two sides; the front wall was lined with latticed windows, and he could see a door leading to a sunny kitchen in the back of the room. A baby grand piano nestled against the far bookcase.

"Please, sit down," she said. "Would you like some tea?"

"No, th—" he began, but Hemming interrupted.

"Yes, thank you. Can I give you a hand?"

"I'll be fine, thanks," she said, swaying gracefully through the low door leading to the kitchen.

When she had gone, Hemming strolled around the room, stopping to look at this and that in a seemingly casual manner, but Jarral suspected he missed little. He wondered if Hemming was looking for something in particular, yearning to know what was going on in the detective's head, but instinct told him not to interrupt. This was their first case together, and the sergeant wanted to make a good impression.

"Here we are," Erin said, bringing in a tea tray loaded with cakes, pastries, and a large blue china pot. She smiled at his surprised look. "People come here not only for books."

"Very good of you," Jarral remarked.

"It's good business. The longer they stay, the more they browse."

"I noticed you have quite a collection of crime books," Hemming said.

"Ever since I read *In Cold Blood*, I've been fascinated by true crime." She looked away, and Jarral had the feeling there was more to the story.

"You said earlier people were talking about us," he said. "Who exactly—"

"Oh, everyone. It's not every day such excitement comes to our sleepy little market town."

"I believe you were present when Mrs. Pemberthy was—"

"Yes, I was at the meeting with everyone else. We were on tea break, and I was talking with Hetty Miller and Pru—Prudence—Pettibone. There was a scream, and Suzanne Becker staggered into the room saying Sylvia was dead."

"Do you remember her exact words?"

"I believe she said, 'Help, somebody please help.' Then, 'It's Sylvia—she's dead.'"

"You have a good memory, do you, Ms. Coleridge?"

"My aural recollection is better than my visual. I'm not great with faces—not a good quality in a shop owner, I'm afraid."

"Do you have any idea who might want to harm Mrs. Pemberthy?" Rashid asked as she handed them each a steaming cup of tea. "Apart from her husband, that is."

"Take your pick. She wasn't the most popular president in society history."

"Why not?"

"Let me put it this way. If she were a Jane Austen character, she would be Lady Catherine de Bourgh."

"Snobbish, standoffish, thinks she's better than everyone else?" said Hemming.

"Exactly. Though Sylvia was hardly nobility—her ancestors were peat farmers. Still, she was quite wealthy."

"'It is very difficult for the prosperous to be humble.'"

Erin clapped her hands. "I love that quote! So you like Jane Austen?"

"It would be unpatriotic not to."

"Mind you, I liked Sylvia—she could be gracious and charming. But I could see how she made enemies."

"I hear there was talk of a coup," said Jarral.

"Society politics was always a bit rough-edged, but things heated up after . . ."

"After what?"

"The former president is a local landowner named Owen Hardacker, and he ran things with a pretty loose hand. Not a lot of rules or regulations, and I guess some people felt it was just too slipshod. There were fewer and fewer meetings, and some people didn't bother to turn up at all. Membership was declining, and some people blamed Owen."

Hemming leaned forward. "And what did you think?"

"I arrived here less than two years ago."

"Yet I hear you're popular."

She blushed, twin patches of red staining her pale cheeks.

"'Everyone comes to Erin's,' or words to that effect," he added.

She laughed, a tinkling sound like wind chimes. "Who said that?"

"Mrs. Appleby."

"I'm glad someone in town thinks I'm popular."

"Surely she's not the only one?" said Jarral.

"People in Yorkshire don't always welcome interlopers with open arms," she said, refilling their cups. "But once you're accepted, you have to do something pretty horrible to make people turn their backs on you."

"Murder, for example?" said Hemming.

The bell attached to the front door of the shop jingled, and Erin rose from her chair. "Will you excuse me for a moment?"

She went through the bead curtain to the front room, and Rashid was mesmerized for a moment by the gentle sway of the curtain and the faint rattle of beads. He heard Erin greet someone—he couldn't make out the words, but he got the impression it was someone she knew. A man, judging by the voice. There was a brief conversation, too low for him to make out; then Erin said, "I'll let you know the minute it comes in."

The man thanked her and left, the bell jingling as the door closed behind him. Erin reappeared moments later through the curtain.

"Sorry about that—a customer checking to see if a book had come in."

"Mind if I ask who?"

"Jonathan Alder. He teaches at the middle school."

Jarral set down his teacup. "Why didn't he just phone, I wonder?"

"You'd have to ask him," she said, and blushed again, crimson spreading upward from the base of her neck. Rashid heard the wind picking up outside, whistling in the ancient eaves. This time of year storms came and went in the North Country, quick as rabbits.

"And you, Ms. Coleridge?" Hemming said, reaching for a hot cross bun. "What did you think of Sylvia Pemberthy's handling of the society?"

"'If things are going untowardly one month, they are sure to mend the next.'"

"You're rather adept at quoting Austen yourself, it seems." Detective Hemming set down his teacup and leaned forward. "Can you recall anyone acting strangely at the meeting?"

"I didn't see anyone slip something into her tea, if that's what you mean."

"Did she put her teacup down at any point that you noticed?"

"I wasn't really paying attention. As I said, I was chatting with Hetty and Pru."

"Oh, yes, you did mention that," Hemming said, as though he had just remembered. Rashid had heard colleagues say the detective's memory was nearly flawless, so why the pretense? Was it to get her to relax her guard, maybe make a slip of some kind?

"Your friend Ms. Appleby said she left her tea on a chair where anyone could have slipped something into it. Rather convenient claim, considering she was on the tea committee that night and admitted to handing Mrs. Pemberthy her tea."

Erin's face darkened. "You've got the wrong end of the stick, Detective. Farnsworth would never—"

"Did she get on well with Mrs. Pemberthy, then?"

"No one 'got on well' with Sylvia Pemberthy."

"Do you happen to know whether Ms. Pemberthy took sugar in her tea?"

"No, but I know why you're asking. The sugar would hide any bitterness from the poison. And arsenic is a white powder that could easily masquerade as sugar."

Hemming's eyes narrowed. "And how exactly *did* you know it was arsenic?"

"I saw the body, Detective."

"And—?"

"It was obviously a fast-acting poison, but there was no grotesque positioning of the limbs suggesting the involuntary muscle contractions typical of strychnine," she said, as if reciting from a textbook. "I considered cyanide, but that's considerably more difficult to obtain than arsenic, which—as I said—is a common ingredient in rat poison. So the odds were on arsenic."

"You seem to know quite a lot about poison."

"I told you, crime is a hobby of mine."

"So you did."

"And before you ask, I don't have any rat poison in the house— though of course you're welcome to look for yourself."

"That won't be necessary."

"As I said earlier, if I were you, I'd look at her husband. He's a first-class wanker."

"I'll keep that mind."

To Jarral's relief, Hemming folded his notebook and slipped it into his pocket, an indication the interview was over.

"Thank you for your time," he said, "and for the tea."

She rose and stretched her lithe, somewhat boyish figure. "I wish I could be more helpful."

"You've been more helpful than you know," he said, and Rashid wondered if he meant to put her off balance by suggesting she had given herself away. Hemming handed her a business card. "Call me anytime if something else occurs to you. By the way, how did you know where to find us this morning?"

"News travels fast in this town," she said, piling the tea things onto a tray.

"I'll remember that. Good day, Ms. Coleridge."

When they were back in the car, Jarral turned to him as they fastened their safety belts. "Surely you can eliminate her from the suspect list?"

"Can I?"

"You don't think she—"

"Everyone in that room theoretically had means and opportunity. And judging by what everyone says, multiple people may have had motive."

"But—"

"It wouldn't be the first time a fair face has served as a mask for dark deeds."

Irritated, Rashid stared out the window at the dun-colored fields as they headed back toward town. He found Hemming's faux Shakespearean pronouncement condescending, and no matter what the detective said, he couldn't imagine lovely, lithesome Erin Coleridge poisoning anybody.

Chapter Eight

As she cleared away the tea things, Erin mulled over the interview. She wasn't sure what she thought of DI Hemming. His reserve and watchfulness were appropriate for a detective, but she sensed something wounded deep inside him, something he kept well guarded. Ordinarily this would have drawn her to him, but these were hardly normal circumstances. They were adversaries—at least until he was convinced of her innocence.

More importantly, she needed to convince him of Farnsworth's innocence. She had not revealed that Farnsworth had phoned her shortly before their arrival, frightened in a way Erin had never seen before.

The phone rang again, and she picked up.

"Are they gone yet?" said Farnsworth. She sounded a little breathless.

"Yes, they just left."

"Did they mention me?"

"We talked about a lot of people who were there that night." Erin didn't think her friend needed any more cause to worry—she sounded as if she was about to jump out of her skin.

"What did you tell them?"

"That you weren't capable of something like that."

Erin didn't point out that any policeman worth his salt would know better than to exonerate a suspect based on supportive words from a friend. She knew of far too many cases where the least obvious suspect had ended up being the killer—the sweet, shy boy next door who mowed everyone's lawn; the cheerful, helpful wife who volunteered at homeless shelters on weekends. The truth was that *anyone* was capable of murder.

But she did her best to reassure Farnsworth that the real culprit would soon be caught. After calming her down, Erin returned to the kitchen to finish tidying up. The steam rising from the sink fogged the windows overlooking the fields behind her cottage.

Seen through the gauze of steam, it looked like something out of a fairy tale: the little bridge with its rustic, hand-hewn wooden handrails; the narrow, winding creek twisting through the rolling landscape dotted with sheep grazing fields thick with gorse, chick-weed, and heather. To her eye, there was nothing more beautiful than a purple ocean of heather in bloom. Now in mid-October, only a few tiny pink blossoms of ling heather clung on bravely as the days grew shorter.

She was drawn to this landscape, forsaking the gentler geography of her native Oxfordshire with its downy mounds and softly rolling hillocks, preferring the grand, tragic sweep of the northern moors. Here she felt wild, free, and a little dangerous. After four years at Cambridge, she had tired of the snobbery and striving, the relentlessly high expectations. And when her mother died, Oxford became a sad place of lost memories.

Finishing the dishes, she went through the living room to the shop, the lingering scent of almond paste and vanilla trailing after her. Detective Hemming might be a tormented soul, but he did like his pastries.

Sergeant Jarral was an entirely different case—open, sunny, even a little naive; his charm flowed like perfume. It was impossible not to like him. But Hemming was diffident—solitary and remote—which made him more intriguing. She unlocked the front door and lugged the heavy OPEN sign outside. It was only Wednesday, but the weather continued warm, so she decided to open the shop, at least for a few hours.

Lifting the sign onto its hooks hanging from the eaves, she checked her hands for splinters before going back inside. She had thought about getting a lighter sign but feared it would be blown to bits in the harsh winter winds. Plywood might do in Oxford, but something substantial was called for in the stark northern clime. It was hard on wooden signs, she thought, but good for building character.

She remembered a favorite quote from *Pride and Prejudice*: "The more I see of the world, the more am I dissatisfied with it; and every day confirms my belief of the inconsistency of all human characters, and of the little dependence that can be placed on the appearance of merit or sense."

But wasn't character a work in progress? she thought as she spied a Moroccan cookbook lurking in the travel section. She slipped it into its proper place next to Jamie Oliver's *15 Minute Meals*. Surely everyone had the chance to improve, she mused as she tidied the art book section, making sure the Cézanne was even with the book on French neoclassicist Jacques-Louis David. But the David book was still poking out of the shelf, and she opened it to *The Death of Marat*, David's portrait of the famed firebrand and scribe of the French Revolution. The painter had caught him lying in his bath, just after being stabbed to death by Charlotte Corday.

Even with the visible stab wound and blood-spattered sheets, the painting had an odd stillness. The expression on Marat's face was almost blissful, as if death had been a deliverance.

On the opposite page was *The Death of Socrates*, the great man undaunted, holding the chalice of poison triumphantly aloft like a torch, his supporters and pupils draped around his deathbed in attitudes of despair. What a fertile subject for artistic contemplation death was, Erin thought as she slid the volume back on the shelf.

And now Kirkbymoorside had its own violent death, closer to Marat than Socrates. Sylvia Pemberthy had not swallowed the poison that killed her willingly or knowingly. And what if Jane Austen was right, that everyone was inconsistent and not to be trusted? If so, Sylvia's killer could be someone who didn't seem capable of such violence.

The front doorbell jingled. "Coming!" she called, hurrying to the front of the store.

Standing near the small wooden table that functioned as her desk, checkout counter, and cash register was Carolyn Hardacker. Elegantly dressed as usual, her slim body was draped in a linen caftan the color of spicy mustard. She wore her thick black hair in a chignon, emphasizing the length of her long, swanlike neck, her glossy skin the color of polished ebony.

She was one of those women who could throw on anything and look like a fashion icon. Of course, the linen caftan looked expensive, as did the gold bracelets and matching earrings, but on someone else they might have looked cheap or flashy. On Carolyn, they were perfect. But her most exotic feature was her emerald-green eyes.

"Hello," Erin said. "So nice to see you."

Carolyn gave a tight smile and fiddled with her gold bracelets. "I hope I'm not disturbing you."

"Never—always a pleasure. Are you looking for a particular book?"

Carolyn glanced out the front window as if she was afraid of being followed. "Actually, I was hoping to talk to you. Is this a bad time?"

"No—come in, please. Would you like some tea?"

"No, thank you."

"Please, sit down," Erin said, pointing to one of the armchairs scattered around the shop.

"Thanks." Carolyn sank into the chair, her lower lip trembling. "It's just Sylvia's death—" Tears gathered at the corners of her eyes. Though the room was dim, her pupils were contracted, and Erin could clearly see the luminous green of her irises.

"You two were close, weren't you?"

Carolyn wiped a tear away, nodding. "I can't help feeling if I'd been at the meeting, I could have done something."

"Don't torment yourself like that."

"She and Owen had words at the meeting, but he could never do something like that. You know that, right?"

"I haven't heard anyone suggest Owen had anything to do with it."

"I heard the detectives from York are questioning everyone."

"They came by to talk to me earlier."

"Did they ask about Owen?"

"You know how the police are—they keep everything to themselves until they're ready to pounce."

Carolyn's eyes widened at the word *pounce*.

"Why?" Erin asked. "What have you heard?"

"Oh, you know how people can be," she said, scratching her left wrist, the bracelets tinkling. "I'm probably overreacting. So you haven't heard anything?"

"Nothing about Owen. If I had, I'd tell you."

"He didn't mean to be rude to Sylvia—it's just that he's concerned about Gypsy, you know."

"Your dog?"

"His dog, really. She's been off her food lately, and he's worried. He apologized to Sylvia afterwards, just before she—"

Erin laid a hand on Carolyn's arm. "I'm sure it'll come out during the investigation."

Carolyn's shoulders relaxed, but the muscles on her face were still taut. "Thank you, Erin—I knew I could count on you."

"Why are you so worried?"

"Well, it's just that Owen and Sylvia have never hit it off, and . . . well, you were there the other day."

"The Sunday meeting?"

"I heard it was pretty bad between them."

"Not that bad," Erin lied, partly to soothe Carolyn's feelings but also to keep her talking.

"And then they fought again the night she—she was . . ." Carolyn bit her lip to keep from crying. "I just can't believe she's gone."

"You missed both meetings. Owen said you weren't well."

"Yes, that's true," she said, pretending to study a volume of Augustan poetry.

"Are you feeling better?" Erin asked, wondering why Carolyn was such a hopeless liar.

"Much better, thank you."

After Carolyn had gone, Erin tucked the poetry anthology back into the shelf. Almost no one was interested in Augustan poetry. Highly stylized and dry, it had emerged before the blossoming of the Romantic era that began with William Blake, reaching its peak with writers like Wordsworth, Coleridge, and Keats. She kept the book just in case a scholar or poetry fanatic dropped in.

What was the real reason for Carolyn's visit? She and Erin weren't particularly close, though she admired the older woman. Carolyn was clearly hoping Erin had some information but was wary of asking for it straight out.

Going to the bookcase next to her stereo system, she pulled a well-worn CD from the rack. When confronted with a problem like this, there was nothing for it except J. S. Bach, or as she called him, The Man. Sliding the disc from its cover, she opened the CD player and popped it in and turned up the volume. She lay on the burgundy sofa with the curved back as the opening passages of Bach's *Mass in B Minor* filled the room. Propping her head up with a couch pillow, she pondered the situation.

Owen Hardacker and Sylvia Pemberthy's lack of amity was deeper than their disagreements within the society. As in *Pride and Prejudice*, their mutual distrust was based on notions of class and breeding. Both were wealthy, but Sylvia affected posh airs, whereas Owen was intent on portraying himself as a man of common sense and working-class values.

Erin tried to imagine Owen as a poisoner. She could imagine him loading someone full of shotgun pellets—he kept a couple of guns on hand to shoot grouse—but even that was a bit of a stretch. Owen Hardacker was quick to anger, but she didn't see him as a poisoner. That required premeditation and a certain coldness of character.

But then, as she knew from countless true-crime stories, given the right circumstances, anyone could be the murderous type. What about Carolyn herself? Had there been a falling-out with Sylvia of some kind? Maybe she'd met Sylvia in the alley where she died and slipped something into her tea.

And what of Suzanne Becker? She had every reason to want Sylvia dead, and she had conveniently discovered the body—perhaps a little too conveniently, Erin thought. It was almost a cliché in crime solving that the person who "discovered" the body might be the killer. Another cliché, of course, was the notion that poison was a woman's tool—but plenty of men had taken that route as well.

As the majestic strains of Bach filled the room, Erin vowed this was one killer who would not escape—she intended to make sure of that.

Chapter Nine

～

Jerome Pemberthy lived in a gracious two-story brick Edwardian on an acre of land at the edge of town. A dark-blue Rover sat in the circular driveway, its highly polished metal gleaming in the pale morning light. As Erin approached the house Wednesday afternoon, the chunky white gravel crunched beneath her feet, and she rapped on the elaborate brass knocker in the shape of a lion's head.

Jerome Pemberthy opened the door. Tall and lean, clad in a black turtleneck, tan slacks, and a beige corduroy jacket with suede elbow patches, he looked the part of a college don, with his square spectacles and distracted air. Erin thought the jacket was laying it on a bit thick. He even had a little brush of a mustache, beginning to gray, and a Meerschaum pipe poking out of his breast pocket.

"But I didn't order a book," he said when Erin presented him with the heavy tome *Medieval Magic: The Origins and Practices of Alchemy*.

"I came across it and thought you might like to have it."

"It's rather expensive," he said, frowning. "Quite a rare edition."

"It's a gift."

Astonishment crossed his face, replaced immediately by suspicion.

"What for?"

"All I want is a few minutes of your time."

"Very well. It's like Victoria station in here today," he added with a sigh.

"I saw the police as they were leaving. What did they want?"

"Oh, you know—the usual nonsense. Did I kill my wife, and if not, who else did?"

"I am so sorry about Sylvia."

Pemberthy gave a short laugh. "Really? Then you're one of the few. I have no illusions about her popularity around here. Why don't you come through and sit down?" he said, leading her into a well-appointed study with potted wood ferns, leather furniture, and built-in floor-to-ceiling bookshelves. A ceiling fan rotated slowly on its axis, the fern fronds waving gently in its wake.

"Sylvia's the gardener," he said, noticing her admiring the flowers. "Or was. Don't know what I'll do with them now. I'm not much good at growing things. So much you take for granted when someone's alive, and then . . . well, enough of that," he said, his voice breaking. Either he was a very good actor or was genuinely upset. "Please, make yourself comfortable," he said, settling his wiry body into a chocolate-colored leather armchair with matching footstool. "Now then, how can I help?"

Erin had never felt very cozy around Jerome Pemberthy—he was a remote, stiff presence who made Mr. Darcy look fuzzy and warm by comparison. But now she felt sorry for him, looking so forlorn among the profusion of potted plants, a reminder of his wife's absence. She perched on a matching brown sofa, the leather smooth and cool against her skin.

"I really am so sorry about Sylvia," she began.

"But you want to know whether or not I killed her."

"I was just wondering if you had any thoughts about who could have done it."

"Poison's meant to be a woman's game, isn't it?"

"Actually, it's more complicated than that."

"You're into that sort of thing, aren't you?" he said, pronouncing *that sort of thing* as if it were an unsavory bit of spoiled food.

"I am interested in crime, yes—"

"Then why don't you help the police sort it out? They strike me as a couple of oafs, Laurel-and-Hardy types."

"I hardly think that's a fair description."

"Can't stand blokes like that," he said, lapsing into a more colloquial accent. "Think they bloody well know everything."

Erin wondered what the accent change meant, or why he was so resentful of the police. "When did you last see your wife?"

Pemberthy plucked the pipe from his pocket and made a rather elaborate show of stuffing it with tobacco. "I was home when she left for the meeting."

"And after that?"

"I was here, grading papers."

"Sylvia was found in the alley next to the church. Someone could have slipped poison into her tea out there."

Pemberthy stopped filling his pipe. "Do you really think I would drive to the church and lurk in the alley on the off chance she might show up there? Not to mention the poison I conveniently thought to bring along in case she happened to have a cup of tea with her?"

"I've read about much stranger crimes than that."

"What a pity for an attractive young woman like yourself to be consumed with such tawdry things."

"You used to live in York, and you still teach there. Why did you relocate to Kirkbymoorside?"

Pemberthy leaned back in his chair and lit his pipe, taking his time about it. He drew from the pipe and exhaled a plume of smoke. "Do you want the reason we gave publicly or the real reason?"

"Both, if you don't mind."

"We told people we wanted a quieter life, which wasn't entirely a lie, but it wasn't the whole truth either."

"What was the whole truth?"

"My wife wanted to be nearer her lover."

Erin had to admit she hadn't foreseen that answer. "And who might that be?"

"Kurt Becker, of course. Oh, I didn't know about it at the time—I doubt I would have agreed to move if I had. But I found out soon enough. And his wife Suzanne found the body. Doesn't conventional wisdom say that more often than not the killer is the one who 'discovers' the body?"

"I didn't realize you had an interest in crime too."

"I *read*, Miss Coleridge."

"Can you think of anyone who might want to harm Sylvia?"

"Apart from everyone in the Jane Austen Society?"

"Really?"

"I'm exaggerating, but you know as well as I do—"

"You teach history, right?"

"Medieval history. Appropriate subject in a town with medieval origins, don't you think?"

The hall clock chimed, breaking the mood. Pemberthy stood and shook the pipe ash from his jacket. "I have a class. If I don't leave soon, I'll be late," he added as his mobile phone rang. Sliding it from his pocket, he glanced at the screen and silenced the ringer.

"Do you need to get that?" she asked.

"It'll keep. Was there anything else you wanted to know?"

Erin took a deep breath. "Carolyn Hardacker."

"What about her?"

"I believe she taught at York Uni as well, didn't she?"

"She used to, yes."

"So you were colleagues?"

"We were in different departments, but I knew who she was."

"Why did she leave?"

Pemberthy ran a hand through his neatly cropped salt-and-pepper hair. He would be an attractive man, Erin thought, if it weren't for his habitually pinched, sour expression.

"Look, I probably shouldn't be telling you this, but rumor was that she was let go."

"Do you know why?"

"No—and I heard it secondhand, so I wouldn't necessarily trust it. University campuses are hotbeds of gossip, you know."

"That's what my father says."

"Your father?"

"He's at Oxford."

"Oh. Well, then," he said, and Erin sensed for a moment she had the upper hand. "Do you think Carolyn had something to do with it?" he asked.

"I'm just trying to clarify some things."

He gave a short laugh. "You sound just like them—the police, I mean."

"I'll take that as a compliment."

"If you insist," he said, not hiding his disdain. "But now I really must go. Mustn't be late for class."

"Thanks for your time."

"Shall I see you out?" he said, looking for something in his jacket pocket.

"I'll manage. Thanks again."

Erin was acutely aware of her footsteps echoing on the highly polished floors as she walked through the narrow hall leading to the foyer. The heavy black door closed behind her with a thunk, and her shoes crunched on the gravel drive as she headed for her car.

Climbing into the Sunbeam, Erin was putting on her seatbelt as Jerome Pemberthy emerged from his house, mobile phone to his ear, in heated conversation. Though she couldn't hear his words, it was clearly an emotional discussion. He seemed oblivious to her presence as he climbed into his car and pulled around to exit his circular drive, still on the phone.

Erin wondered what was so important that he would break the law and risk getting a traffic ticket. She knew just how hefty the fines were, having received one herself for using her mobile at a stoplight. After cranking the Sunbeam's engine, she drove the little sports car around the driveway. When she reached the street, she turned in the direction of Farnsworth Appleby's house.

Chapter Ten

~

"Sounds like Jerome Pemberthy was being a wanker, as usual," said Farnsworth, pulling the kitchen curtains closed. The sun had long since set, and the warm day had given way to a considerably colder evening. Drafts seeped in through the farmhouse's ancient walls, and the thin flowered curtains did little to dispel the chill in the air.

Erin leaned her elbows on her friend's cluttered kitchen table. "That's not what bothers me."

"What bothers you?"

"The fact that he wasn't very curious about who killed his wife. Either he doesn't care enough to wonder who did it, or he already knows."

"So Carolyn Hardacker was fired?" Farnsworth said, sitting heavily into one of the sturdy oak chairs at the table. "I thought there was something wonky going on with her."

Erin looked at the ceramic bowls heaped with bits of string, empty pouches of catnip, loose batteries, spare change, rubber bands, and pieces of broken china plates. Erin was used to her friend's ways, though sometimes she had an urge to dive in and clear the cobwebs and clutter from the rambling, ramshackle farmhouse. But Farnsworth seemed so content with her life that it seemed churlish to question her housekeeping. Erin liked her own orderly habits but tried not to judge her friends, though with Farnsworth it was a struggle.

"Did Jerome say where he heard this?" Farnsworth said.

Erin plucked a rubber band from one of the bowls and twisted it around her fingers. "No, but he admitted it was just gossip."

"Still, it would explain a lot," Farnsworth said, stroking a glossy black cat that jumped onto her lap the moment she sat down.

"What do you mean?" Erin said, a nudging emptiness in the pit of her stomach as she realized she had been trying hard not to acknowledge her own suspicions about Carolyn.

"Don't tell me you haven't noticed her erratic behavior and mood swings? And you told me she was acting strangely when she came to see you."

"I put it down to being worried about Owen, but now I'm beginning to think—oh."

"What is it?" said Farnsworth, leaning forward so that she nearly knocked the black cat from her lap. The animal protested with a loud meow, digging its claws into to her ample thighs. "Ouch!" she said. "Stop it, Lady Catherine! So what *is* it?" she repeated.

"Her eyes," said Erin.

"What about them?"

"I noticed it at the time, but I was just thinking about what a beautiful color they were."

"Noticed *what*?"

"It was dim inside the store, because I had turned off most of the lights, but her pupils were tiny. I was too busy admiring how green her eyes were to realize that—"

"Pinprick pupils are a sign of opioid addiction."

Erin cocked her head to one side. "How did you know that?"

"I used to be a nurse, remember?" Placing the black cat gently on the floor, she rose and lumbered to the sink. "This, I think, is a three-pot problem," she said, filling the kettle with fresh tap water.

"Very clever," Erin said, recognizing the famous quote from *The Hound of the Baskervilles*. "Conan Doyle would be pleased."

"He's more likely to be turning in his grave—he'd be much happier if I were quoting *The White Company* or another of his 'serious' novels."

Erin smiled. "If I were him, I'd be glad to have created one of the most memorable characters in all of fiction."

"Quite right," Farnsworth agreed, spooning tea into a pink rose-petal teapot. "And don't let it get around that I quoted someone other than Jane Austen, or I shall be summarily ejected from the society."

"My lips are sealed. Though I wonder what will become of the society now."

"There's to be a meeting tonight to decide what to do next."

"Last time I looked, there was crime scene tape everywhere."

"They just took it all down."

"So it's no longer a crime scene?"

"Apparently not, so Pru and Hetty are putting together a meeting. I told them I would let you know. They were originally going to do it over the weekend, but Reverend Motley couldn't attend—he's going to some retreat or other."

"Lucky us."

Farnsworth gave an evil smile. "I think he's sweet on you."

Erin rolled her eyes. "You *think*?"

"Play your cards right and you could be the next Mrs. Reverend Horace Motley."

"'Oh joy, oh rapture unforeseen.'"

"I'm afraid I'm going to have to insist that we quote only Jane Austen from now on," Farnsworth said, getting up as the teakettle came to a boil, its shrill whistle piercing the air. "Gilbert and Sullivan are nice, but we must get in the mood for tonight's meeting."

"But you just quoted Conan Doyle!"

"A lapse of judgment on my part, for which I shall atone by

forgoing sugar in my tea—at least the first cup." She returned to the table with the teapot and two matching china cups and saucers. "I'm sorry I don't have any biscuits. So what are you going to do about Carolyn?"

"I don't know. It's not like I'm going to tell the police she's an addict. We don't even know that for a fact."

"That's probably why she didn't show up at the meeting," Farnsworth said, an edge of bitterness in her voice. "And if I hadn't volunteered to take her place, the police wouldn't be focusing on me."

"You can't think like that. It'll drive you crazy."

"You're right, of course," said Farnsworth. "But it's bloody hard being under suspicion for a crime you didn't commit. You see it on the telly all the time, but when it happens to you . . ." She stopped, her voice breaking.

"I'll find the real killer—I promise," said Erin. She hated seeing her friend like this. In spite of her reputation as the Woman Scorned, Farnsworth Appleby was proud, not given to self-pity.

"I know you will, pet." Grabbing a rubber band from one of the ceramic bowls, Farnsworth snapped it at a lanky gray tabby trying to climb onto the kitchen table. "Not now, Bingley!"

"You named him well."

"Yes, he's quite silly. Now, then, shall I be mother?"

"Yes, please," said Erin, but the gnawing feeling in her stomach had returned. She wondered if she would be able to make good on her promise. She was beginning to realize that it was one thing to read about crime in books but quite another to tackle crime solving in real life. "You know," she said as Farnsworth handed her a steaming cup of tea, "there's something off about Jerome Pemberthy. I don't trust him."

"The august Professor Pemberthy, guilty of uxoricide?" Farnsworth said, raising her eyebrows in mock surprise.

"Ux—what?"

"The killing of one's wife."

"How did you—"

"I looked it up. Actually, years ago, when I was having murderous thoughts towards you know who."

"Dastardly Dick?"

Farnsworth nodded. "I didn't seriously contemplate killing him—good thing, too, since the universe dispensed its own form of karmic justice."

"You really believe in all that?"

"No, but it sounds good. And killing one's husband is mariticide, not to be confused with matricide."

"How commendable of to you to educate me whilst serving me tea, Miss Appleby," Erin said, affecting a posh Surrey accent.

"How kind of you to remark upon it, Miss Coleridge," Farnsworth replied, catching on immediately. It was a little game they played, adopting the manner and speech of Jane Austen characters.

"This tea is most excellent, by the way," Erin said. "May I inquire as to what it is?"

"It gratifies me that you find it so—as a matter of fact, it is a rather rare blend of Darjeeling."

"How gracious of you to serve me your best tea. I am humbled by the honor."

"And I am honored by your presence."

They drank in silence for a moment, and then Farnsworth said, "Do you really think old Professor P might have done it?"

"He is the obvious choice—too obvious, maybe."

"How so?"

"With married couples, you look first at the spouse."

"That seems reasonable."

"But if it was Jerome, why would he do it in public, where he has so much less control, and so many potential witnesses?"

"Because they're also potential suspects."

"It's still awfully risky. The vast majority of spousal poisonings take place at home. I can't think of one in a public place."

"There's always a first time. Stop it, Mrs. Bennet!" Farnsworth said to a portly calico trying to pull the tablecloth from the round oak table. The cat glared at her, then dashed out of the room. "She's a real busybody," Farnsworth sighed, straightening the tablecloth. "Always poking her nose where it doesn't belong."

"Which is exactly what I'm going to do," said Erin.

"Mind you don't get it nipped off. Oh, look, it's getting late," Farnsworth said, looking at the ceramic pumpkin clock on the kitchen fireplace mantel. Like many things in her house, it was both quirky and gloriously tacky. "Nearly time for the meeting."

"Shall I help you wash up?" said Erin.

"No time for that—you can drive, though. No point in taking two cars."

"Right," Erin said.

Putting on their coats, they hurried from the farmhouse, leaving the tea things on the table. The unusually warm weather having given way to an autumn snap in the air, their breath was visible in thin white clouds of vapor as they headed for the Sunbeam, parked just a few yards from the kitchen door. As she opened the driver's side door, Erin glanced back at the house to see half a dozen pairs of eyes, yellow, green, and in between, peering out at them from downstairs windows. She shivered a little as the car doors closed with a *thunk*. Starting the engine, she drove away from the safety of her friend's house and into the waiting night.

Chapter Eleven

～

"Order! Let's come to order," Owen Hardacker said as Erin and Farnsworth entered All Souls' conference room. The turnout for the meeting was good—besides the usual stalwarts, there were a few less-familiar faces, though not nearly as many people as on Monday night. The two women took seats in the back of the room—the church basement was drafty, and the temperature outside continued to drop.

They settled into the metal folding chairs, Farnsworth wrapping her long red shawl around her shoulders. Clad only in a long skirt and turtleneck, she looked perfectly comfortable. Erin was already chilly; she could feel the cold metal of the chair under her yoga pants. She buttoned her wool jacket, wishing she had worn a long coat.

Seated two rows in front of them, Reverend Motley turned around to grace them with a smile. Farnsworth gave Erin a little nudge, which she ignored. She spotted Prudence Pettibone in the front row, flanked by Hetty Miller and her husband Winton, his wig listing to one side like a drunken badger. Kurt and Suzanne Becker sat off to the side in the row behind them. Suzanne's hands were folded quietly in her lap, her husband's arm draped around her in a protective—or controlling—gesture.

"I feel more relaxed already with Owen in charge," said Farnsworth.

She had a point. Tragic as Sylvia's death was, there was no

question her presence had increased the aura of tension. Owen Hardacker might not be cuddly, but he was less tightly wound than Sylvia.

At the podium, he shifted his weight and cleared his throat. "Right, then. It were suggested that as former president, I should conduct this meetin'. So the sooner we get this sorted, the sooner we can get to pub, eh?"

His remark was greeted with nods of agreement and a few nervous chuckles. A couple of people glanced back to see Reverend Motley's reaction. Erin thought his shoulders stiffened a little, but like most people in town, the reverend respected Owen—besides, the cleric was known to enjoy a pint or two himself.

"First order of business is t'express our profound sorrow over the tragic death of our late president—" He paused to acknowledge general murmurs of "Hear, hear" and "Well said," as well as a couple of groans. "I'd appreciate if you'd save comments for later," he continued, fixing the groaners with a stern glare. Sitting toward the back, Erin couldn't see where they had come from—someone near the front, she thought. She heard a stifled sob behind her and turned to see Carolyn Hardacker sitting in the backmost row, looking wan. Even without makeup, her face was handsome as ever, but her eyes were dull. She looked ill, and Erin wondered why she had come to the meeting.

"Is Sylvia's husband here?" Owen said, scanning the crowd.

"He had to teach a class," said Erin.

Owen looked surprised. "I see." His tone suggested he did not approve. Did he think Jerome Pemberthy should immerse himself in grief and recrimination? Erin wondered.

She felt another elbow in her ribs, and turned to Farnsworth.

"Don't-look-now-but-someone-is-trying-to-get-your-attention," Farnsworth whispered, nodding her head toward the far side of the room. Erin turned to see Jonathan Alder smiling and waving at her. She smiled in return and turned back to see Owen fumbling with a pair of glasses, struggling to read a sheet of paper on the podium.

"Next item ont' agenda is to elect interim president pendin' general election."

"I nominate Owen Hardacker," Hetty Miller called out. She alone seemed oblivious to the chilly weather, clad in a tight yellow dress and matching three-inch heels, in full makeup. Erin had to admire her consistency—Hetty's wardrobe didn't seem to have a "casual" setting.

"I second the motion!" Prudence Pettibone chirped. Seated between Hetty and her husband, she looked prim and protected.

A few people called, "Hear, hear."

Owen's lean face flushed, and he cleared his throat again. "Are there any other nominations?"

There was a brief silence. Owen persisted. "Would any other candidates care t'come forward?"

"Not unless they want to be poisoned," Farnsworth whispered, and it was Erin's turn to poke her elbow in her friend's ribs.

"All in favor of Owen Hardacker," Prudence shouted shrilly. She was met with a chorus of "Yeas."

"The yeas have it!" Hetty crowed.

"That's odd," Farnsworth whispered to Erin. "I thought Pru was keen for the post."

"The motion is carried," Owen said, looking uncomfortable. Erin couldn't blame him—this was hardly the way a man like him would want to regain power, through the untimely death of his rival. Unless, of course, he was responsible for her death. If he was, she thought, he was doing a good job of playing the reluctant hero. His hands shook slightly as he read from the list. "Next item ont' agenda is public relations."

"Public relations?" said Jonathan Alder. Half a dozen pairs of female eyes turned in his direction. He did look handsome in his school tie and jacket, a blue blazer tailored to fit his slim figure, and Erin felt a tingle in her stomach at the sight of him.

"Since when are we concerned about public relations?" Farnsworth echoed.

"Since Monday," Owen replied grimly. "If press take interest in Sylvia's death, we need publicity director."

"And we don't want the society's image tarnished before the Christmas ball in York," Hetty pointed out. "It's the ten-year anniversary."

The elegant eighteenth-century Twelfth Night ball was the society's biggest fund-raising event, receiving wide press coverage both locally and nationally. Sylvia had been instrumental in creating it and had been inordinately proud of her role in raising the society's prestige and visibility.

"I nominate Prudence Pettibone," Hetty called out.

"I second the motion," Winton said immediately.

Their responses were so perfectly timed, they seemed rehearsed. Farnsworth noticed it too. "So *that's* their plan," she said under her breath.

A couple of attempts were made to put Jonathan forward for the post, but he demurred, and in the end, Pru's nomination prevailed. She pretended to be surprised, but even seated behind her, Erin could see the satisfied set of her shoulders.

The meeting broke up sooner afterward, with an agreement to keep members updated via email regarding the investigation into Sylvia's death. Prudence stood by the exit, armed with a legal pad, collecting any missing email addresses from the members as they filed out the door. She appeared to be enjoying herself hugely, a smug smile on her pinched face. Her husband stood nearby, watching serenely, hands at his sides, wearing a bulky gray tweed jacket circa 1955. They were not a glamorous couple, Erin thought, but they were a happy one.

"No tea break," said Farnsworth as she and Erin sat watching the room clear out. "Just as well, I suppose."

"Hello, ladies."

Erin looked up to see Reverend Motley approaching them, weaving through the rows of chairs like an ocean liner cresting the waves. Clad in his usual long cassock with shiny brass buttons down the front, his balding pate shone with oil, his small blue eyes moist behind round spectacles.

Farnsworth stepped forward, extending her hand. "Why, Reverend, how nice of you to make time in your busy schedule to join us."

Clearly she was playing at something, but Erin wasn't sure what—maybe trying to save her from unwanted attention?

Reverend Motley looked puzzled but quickly broke into a broad smile. "Ah, Miss Appleby." He beamed. "'There is nothing I would not do for those who are really my friends. I have no notion of loving people by halves, it is not my nature,'" he said, with a glance at Erin.

"How clever of you to quote Austen so astutely!" Farnsworth said. "Prudence would be quite envious of your literary prowess."

"Oh, she is the acknowledged maven of Austen quotes," he replied modestly, turning once again toward Erin, but Farnsworth seized his arm.

"I wonder if you might have a moment to clarify a point of scripture I have always wondered about," she said, pulling him away.

Irritation flickered across his pudgy face, quickly replaced by an unconvincing smile. "Of course—how can I be of service?"

"It's about a certain passage in Genesis," Farnsworth said.

Gripping him firmly by the elbow, she dragged him toward the other side of the room. Erin watched them go with amusement, musing that he was nearer Farnsworth's age than her own—not to mention closer to her girth. She hoped her friend had not done her job so well that she would find herself in the reverend's sights.

"That was a narrow escape."

She turned to see Jonathan Alder approaching her.

"Escape?" she said, feeling her neck becoming warm.

"Don't tell me you didn't see what the reverend was up to—or how your friend so deftly saved you. I could see it from across the room."

"Saved me from what?"

Jonathan shook his head, and Erin couldn't help noticing how his dark curls bobbed. "No wonder men are such basket cases around women! We think we're being obvious, but it turns out—"

She laid a hand on his arm. "I was just teasing. I knew what he was up to, and I appreciate Farnsworth's intervention."

"Perhaps you shouldn't be so keen to spurn his advances. After all, he does have the weight of the Church of England behind him."

"And who knows?" she said. "He might make a remarkably attentive husband."

"I should think any man would be attentive to you," he remarked, one lock dark hair falling onto his forehead.

"I believe that the reverend 'thinks it a right thing for every clergyman in easy circumstances (like himself) to set the example of matrimony in his parish.'"

"Touché," Jonathan said, clutching his side. "Fending off my compliment with an Austen quote."

"I've been told I'm not good at accepting compliments."

"A correct diagnosis, I believe."

"I shall endeavor to redress that shortcoming."

"As you are one who must receive a fair number of compliments, I suggest you begin your reformation efforts at once," he said, smiling to reveal small, pearly teeth.

"I shall apply myself to the discipline with fervor."

"To quote your august ancestor, 'Love is flower like; Friendship is like a sheltering tree.' Do think of me if ever you're in need of shelter," he said, tipping his cap politely.

Watching him go, Erin felt her heartbeat slowly return to normal. He had adopted the same tone of playful banter she and Farnsworth used, displaying appealing wit and intelligence. He certainly knew how to pique her interest. As she stood admiring the graceful way he walked, the bounce of black curls with every step, she had to admit she was intrigued. The question now was what she was going to do about it.

Chapter Twelve

❧

Thursday morning went by without any customers, so Erin took down the OPEN sign and sat down at the piano, determined to conquer (or at least come to a draw with) Bach's C minor prelude from *The Well-Tempered Clavier*. She had not played since before Sylvia's death, and her fingers felt stiff and rusty. After struggling with it for half an hour, she finally nailed the fingering in the section leading into the coda. Playing Bach was like entering a deep, lush forest—the canopy of trees was lovely, but it was easy to lose your way.

She played a little Mendelssohn as a reward, then a few George Shearing tunes, and called it quits after an hour or so. She looked at the kitchen clock—it was just past eleven, a perfect time to drop by Kurt Becker's bakery. The morning rush would be over, and the lunchtime rush wouldn't start for at least an hour.

Pulling a clingy blue cotton dress over her ubiquitous yoga tights, Erin drove into town, pulling up in front of Fresh and Hot bakery. The young girl at the front counter directed her to the back of the store, where Becker was sliding a rack of hot cross buns into the oven.

Dressed in a long white apron, bits of flour clinging to his fingertips, Kurt Becker looked innocuous enough. His spiky blond hair, teased into points with plenty of gel, gave him a hipster vibe, reinforced by his square black glasses. Turning to see her, the baker gave a tight little smile. He looked as if he hadn't slept much—his eyes were rimmed with red and his skin had a pasty pallor.

"Hello, Erin. Please, sit down," he said, pointing to a chair at a large rectangular table. Made of polished blond wood, it was waist-high, covered with a fine dusting of powder—the baker's main workstation. Several large blue ceramic bowls sat at one end, covered with dampened dishcloths. Erin was transported to her mother's kitchen, watching her bake bread—the sweaty, yeasty aroma of rising dough erasing the intervening years in an instant.

"I brought you a book," said Erin, taking it out of her knapsack.

"*Die Sonette an Orpheus*," he said, looking at the cover, "by Rainer Maria Rilke. *Sonnets to Orpheus*. How did you know?"

"You were looking at it last time you were in the store, so I thought you might like to have it."

"That's very thoughtful of you." His eyes welled with tears, and he turned away to brush some flour from his apron.

"I like Rilke too," she said.

"'*Wer, wenn ich schriee, hörte mich denn aus der Engel Ordnungen?*'"

"'Who, when I cry, would hear me among the angelic orders?'"

"Your German is very good."

"I'm cheating. It's probably his most famous line of poetry."

"Still," he said, turning the book over in his hands. "Do you know that an ancestor of mine once painted his portrait?"

"Oh?"

"Paula Modersohn-Becker. She was an early expressionist. You are a descendent of an English poet yourself, correct?"

"From a cousin of his, actually."

"Mind if I work while we talk?" Becker said. Taking the towel off one of the ceramic bowls, he slid the raw dough onto the table and sprinkled flour over it.

"Of course," she said, noticing that white flour looked exactly like powdered arsenic.

"I actually wanted the book to give to Sylvia, as a present," he said, slapping the dough to flatten it. He gave a little cough to cover what sounded like a sob. "Sorry. It's been a bad few days."

"There's a rumor going around that you—"

"I would think it's more than a rumor," he said bitterly. "I suppose some people think I'm behind her death."

"Like who?"

"For all I know, half the town thinks I'm guilty."

"Are you?"

"Of adultery, yes," he said, working the dough with his strong hands. "But not murder. I cared for Sylvia, and her death . . . as I said, it's been a difficult week."

"Were you and Sylvia in love?"

"People here bandy that word about a lot, but I'm never quite sure what they mean by it. She wasn't planning to leave her husband, as far as I know, and I wasn't planning on leaving my wife. But we did care for each other."

Erin watched the baker pummel the dough, kneading it with his palms before sprinkling it with more flour.

"Surprisingly violent, isn't it?" he said. "Dough has to be treated firmly—like women." When she didn't respond, he stopped and wiped some sweat from his brow. "I hope you recognize a joke when you hear it. I thought you English were fond of humor."

"And Germans aren't?"

"That is our reputation."

"Perhaps this isn't a good time to be making jokes about harming women."

"One of your British playwrights said, 'Women should be beaten regularly, like gongs.' Or something like that."

"It was Noel Coward. The quote is, 'Certain women should be struck regularly, like gongs.' It was a character speaking of his ex-wife."

"Ah—so not the writer's views, then."

"And it was another time period."

"Timing has never been one of my—how do you say—strong suits. Oh, *Scheisse!*" Dropping the dough onto the table, he rushed over to the oven, which was beginning to smoke. Grabbing a thick pair of hot pads, he opened the oven door and pulled out the tray of hot cross buns.

"I came within seconds of burning them," he said, sliding the tray onto the top shelf of a metal rack next to the oven. "That's what comes of not setting the timer. Baking is a precise science—any distraction can be disastrous."

"I'm sorry if my presence is a distraction."

He picked up a towel and waved it over the steaming buns. "I've always liked you, but why are you asking all these questions?"

"Because the police think Farnsworth did it."

A laugh escaped him—a short, sharp sound closer to a bark. "*Unglaublich.* Why would they—"

"Because she served tea that night."

"So you're working to clear your friend's name? *Sehr ehrenvoll.*" He removed a ball of dough from another of the bowls and flung it onto the table, pressing it into the wood with his palms.

"It doesn't feel especially noble."

"I told the police and I'll tell you too. Sylvia and I were both about to break it off—"

"You were getting tired of each other?"

"I had my wife to consider. Suzanne is . . . fragile, and my actions were causing her pain. I was finding it hard to live with myself."

"So you didn't poison Sylvia because she dumped you?"

"I wasn't even near Sylvia when she—" Again his eyes welled with tears, and he took a deep, shuddering breath. "*Gott im Himmel*, if she was killed because of me, I—" Stopping abruptly, he went back to kneading the dough, pounding it violently with his fists.

"You'll what?"

He stopped his work and looked Erin in the eye. "Someone needs to pay for this."

"They will," she said. But the words felt hollow as they rolled off her tongue, and she sensed the enormous gap between desire and deed.

As she left the shop, Erin had a sudden impulse to look in the alley next to the building. Walking through the narrow passage dividing the bakery from the insurance company next door, she saw a row of rubbish bins along the high wooden fence. Lifting one of the lids, she poked around inside and saw household trash, takeaway containers, industrial-sized yeast packets. Just as she was about to replace the lid, a flash of red caught her eye. Reaching in, she carefully extracted an empty red-and-yellow bag. Her heart pounded as she read the label. THE BIG CHEESE PROFESSIONAL STRENGTH RAT & MOUSE KILLER.

She hesitated. Was this evidence, and if so, should she turn it in to the police? Or had they already seen it? But surely Kurt Becker was too intelligent to leave the empty bag if he had in fact poisoned Sylvia . . . or, like a lot of killers, was he simply arrogant and careless? As she was debating, her mobile phone rang. She dug it out of her pocket, nearly dropping the phone in her haste.

"Hello?"

"Just wanted to let you know the coppers are on their way over to interview Pru and Winton," said Farnsworth.

"How do you know?"

"I was having lunch at the Kings Head just now, and I overheard them talking about it."

"Well done—I'll head over there."

"What are you going to do?"

"I'll find out when I get there."

"Be careful, pet."

Erin smiled as she slid the phone back into her pocket. They both knew being careful was not her strong suit. She hesitated before carefully replacing the poison bag in the rubbish bin. Best to disturb the scene as little as possible—if indeed the bag did turn out to be evidence.

*　*　*

Prudence Pettibone lifted her kitchen curtain to peer out the window as a battered blue Citroën pulled up in front of the house. She'd known a visit was inevitable but felt nervous all the same. She let the curtain fall and dithered, trying to decide whether to change out of the comfortable slippers she wore around the house. Winton never seemed to mind, bless him—no matter how she dressed, he always said she looked beautiful. She knew it wasn't true, but she loved him for it.

"Here come those blasted policemen," she muttered as he strolled into the kitchen, newspaper in hand. Many of her friends got their news online or on the telly, but Winton was old-fashioned and liked his morning paper with a good strong cup of tea. He stood in the doorway, mug in one hand and paper in the other. Dressed in a gray cardigan over a red flannel shirt and black wool pants, he didn't look that different from the day they were married—except for the horrid toupee, of course. She knew people made fun of it, and it did look like a groundhog nesting on his head, but if it made him happy, she wouldn't be one to nag him about it. Over the course of their marriage they had found ways around each other's sharp edges, nestling into the soft places, until they fit together like a well-made piece of furniture.

"Do you think I should change?" she asked. "Or is it better to just be casual with them?"

"I don't see why it matters," he remarked mildly. "You haven't done anything wrong."

"But my heart's fluttering just at the thought of talking to them."

He drained the rest of his tea and set the cup in the sink. "They've a job to do, Pru—just let them do it, and try not to fuss too much."

"Oh, Mr. Bennet," she said, hugging him impulsively. She sometimes called him Mr. Bennet because he was so sensible, so calm and wise. "Whatever would I do with you?"

"I've no earthly idea," he said as the doorbell rang.

Chapter Thirteen

Erin Coleridge stood on the Pettibones' doorstep for several minutes before ringing the doorbell. DI Hemming's blue Citroën was parked in front of the house, so she knew he was in there. She had hoped to overhear some of the conversation, but the house's thick walls made eavesdropping impossible. She would have to go inside. It was risky—he might conclude she was following him, which was sort of true.

She rang the bell. The sound of footsteps was followed by the sound of a deadbolt sliding open. The door opened to reveal Prudence, dressed in her usual mishmash of ill-fitting clothing, her mouse-colored hair pulled back in an untidy bun. Her face brightened when she saw Erin.

"Hello, Erin—come to rescue me, have you?"

"From what?" Erin said, as Detective Hemming appeared behind Pru.

"Just kidding," Prudence said nervously, holding the door open. "Come in, please."

"Hello, Detective," Erin said, wiping her feet on the mat.

"You do get around, don't you, Ms. Coleridge?" he said, standing in the entrance to the foyer with his arms crossed. Erin couldn't help noticing the solid outline of his muscles, even under the wool jacket.

"I just dropped by to tell Mrs. Pettibone—Pru—that the book she ordered came in."

Pru frowned. "But I didn't—"

Erin glared at her. "You know, the one on *orchids*."

"Oh, yes, of course!" Pru said, catching on. "How lovely it's arrived."

"Why didn't you bring it with you?" Hemming asked.

"What a nice coincidence running into you, Detective," Erin said.

He cocked his head to one side. "Is that what it is, Ms. Coleridge—a coincidence?"

"You're not suggesting I'm *stalking* you?"

"What I'm suggesting is—"

He was interrupted by the appearance of Winton, who padded soundlessly in from the parlor. He stood behind Hemming, hands in his pockets.

"Hello, Winton," Erin said.

"Hello," he said, a smile following his words with just enough of a pause that it was clearly the product of practice rather than a natural impulse. *On the spectrum*, Farnsworth liked to say. Erin was drawn to people like Winton and felt protective of him, maybe because he reminded her a little of her father.

Winton turned to Hemming. "Did you have any more questions for us?"

The detective looked at Erin, then back at them. "I suppose that's enough for now. But I may need to talk to you later. I'd appreciate it if you don't leave town."

Prudence smiled. "The last time we left town was in 2008."

"It was 2009, I think," said Winton. "My niece's wedding."

"In Surrey," said Prudence. "They have a wonderful society branch down there—very elegant."

"Bit fancy for my taste," said Winton. "Fussy, you know. They—"

"Thanks for your time," Hemming said, backing toward the door.

"Wait—I'll walk you to your car," said Erin.

"Wouldn't you like to stay for tea?" Pru asked, sounding disappointed.

"I'll be right back," Erin said, following the detective out.

They stood on the front stoop, the soft October sun glinting off the rooftops behind them. A slight breeze ruffled Hemming's blond hair, and Erin wondered what it would be like to run her hand through the thick, wavy locks.

"There is no orchid book, is there?" he said, looking her in the eye.

She returned his gaze. Finding it impossible to lie to him, she said nothing.

"What do you want, Ms. Coleridge?"

"I want to find out who killed Sylvia."

"Why don't you leave that to the professionals?"

"Because you're already on the wrong track! Farnsworth could *never*—she's not capable of—"

"If Ms. Appleby is innocent, that will become clear in good time."

"Meanwhile, she's just supposed to squirm in her shoes? Do you have any idea what it's like being suspected of being a criminal by the police?"

"I do, as a matter of fact."

That brought her up short. She stared at him, hoping for an explanation, but he pulled on his hat and started toward his car.

"Kurt Becker has a bag of rat poison outside his shop!" she called after him.

He stopped walking and turned around. "How do you know?"

"I saw it."

"When?"

"Today, just before I came here."

"Thanks," he said, climbing into his car.

"It's in the alley!" she called as he started the engine. She wasn't sure if he heard her or not. With a puff of smoke, the old car rolled forward, rattling off down the road.

Detective Hemming had an air of world-weariness she found appealing. She couldn't help noticing other details: he could do with a haircut, the collar of his tweed jacket needed turning, and his shoes hadn't seen polish for some time. She concluded he was accustomed to a woman's presence but had none in his life at the moment. The absence of a wedding ring was confirmation of her theory—men like him always wore one if they were married. She concluded he was divorced, recently enough that he hadn't yet adjusted to living alone.

She gazed at the darkening sky as she waited for the Pettibones' front door to open in response to her knock. Rain clouds glowered in the distance, and a wind had picked up, scattering dead leaves at her feet.

Winton opened the door and beckoned her in.

"Pru's just put the kettle on." It was as if he was reciting rehearsed phrases rather than making up his words on the spot. "Please, come through," he said, ushering her through the foyer into the living room. Dominated by a huge stone fireplace, it was small but cozy, the low ceiling boasting lovingly restored oak beams, and had wide plank hardwood floors. The old house smelled of oiled wood and pinecones.

"Make yourself comfortable," he said, pointing to an over-stuffed burgundy armchair.

"Thanks. I know you've told me, but what year was this built?"

"In 1591," he said, beaming. "The original structure, at least, which we're in now. The kitchen wing was added a century later."

"You've done such wonderful work restoring it."

"No trouble, really, when it's your passion. I'm a thatcher, y'see, born and bred. My father afore me, and his father—it's in the blood, y'might say." It sounded like a phrase he had repeated many times. "Here," he said. "Take a look at this." Removing a penlight from his pocket, he aimed it at the thick wooden beam over the fireplace, revealing half a dozen vertical nicks carved into the wood. "Legend has it these were left by Robert the Bruce hisself—one for ev'ry British officer he killed."

"Impressive," Erin said. She wasn't about to challenge Winton on it, whether she believed it or not. "Don't you find old houses tend to attract rodents? Mine's not as old as yours, but I know they like to creep inside as soon as the weather turns cold."

"Whole town's had a problem lately, hasn't it?"

"Farnsworth says her cats keep them away."

"Pru has allergies, I'm 'fraid. No cats here."

"Here we are," said Pru, entering the room carrying a huge silver tea tray. Tarnished and stained, it looked as old as the house itself.

"Let me do that, love," Winton said, taking it from her and putting it on the coffee table.

"Terrible business, Sylvia's death," Pru said, clucking her tongue as she perched on the edge of a well-worn plaid sofa. "It's put the fear of God into us—hasn't it, Winty?"

He nodded placidly. "Indeed it has."

"Poor Sylvia, so full of life—she didn't deserve this," Pru said, her face tragic.

"You did recognize her, uh, good qualities, love," Winton, said, shifting uneasily in his chair. Clearly he was not comfortable improvising dialogue.

"Well, she could put on airs," she said, handing Erin a cup of tea, "but I'm *hardly* the only one in town who thinks so."

Erin turned to Winton. "You were on the tea committee that night."

"And a busy time we had of it. Never saw such a crowded meeting. Workin' fast as we could, afraid we'd run out of supplies."

"So you didn't see anyone slip anything into Mrs. Pemberthy's tea?"

"Didn't have time t'notice much of anything. She were int' alley for quite a while—couldn't someone have done it then?"

Erin frowned. "That hardly seems likely."

He turned to his wife. "You said you were int' alley when Sylvia came out."

Color flooded Pru's pale cheeks. "Well, yes, I—I stepped out for some air, but as soon as I saw her, I marched right back inside."

"I didn't know you saw her out there," Erin said.

"It was only for a moment, as I said."

"Did you notice anything suspicious?"

"Well, no . . . not that I recall," Pru replied, avoiding her gaze. "Oh, dear, is that the time?" she said, looking at the clock over the mantel. "I really must be getting dinner on."

"Thanks for the tea," Erin said, rising from her chair.

"I'll see you out," Winton said.

As Erin headed to her car, the clouds parted to reveal a gentle, lemony light falling over the town of Kirkbymoorside. Starting the engine, Erin resolved that though she might not endear herself to DI Hemming, she wasn't going to let him intimidate her into backing off. She turned the Sunbeam toward town as the last rays of sunlight sank behind the buildings, followed by a brief flash of green.

Chapter Fourteen

By the time Erin arrived home, it was dark. Driving up the long, muddy driveway, she parked the Sunbeam next to the front entrance, which led through the shop. She shoved the key into its metal slot and twisted, the deadbolt sliding open with a hollow click. She usually enjoyed her cottage, but tonight, walking through the darkened rooms, switching on lights, she felt jumpy and unsettled.

Peter Hemming's face appeared in her mind's eye, a damp lock of blond hair falling over his forehead. She didn't want to admit it, but his nearness had created a deep longing she hadn't felt in a while. Grabbing a pen and scrap of paper, she jotted down a line: KINGDOMS HAVE BEEN LOST FOR A LOCK OF HAIR, A SIDELONG GLANCE, A HOPE OF HEAVEN IN A FAIR FACE. She might use it later to construct a poem around.

It was near dinner time, but she wasn't hungry yet, so she decided to arrange some books in the shop. She tried to do a different section every week, partly to keep things in order, but also to remind herself of books in stock in case customers asked for something specific. The best bookstore owners seemed to have a photographic knowledge of their inventory—lacking that, Erin did her best to refresh her memory. It had been a while since she had reviewed her forensic section, so she decided to start there.

It was in pretty good order, but when she got to the *P*s, she realized one of her favorites, *The Poisoner's Handbook*, was missing. She nearly always had a copy in stock—it was a lively, well-written book, and sold well. She went to the sales ledger she kept in her little desk by the front door, but no one had bought a copy recently. As she was pondering this, her phone rang.

"Hello," she said as a yawn fought its way up her throat.

"Did I wake you?" Her father sounded surprised, and a little disapproving.

"No, I was just taking inventory."

"Ah, I see." His amused tone suggested he didn't believe her. "I'm just checking in, since I haven't heard from you."

"Sorry—we had a bit of bad news this week." *"A bit of bad news." Good lord, how British can you get?*

"What happened?"

"Sylvia Pemberthy. She . . . died." *Why couldn't she just come out and say murder?*

"Wasn't she the new society president?"

"Yes," she said, going through the beaded curtain separating the shop from her living quarters.

"How did she die?"

"She was poisoned."

"On purpose?"

"I'm afraid so. The police are investigating."

"Good lord. Are you all right?"

"I'm fine," she said, flopping back onto the living room couch.

"Now I'm worried."

"'Do not give way to useless alarm; though it is right to be prepared for the worst, there is no occasion to look on it as certain.'" Erin's ability to quote Austen was easily equal to Pru's, but Erin didn't believe in showing off every chance she got.

"No doubt Jane Austen is very wise, but I'd fret less if you were safely married."

"I could say the same about you."

"Ah, but you're young yet."

"And you're the most eligible bachelor in Oxford, Mr. Bennet."

"You flatter me. I'm nowhere near as sensible as he is."

She imagined him in his study, leaning back in his swivel chair, feet up on the desk, a hole in the toe of one Argyle sock, smoking his weekly cigarette, a Sobranie Black Russian. He kept only one picture on his desk, of Erin and her mother, taken when Erin was eleven. They were standing arm in arm in Piccadilly Circus, her mother radiant, confident, glimmering with zest for life. Erin was squinting into the camera, apprehensive but glad to be with her mother, clutching her arm tightly. The location was appropriate; life with her mother was a circus—a big, happy merry-go-round that had stopped abruptly, leaving her and her father reeling with residual centrifugal force.

"Tell you what," Erin said. "I'll get married if you will."

She waited for his usual response. *No one could ever measure up to your mother.* A lousy excuse, but he still trotted it out like a washed-up racehorse.

Instead he said, "Do the police have any leads?"

"They haven't finished interviewing all the witnesses," she said, wrapping herself in the afghan from Farnsworth. She went on to tell him of the contentious meeting and the ensuing chaos in the society.

"Good lord," he said when she finished. "It's like a bloody soap opera. Wouldn't be surprised to hear Sylvia has an evil twin somewhere."

"There must be nearly as many suspects as witnesses, but so far no one seems to know anything."

"There's at least one person who does," he said.

Even wrapped in her afghan, Erin shivered. She had been thinking the same thing. Outside, the barn owl screeched, the harsh sound of a predator stalking its prey.

Chapter Fifteen

～

An hour later Erin stood at the takeout counter of Moorside Fisheries, a small shop on Church Street, waiting for her order of fish and chips. Thursday was her night to indulge in the crispy fried treat; the fish was always fresh in preparation for the big Friday rush. Kirkbymoorside was home to only a small percentage of Catholics, but half the town seemed to come in on Friday. The village boasted two excellent fish-and-chips shops, and Erin toggled between them—next week she would go to the Lemon Tree.

Rain pummeled the streets outside, wind flipping the canvas awning up and down furiously. A storm had whipped up from the coast, blown inland, and looked to be settling in for a few days. Pools of water gathered in the roads, creating pockets of impassable crossings and rivulets of rushing rain water. Umbrellas were useless, ripped to shreds by renegade gusts of wind. Erin watched out the window as people dodged puddles, hopped over eddies, dashing in and out of doorways. She was grateful to be relatively dry, having found a parking spot just outside the shop.

She watched as the owners worked alongside their two employees. Helen manned the cash register, while her husband Ravi fried long strips of battered cod to a golden brown. Erin's mouth watered as she watched the boiling oil bubble and burble around the fish, imagining the tender, flaky cod inside the eggy batter.

"Hungry?" Ravi said, seeing her stare at the fryer. He was a sweet-faced Indian with a scraggly beard, black eyebrows, and a bald head.

"Starving."

"Here's an extra piece for you," he said, sliding another piece of cod on top of the already generous serving. That wasn't unusual—Ravi and Helen were popular with their customers because of not only their excellent food but also their friendliness and generosity.

"Cheers, Ravi," she said, knowing it was useless to protest. Ravi enjoyed taking care of his customers but was also a savvy businessman.

As she went up to pay for her food, she saw Detective Hemming enter the shop. He didn't see her, so she had a chance to observe him as he studied the menu. He wore a long dark raincoat, sleek with rain, no hat or gloves. His profile was classic, with a long, straight Viking nose, full lips, and firm chin. She didn't know if it was a Viking nose, of course, but there was something distinctly Nordic about him—with his high forehead, blond eyebrows, and blue eyes, he looked like he belonged aboard a seagoing vessel.

"Six pounds twenty, please," Helen said, snapping her out of her reverie.

"Sorry," she replied reflexively, true to the British character—when in doubt, apologize. *We're a race of sorry sods*, she thought.

"Bit of a looker, innit?" Helen said with a glance at the detective. She was originally from Saltburn and had a round, open face framed by dark-brown curls.

"I suppose," Erin said, feeling the color spring to her cheeks.

"Wouldn't mind bein' questioned by the likes a' him," Helen added with a wink as she handed Erin her change.

As Erin pocketed the coins, Detective Hemming saw her and

gave a little wave. She waved back, and was about to leave when he walked over to her.

"You really *are* stalking me."

"I come here every other Thursday—ask anyone."

"What do you recommend?"

"I usually get the cod."

"A codpiece for me, then," he said, smiling.

What was with the Shakespearean pun? And why was he so friendly? Just a few hours ago he'd been telling her to sod off. Her glasses were beginning to fog over, and she removed them to wipe them off.

"Are you related to Samuel Taylor Coleridge?" he said, apparently in no hurry to place his order.

"I'm descended from his second cousin."

"So owning a bookstore was a natural choice for you. I'm surprised anyone can make a go of it these days."

"I do most of my business online. I deal in a lot of rare books."

"I've always enjoyed Coleridge."

"Anything in particular?" she said, half hoping to catch him in a lie.

"'Christabel'—it's so erotic."

"And terrifying."

"'Tis the middle of night by the castle clock, And the owls have awakened the crowing cock.'"

"Well done," she said, surprised.

"Do you know he was influenced by the feminist philosophy of Mary Wollstonecraft?"

"Yes, I did," she said, even more astonished he knew of Mary Shelley's less famous mother.

"Ready to order, sir?" Ravi said from behind the counter. The shop was filling up, and several people had lined up behind them, clumping in wearing muddy green Wellies and sodden jackets. The front window was completely fogged over by now, the air steamy from the fryer and the bodies jammed into close quarters.

"Cod and chips, please," Hemming said.

"Tartar or curry sauce?"

"Tartar, please."

"The curry sauce is quite good as well," Erin said.

"I'm too set in my ways, I guess."

"Any promising leads?" she said as he waited for his food.

"I can't really discuss—"

"An ongoing investigation," she finished for him, noticing a slight smile that he tried to hide. "I'll tell you something, then."

"What's that?"

"Jerome Pemberthy knew about his wife's affair."

"Did he tell you that?"

"He did. Cheers," she said, and was out the door before he could say *iambic pentameter*. Clutching her now somewhat soggy bag of fish and chips, she dashed across the street and climbed into her car for the short drive to her cottage.

She slipped a CD into the player—she had recently discovered the work of the Welsh composer Karl Jenkins and had fallen in love with *The Armed Man*, probably his best-known work. She sat back, her mind floating along with its mysterious melodies and haunting harmonies.

The little sports car had good traction and did well in bad weather, but the storm increased, rain pelting the windshield so hard she couldn't see, so she pulled over near the entrance to Owen Hardacker's farm. She couldn't make out the house through the downpour, but she could see all the lights were on, blazing brightly through the rain and mist. She wondered if they were entertaining—Carolyn enjoyed throwing parties—but that would be odd so close to Sylvia's death. Erin had always had the impression she and Carolyn had been pretty tight.

A couple of sodden sheep huddled near the gate, looking miserable, their oily coats shiny with rain. Owen had a nice big barn, so she wondered what they were doing out in this weather. Sheep weren't very bright, but even so, Erin was surprised to see them. She had half a mind to tell Owen, but feared he might find it intrusive. He had the temperament of a typical Yorkshireman—independent and stubborn.

The rain finally abating, she started to turn the key, preparing to drive away. But something about the way the sheep were standing struck her as odd—they seemed to be sniffing at something on the muddy ground. Rolling down the car window, she poked her head out to see if she could make out what it was. It was too dark, so she pulled the torch from the glove box and got out to have a look.

Glad to be wearing her Wellies, she squished through the muck to where the sheep stood, huddled side by side. They watched her as she approached, the beam from the torch reflecting off their horizontal pupils, which contracted as the light hit them. They stepped aside to make room for her, watching her with mild eyes. Aiming the beam at the spot on the ground they had been sniffing, she saw, half buried in the mud, a familiar red-and-green tweed cap. She bent down to pick it up. Wiping off the caked-on dirt, she saw that it was Owen's tweed cap, the one he wore wherever he went. Shoving it into her pocket, she turned and slogged back to her car.

The rain was accelerating again as Erin pulled her collar closer around her, tucking the torch into her jacket to keep it dry. It pelted her head and shoulders as she sloshed back to the car, hunched over to keep the rain from her face, cursing herself for leaving the umbrella in the car.

Inside the car, she sat for a moment, her brain working, her warm breath fogging the windows. Finally she cranked the engine and put the little Sunbeam in gear, the tires spinning in the mud as she turned toward home, away from the big farmhouse on the hill.

Chapter Sixteen

～

The funeral, scheduled for two o'clock Friday afternoon, was delayed due to the large crowd filing into All Souls. The pews were already packed when the policemen arrived—not so much a tribute to the deceased as curiosity about her lurid death, Peter Hemming thought. He and Detective Sergeant Jarral were forced to stand in the back, next to Chief Constable McCrary, looking uncomfortable in a stiff dark-blue suit, his sparse hair combed back severely, his abundant mustache gleaming with wax. He gave a curt nod and glared at the backs of the attendees' heads, as if he could glean the murderer's identity by the way they parted their hair.

The altar was festooned with an abundance of gardenias, the air thick with their heavy scent, and Hemming felt his nasal passages swelling. He fished a damp handkerchief from his pocket as the minister began his invocation. It was a formal, old-fashioned Protestant service, sprinkled with standard funeral hymns such as "Abide With Me," "All Things Bright and Beautiful," and "Jerusalem."

It was not an open coffin. Hemming remembered attending the service of an elderly Catholic aunt as a boy. Though warned by his mother to expect an open casket, nothing could have prepared him for the ghastly waxen apparition he saw when he peered over the side of the box. Having heard people murmur things like "so life-like," he was struck by how utterly *un*lifelike she looked. She looked dead, like a *thing*, and he wondered why anyone would want to be preserved as an object when the force that had illuminated them in life was clearly gone.

He was glad to see there would be no teary-eyed remembrances or invitations to share touching anecdotes about the recently departed, the kind of emotional free-for-all Americans were so fond of. Hemming had seen too many people succumb to the temptation of a captive audience and had sat through flowery speeches—often fueled by alcohol—that devolved into rambling, self-indulgent monologues.

After the hymns, Reverent Motley stood to deliver the eulogy. His bald head reflected the afternoon sun streaming through the stained-glass windows, giving the appearance of a halo. He cleared his throat officiously, regarding the crowd through wire-rimmed spectacles.

"We come here today to honor our beloved sister Sylvia, who was so rudely torn from our midst. She was a loving wife, faithful friend, and loyal supporter of All Souls." He paused, and Hemming thought he heard someone snicker. Undeterred, the reverend soldiered on.

"Her untimely death serves not only as a reminder of how precious life is, but also a warning that while God may forgive the sinner, He does not condone the sin." Surprised, Hemming looked at Constable McCrary, who looked equally nonplussed.

"Therefore," Reverend Motley continued, "I urge any of you with knowledge about Sylvia's death to come forward as soon as possible before something else dreadful happens." This was met by a general murmur from the assembly, and Hemming heard someone weeping. Craning his neck, he saw the sound was coming from Carolyn Hardacker. Seated next to her husband, head bowed, she was sobbing quietly, a handkerchief pressed to her eyes.

The rest of the eulogy went on to praise Sylvia's qualities and accomplishments, but Hemming was only partially listening. He was wondering what, if anything, the reverend knew, and why Carolyn Hardacker seemed so cut up about Sylvia's death.

The eulogy was followed by a rendition of Schubert's "Ave Maria," sung by a sturdy-looking soprano in a powder-blue gown. As her tremulous tremolo filled the church, Hemming fished around in his pocket for his handkerchief. The gardenias were making his eyes water, and he hoped to forestall a sneezing fit.

Sergeant Jarral appeared to share Hemming's views on funerals.. He shifted his weight impatiently as the wavering warbler geared up for a second verse. When it was over, he brushed a bit of lint from his lapel and yawned.

The one concession to modern custom was a bulletin board filled with pictures from Sylvia's life. After silently observing the line of people filing past the display, the two policemen stepped up to look at the pictures.

Judging by the photos, Sylvia was quite the animal lover—hardly a unique trait in an English village—but Hemming had seen no sign of pets at the house she shared with her husband. Yet the board was littered with pictures of Sylvia on horseback, hugging a grinning spaniel, and, as a young child, clutching an enormous white pet rabbit.

Jarral seemed to be reading the detective's mind. "Odd, isn't it, sir?" he said, studying a photo of Sylvia astride a handsome chestnut, resplendent in creamy jodhpurs and shiny black riding boots. "I didn't see any sign of pets at her house."

"Yes," Hemming agreed. "Not so much as a wisp of cat hair."

"I wonder what changed in her life?" Jarral mused, looking at a photo of a young Sylvia on a couch holding a large orange tabby. "Allergies, perhaps?"

"Ah, gentlemen—I'm *so* glad you could make it!" a cheery female voice behind them said.

Hemming turned to see a tall, angular woman with vermillion lips and matching fingernails. She was a clash of reds, from her dyed hair to her bright cherry-colored frock and floral scarf, attire more appropriate for a cocktail party than a funeral. Her age was impossible to guess, but he would have put money on the fact that the skin stretched tightly over her cheekbones was the work of a surgeon's scalpel. She was such an odd apparition he couldn't help staring, which apparently she took as a sign of interest. She lowered her head and gave a sly smile from beneath mascara-smeared lashes.

"No one told me what attractive emissaries the York Constabulary sent us. I heard you were in town, but I must say, the reports did you no justice."

Taken aback by such blatant flirtation, Hemming glanced at Sergeant Jarral, who stood there slack-jawed, apparently also thrown off by the onslaught of feminine charm.

"Hetty Miller," she said, extending a slim hand. "Please, call me Hetty."

Looking at the crimson talons, Hemming hesitated before shaking her hand. Her grip was surprisingly firm, the fingers thin but strong.

"Detective Inspector Hemming," he said. "And this is Detective Sergeant Jarral."

"Delighted," she said, swiveling her slim hips to face the sergeant. "I spent some time in Pakistan myself—charming place. The men are *so* handsome. Is your family from the Kashmir or Punjab branch of the Rajput tribe?"

The sergeant's lifted eyebrows registered his surprise. "We're, uh, Punjabi."

"I *thought* so! The men are better-looking there. Will you be attending the reception?"

"Yes," Hemming replied.

"Good. And to save you the trouble of asking: no, I didn't particularly care for Sylvia, but I didn't kill her. I wish I knew who did, but I'm afraid I can't help you there. Any other questions, I will of course be only too glad to answer. Toodle-oo—see you at the reception!"

And with that, she turned on her spiky high heel and strutted away in a trail of lily-scented perfume, joining the mourners filing into the narrow hallway leading to the reception room behind the sanctuary. Her perfume made him sneeze, but Hemming had to admire how she had managed to control the entire encounter. Normally he would consider it suspicious behavior, to say the least, but Hetty Miller seemed so genuinely wacky that he had to wonder what motivated her.

"Punjabi, eh?" Hemming said. "How the blazes did she know that?"

"Either she's done her homework or has spent time in Pakistan. The Jarrals are a Rajput tribe from those two areas of Pakistan: the Kashmir, which is just north of India, and the Punjab, to the west."

"She could have learned that easily enough on the Internet."

"But why do all that research just to trot it out for us?"

"Good question."

He turned to see Chief Constable McCrary coming toward them, looking uncomfortable, trapped in his wool suit. Even his prodigious mustache seemed to droop. "I hope you're planning t'attend the reception," he said. "We'll not find a more concentrated gathering of potential suspects. And the food will be brilliant."

"Lead on," said Hemming.

"I'm famished," Jarral added.

The aroma of roast lamb and potatoes floated through the hall as they turned the corner leading to the spacious reception hall. Hemming's stomach contracted with hunger pangs—it had been a long time since breakfast, and they had worked straight through lunch.

*   *   *

Erin Coleridge stood in the back of the church watching the line of mourners waiting to get into the reception room. Cursing herself for arriving so late—she'd missed the first few minutes of the service—she was determined to make up for it by doing a little spur-of-the-moment sleuthing.

She hadn't yet seen Jerome Pemberthy, so she decided to prowl the nooks and crannies of the church in search of him. Walking through the sanctuary, she ducked into a side hall leading to the vestry. In the cloakroom she saw Reverend Motley changing out of his clerical robes. Taking a deep breath, she put on an impersonal but friendly smile.

"Beg pardon," she said, "but have you seen Jerome?"

Startled, the reverend turned, and his expression changed from annoyance to delight when he saw her. "Why, hello there," he said, his watery blue eyes shining.

"Hello," she replied coolly. "Do you have any idea where Jerome is?"

"I believe the grieving widower stepped out for a breath of air," he said in a lugubrious voice.

"Cheers," she said, and fled before he could say anything further.

The side door was just down the corridor and led to the small garden to the east of the church. Pushing it open, she saw Jerome leaning against a pin oak, phone to his ear. She didn't need to hear his words—his body language said it all. From the tilt of his head to the smile on his face, it was clear Jerome Pemberthy was talking to an intimate, probably a lover. Quietly she slipped back into the building and, without a word to the reverend, hurried back through the sanctuary to the reception.

The buffet table was crowded, so she lingered at the entrance, scouting the room. Her eye was caught by Jonathan Alder and Carolyn Hardacker, huddled together in the back of the room. He was listening intently to something Carolyn was telling him, and Erin burned to know what they were saying. She took her phone from her clutch purse and pretended to be engaged in looking at it. Hugging the wall, she sidled toward them, all the while gazing at her phone. When she was a few feet away, she stood on the other side of a ficus tree and listened to their conversation.

Carolyn was saying, "It's a small sum—to me, at any rate."

"Does Owen approve?"

"I do have my own money, you know."

"I'll do my best to earn it."

"I'm tired of living selfishly."

Jonathan smiled. "Perhaps in practice, but surely not in principle, as Mr. Darcy would say."

"Listen to us!" Carolyn said, tears springing to her eyes. "Consoling ourselves by quoting Jane Austen, as though that could save us. But I fear I am lost."

"Nonsense!" he said, taking her hand. "Stop such foolish talk."

"We are all fools in love," she said sadly. "There I go again—I'm afraid Prudence is rubbing off on me."

"The important thing is that there was—is—love," he said earnestly. "Surely that counts for something."

"You won't tell anyone?"

"Cross my heart and hope to die."

"There has been enough death already."

Listening to them from her perch on the other side of the fig tree, Erin had to agree.

Chapter Seventeen

"That smells brilliant," Sergeant Jarral remarked as the policemen joined the line of people gathering around the remarkably lush buffet. In addition to the lamb and mashed potatoes, there were salads and platters of fresh fruit as well as hot and cold hors d'oeuvres. The shrimp cocktail platter alone must have cost a fortune. There was even a platter of haggis, and a roast beef with Yorkshire pudding, as well as the inevitable chicken tikka masala.

As the men loaded their plates, Hetty Miller swooped down on them like a bird of prey.

"One thing about Kirkbymoorside," she said, chewing daintily on a maraschino cherry, "we do brilliant funerals. It's like a competition—people expect a spread fit for a king. It's our tradition."

"Well," the detective replied, spearing a slice of pineapple from an elaborate fruit display. "It looks like you've outdone yourself."

"Remind me not to die here," Sergeant Jarral muttered when she had gone. "I can't afford it."

"No one else is going to die here if I can help it," Hemming said, studying the crowd as they joined Constable McCrary at one of the large round tables covered in pale-pink tablecloths.

"What, no haggis?" Sergeant Jarral said, looking at the Scotsman's plate.

McCrary shuddered. "Ach, no—vile stuff!"

"But it's the Scottish national dish."

"Aye, all the bits the landlord didn't want. Stomach, intestines, an' all that. I'll stick to roast beef and Yorkshire puddin'."

"This is the true British national dish," Hemming said, taking a bite of chicken tikka masala. "At least according to the British foreign secretary." It was delicious—spicy and creamy and sweet, with a generous amount of cardamom.

"Aye," said McCrary. "Though it comes from Scotland."

"What?"

"He's right, sir," said the sergeant. "It was invented by a Pakistani chef at the Shish Mahal restaurant in Glasgow. I've been there—quite a good place, actually. Very similar to the dish my uncle makes."

"Is there anything your family *doesn't* do?" Hemming asked.

"We're not terribly good at football, though I do have one cousin who played on the Welsh national team."

"Of course," said Hemming.

He looked around the room. Prudence and Winton Pettibone shared a table with Hetty Miller and Farnsworth Appleby. Hetty was laughing at something Farnsworth had said, a bit of spinach dangling from her teeth. The Pettibones seemed lost in their own little world, Prudence whispering something to her husband, who listened with the same placid expression the detective had noted earlier. He had to admire the couple's devotion—they were both such odd ducks they were lucky to have found each other.

The detective was helping himself to more shrimp at the buffet when he saw Erin Coleridge walking toward him. Clad in a black form-fitting full-length dress, strawberry-blonde hair piled on top of her head, she cut an elegant figure, more glamorous than the young woman in yoga pants and sandals he had met earlier.

"You clean up well." It was something his father used to say, and he had no idea why it suddenly popped out of his mouth. He'd never cared for it when his father said it.

Judging by the look on Erin's face, she didn't either. "I'm guessing you meant that as a compliment."

"I meant to say you're the best-dressed stalker I've ever seen."

"Have you seen many?"

"More than I'd like."

"By the way, how was the cod?"

"Very good, thanks."

"Next time try the haddock."

"I might even make a haddock out of it."

Erin groaned.

"One of my more irritating traits, I'm afraid—making bad puns."

"What did you make of Reverend Motley's eulogy?" she said, spearing a kiwifruit with a toothpick. The deep green complemented her strawberry-blonde hair. "I think he knows something. Have you interviewed him yet?"

"You're thinking the cleric did it?"

"I just think he knows more than he's letting on."

"Pastor future?" he said, and she groaned again. "Sorry, but I did warn you."

"Poisoners tend to be specific types," she said, reaching for a slice of mango. "Are you narrowing your search based on that?"

She was, as his father would say, an original text. "Have you tried the tikka masala yet?" he said. "It's excellent."

But she would not be swayed. "There's a cluster of personality traits they tend to exhibit, such as cunning, secretiveness, vanity—"

"If our government were as single-minded as you, the sun would still not be setting on the British Empire."

"It's my hobby, remember?"

"Maybe you should take up backgammon."

"You have a little smudge of sauce on your chin."

"Oh, saucy Wooster."

She made a face. "You're right—your puns really are terrible."

"Better?" he said, wiping his face with his napkin.

"Not quite. Here, let me," she said, and before he could stop her, she swiped his chin with her napkin. Her touch was gentle, and—lingering? Or did he imagine it?

"Thanks," he said. "How did you get so interested in crime?"

"My father is a minister. I went in the other direction, maybe as a form of rebellion. What about you?"

His collar suddenly felt too tight, and he was aware of perspiration gathering around his neck. A piece of shrimp seemed to be stuck in his throat. He gave a little cough to dislodge it.

"Why did you become a policeman?" she asked, spearing a piece of honeydew melon with her toothpick.

He gulped down some beer, swallowing the stuck piece of shrimp.

"My parents were murdered."

"Oh my God," she said. "I'm so sorry."

"I'm afraid it's a bit clichéd, my becoming a detective, but there you have it."

"Did they catch whoever did it?"

"No. The case is still open."

"What did your parents do for a living?" she said, frowning. Her eyebrows were blonde over deep-set eyes, with long pale lashes beneath the thick-rimmed glasses.

"They were on the faculty at Edinburgh Medical School."

"Oh, god. How awful."

"It was a long time ago." The concern in her eyes made his stomach jump a little, not unpleasantly.

"There's Owen and Carolyn Hardacker," she said, pointing to the far side of the room, where the couple sat in deep conversation, a half-empty bottle of Glenlivet in front of them. "I wonder what they're talking about."

"Is your friend Ms. Appleby still here?"

"She had to leave, I'm afraid."

"Erin?" said a child's voice behind him.

He turned to see a gangly, pale girl of about ten, holding the hand of a boy who could only be her brother. He appeared to be a year or two younger, the family resemblance unmistakable—the same white-blond hair, freckled skin, and pale-blue eyes. It was as if the painter who created them had swept the canvas with water, washing any vivid colors into a pastel version of the original. Their dark clothes emphasized the effect—the girl wore a black velveteen dress with a little red bow (probably her Christmas frock), the boy dapper in a dark-blue suit and clip-on tie over a crisp white shirt, a pair of oversized horn-rimmed glasses giving him a studious look. His mother would have approved, Hemming thought wistfully—she liked it when children were "properly turned out."

"Hello there," Erin said, greeting the children warmly. "Are you getting enough to eat?"

The girl rolled her eyes. "James Chester had three helpings of tikka masala. Father said if he has any more, he'll burst like a tick."

"What a charming image," Erin said, wrinkling her nose, which Hemming noticed was thin and straight, delicate but not too short. "This is Detective Inspector Hemming," she told the children. "And these two rascals," she said, turning to him, "are Polly Marlowe and her brother James Chester."

"You're a real-life *detective*?" James Chester said, hopping up and down. "Like on the telly?"

"Of *course* he is," Polly said disdainfully. "But those are just *actors*—he's for real." She turned to Hemming. "You'll have to excuse my brother—he's *different*."

"Am not!" he protested.

His sister rolled her eyes. "Don't have a tantrum right here on the spot."

Erin gave her tinkly wind-chime laugh. "Isn't sibling rivalry delightful? Their father is a butcher—I mean—" she said, reddening.

"I know," Hemming said, smiling. "He owns a shop."

"His name is James Marlowe—everyone calls me James Chester so it doesn't get confusing," the boy interrupted, rocking back and forth. His speech was rapid, with a peculiar flat affect, and Hemming noticed he didn't make eye contact with the adults.

"Where is your dad?" Erin asked.

"He's around here somewhere," Polly said. "Probably chatting up the ladies. Our mother died tragically young," she informed Hemming, obviously reciting a phrase she had picked up. "So our father is on the lookout for a replacement."

"Have you ever met a *murderer*?" James Chester asked him.

"Loads of them."

"*Really*? What are they like?"

"They're like everyone else, silly," his sister scoffed. "You can't tell someone's a murderer just by *looking* at them."

"Sometimes you can," said Hemming.

"H-how?" James Chester said, his pale eyes wide.

"Yeah—how?" his sister echoed. Dropping her superior attitude, she chewed on her right thumbnail.

"Time for all good children to go home," said a tall, loose-limbed man Hemming assumed was their father.

"But we're *not* good children!" Polly said, thrusting her chin out defiantly.

"Another reason you should go home now," he said. His somewhat rounded face was lent some gravitas by a pair of wire-rimmed glasses; he had the same fair skin as his children, with a spray of freckles. His hair was darker than theirs, thick and wiry with a reddish tint, severely combed to one side, which failed to tame its unruly waves. Though tall, he wasn't especially athletic looking, with the sort of soft body likely to go to seed in a few years. But Hemming could see how, in the right light and minus the glasses, some women might find him attractive.

"James Marlowe," he said, offering his hand. "You must be the policemen everyone is talking about. And I'm afraid these two rapscallions are my offspring."

His hand was big and bony, the knuckles protruding, and his clasp was strong, the grip of a man who used his hands.

"Detective Inspector Hemming, York Constabulary."

"Please let me know if I can be of any assistance in solving Sylvia's murder," he said. "She may not have been a saint, but no one deserves that."

"How did you get on with her?" Hemming asked.

Marlowe ignored the question. "Any of these people could be the killer, right?" He gave a nervous laugh and ran a hand through his wavy hair. "Well, time to get these little munchkins home before someone turns into a pumpkin."

Peter, Peter, pumpkin eater, had a wife and couldn't keep her. The children's verse ran through his head. Had Jerome Pemberthy killed his wife out of frustration at not being able to keep her at home?

"Let us stay a while longer, please, Daddy?" Polly begged, pulling at the sleeve of his jacket, which was barely long enough to cover his bony wrists. Marlowe definitely had the look of a man without a woman in his life—a look Hemming knew all too well, being himself a member of that pathetic tribe.

"*Please*—he was telling us about *murderers!*" James Chester pleaded, latching onto his other sleeve.

"I'm sure Detective Hemming has better things to do," his father said. "And I'm sure you both want to go to the bonfire later this month, so I suggest you behave."

"You see how he resorts to threats against us?" Polly told Erin.

"He's right," she said.

Polly crossed her arms and scowled. "You grown-ups *always* stick together!"

"You see what it's like having children?" Marlowe said, adding hastily, "Not that I'd have it any other way—they're good kids, really."

"And good children go home when their father says it's time, don't they?" Erin said.

Polly groaned dramatically, arching her back as she clung to her father's hand, while James Chester attached himself to Marlowe's leg, burying his face in the thick tweed jacket.

"We're *not* good," he whined, echoing his sister.

"Come alone, then," James Marlowe said, unmoved by theatrical gestures. "Say good-bye to the nice detective."

"Good-bye, nice detective," Polly said, punctuating it with another eye roll.

"Good-bye, nice detective," her brother repeated, giggling, as their father hauled them both off, one in each arm.

"They are good kids—really," Erin said.

"In spite of their protestations to the contrary," Hemming answered, watching them walk away, wondering why Marlowe had ignored his question. "If you'll excuse me, I must mingle."

"Yes, of course," she said, a flush creeping up her neck. "Good seeing you again. Sorry about the stalking."

"I was rather beginning to enjoy it."

"Ouch!" a voice said as he collided with the person behind him.

"Sorry," he said, turning to see Hetty Miller, a wine glass in her manicured hand.

"No worries," she said sweetly, giving him a toothy smile. With her red cocktail dress two sizes too small, lips and fingernails painted the same fire-engine shade, she resembled an over-the-hill madame. Lowering her voice to a conspiratorial level, she added, "I suppose you're casing the joint for potential suspects?"

Good lord. Was everyone in this town marinated in police show clichés? "Everyone is a potential suspect," he replied, "including you."

To her credit, she rebounded quickly. "Of course I am," she said sharply. "And don't you forget it!"

She spun around and stalked away. Hemming watched her teeter off on four-inch stilettos, her backside swaying in its snug cocoon of red satin. He sighed. Why did he feel so protective toward Erin Coleridge, whereas something about Hetty Miller goaded him into rude behavior? He'd apologize later; he'd had enough for today.

Draining the rest of his beer, he spotted Sergeant Jarral across the room, surrounded by a gaggle of admiring women. Hemming frowned—their job wasn't to entertain the townsfolk. He shouldered his way through the crowd, ears tuned to catch stray bits of conversation, a technique he had honed over the years. You never knew what might be useful—he'd once tracked down a murderer based on a stray remark overheard in the local post office.

"My cousin has a dog like that," Jarral was saying to a comely young woman with dark braids as Hemming approached. "After a while, he started to look just like his dog."

The assembled females giggled and gurgled and tossed their curls. Hemming had to admit Jarral had something—he didn't exactly understand it, but then he wasn't a fresh-faced village girl whose main impression of the police was crusty, remote Constable McCrary.

Rashid flashed his pearly teeth as a silver-haired old dear in a flowered frock slipped her arm around his.

"I feel ever so much safer knowing you're here watching over us," she declared, as the other ladies murmured their consent.

"It must be terribly exciting being a detective," said the brunette with the braids, eyes glistening with the fervor of youth.

"Not really," Hemming said, stepping between Jarral and his admirers. Time to put a stop to this nonsense.

"Ah! There you are, sir," Jarral said in a friendly voice, but he looked disappointed. Hemming felt a little bad about interrupting, but they weren't there to boost Rashid's social life.

"May I have a word, Sergeant?"

"Certainly, sir," he said, gently disengaging from the old dear clinging to him like a barnacle.

As the two men stepped away from the throng of women, Hemming noticed everyone else was looking toward the back of the room. Following their gazes, he saw Jerome Pemberthy stumbling toward Kurt Becker, clutching a beer bottle in his right hand.

"You bloody Kraut," Pemberthy snarled, his eyes bleary with liquor. "Why don't you go back to where you came from?"

Owen Hardacker reached for his arm, but Pemberthy shook him off.

"Don't you think you've had a bit too much, Jerry?" Hardacker said.

"Oh, we've *all* had too much," Pemberthy snapped. "Too much of bloody foreigners, with their snug little shops and snide little wives." He wheeled around to face Becker. "That skinny wife of yours couldn't satisfy you, so you had to mess around with mine!"

Kurt Becker had been listening calmly, barely moving a muscle, but now he launched himself at Pemberthy, bringing them both down on the floor, hard. Bones crunched against the wooden floorboards as the two rolled around in a chaotic tumble, limbs askew, clutched in each other's arms. Pemberthy's beer bottle clattered to the floor, rolling underneath a chair. Becker staggered to his feet, only to have Pemberthy kick him viciously in the shins, bringing him down again. This time the younger, fitter-looking German got the upper hand, aiming a few swift punches at Pemberthy's face— to Hemming's eye, hitting not nearly as hard as he might have.

By that time, Hemming and Jarral had crossed the distance between the two combatants and were pulling them apart with the help of Owen Hardacker and Constable McCrary. The four of them dragged the two men toward opposite corners of the room.

Blood trickling from the corner of his mouth, Pemberthy looked dazed, but as the policemen released their hold on him, he charged with a roar toward the German. Stooping to grab the discarded beer bottle, he held it by the neck and smashed it against the chair. Pointing the jagged shards toward his opponent, he lunged for Becker.

Rashid Jarral responded with a perfectly timed rugby tackle. Coming in low, he wrapped his long arms around the professor's knees, bringing him down as the broken bottle skittered across the floor. The time when Pemberthy hit the ground, he stayed down, until Jarral pulled him up by the scruff of his neck and flung him into a chair, as easily as if he were made of straw. Hemming appreciated for the first time how powerful the sergeant was, how smooth and graceful his movements.

"Well done," he murmured as Jarral slapped the dust from his clothes.

"Where'd ye learn tae tackle like that?" asked McCrary.

"I was captain of the firsts' rugby team at school."

"Good on ye, mate," said the constable, patting him on the back.

"Are you all right, sir?" Jarral asked Kurt Becker, who appeared not so much frightened as furious.

"Thank you for your assistance," the German answered stiffly. Hemming thought he probably would have preferred a pummeling to being rescued, but the detective didn't relish the thought of Becker's face slashed to bits. He knelt to pick up the jagged beer bottle from beneath the buffet table, where it had landed. As he stood, he came face-to-face with Erin Coleridge, her blue eyes wide with alarm.

"Are you all right?" she said.

"I'm fine," he said, turning back to the men waiting for him. As he did, he felt her eyes boring into him. *Are you all right?* she had said, not *Is everyone all right?* His skin tingled at the thought that there might be something more between them than was probably good for either of them.

Chapter Eighteen

During the warmer months, Saturday was a busy day at the bookstore, but Erin expected the moody October drizzle to scare off customers and was hoping to curl up with a book and a cup of tea, write poetry, or watch old Ealing comedies. The landline rang at precisely ten, just as she was filling a hot water bottle to put on her aching head. Before Erin could say hello, Farnsworth gave her customary greeting.

"Good morning, pet. Not dead yet, are we?"

"Does a wicked hangover count?" she said, looking out the window at the slate-gray sky hanging heavily over the moors, listening to the steady ping of raindrops on the eaves.

"I hope it was worth it."

"That remains to be seen," she said, testing the tap water to see if it was hot yet. The old pipes rumbled and creaked as the water heater cranked to life. "I'm working on the antidote to a bottle of Montrachet."

"I hope at least you shared it with the right person."

"You cut out early last night," Erin said, cradling the phone receiver between her right ear and shoulder, holding the water bottle under the kitchen faucet.

"Had to get home to my felines. They don't stop needing to be fed just because Sylvia died, you know."

"Poor Sylvia—no respect, even in death."

"Pish tosh. Funerals are for the living, not the dead. And

I wasn't keen to hang about with those detectives staring at me. Did I miss anything?"

"As a matter of fact, you did," she said, describing the fight between Jerome Pemberthy and Kurt Becker.

"I'm glad no one was seriously hurt."

"An ego or two sustained a few bruises."

"It's hard to imagine stuffy old Professor Pemberthy indulging in fisticuffs. It must have been glorious."

Erin laughed, groaning as her head throbbed more violently.

"Wish I were there to make you chicken soup, pet."

"That is extremely considerate of you, Miss Appleby," Erin said, slipping into the posh accent she and Farnsworth used when mimicking Jane Austen characters. "I cannot think why I imagined overindulging in spirits would have agreeable consequences."

"It is a marker of youth to imagine agreeable outcomes for the most foolish behavior," Farnsworth said. "Those of us who should be inured to such wishful thinking are sadly in want of it all too often."

"I will endeavor to apply that lesson and improve my judgment in the future."

Pressing the water bottle to her head, Erin leaned against the sturdy wooden door frame separating the kitchen from the parlor, dark from years of smoke from the fireplace. The wood was warm, yielding to her touch. Sometimes she thought she could feel the tree it had been hewn from centuries ago. Her father labeled moments like that her "spooky self."

"So do you think Jerome Pemberthy killed his wife?" Farnsworth said.

"'We all know him to be a proud, unpleasant sort of man,'" Erin remarked, quoting Mr. Bennet on the subject of Mr. Darcy. "But he seemed genuinely upset when I went to his house. And if he

killed her, why attack Kurt Becker? He drew attention to himself—
the real killer would want to stay out of the spotlight."

Farnsworth snorted. "He's such a tosser."

"That doesn't make him a murderer. I did overhear one interesting conversation, though."

"Pray tell!"

Erin told her about eavesdropping on Jonathan and Carolyn.

"Sounds like he has money worries," Farnsworth said.

"Perhaps he's more like Mr. Wickham than Mr. Bingley."

"Watch yourself with him, pet."

"I'm going to forget about everything and curl up with a good
book for a few hours."

"Emma, get off that!" Farnsworth yelled. "Stop it! I'm sorry,
Erin," she said into the receiver. "One of the cats is about to topple
the—Emma, no!" Erin heard what sounded like a heavy object
crashing to the floor. "Sorry—I must go!"

Erin was about to ring off when she heard call waiting. She
pressed the receiver once. "Hello, Dad." Her father usually called
on Sunday, after the early-morning service.

There was a brief silence, then the sound of someone breathing
into the phone.

"Hello?" she said, a feeling of dread threading its way up her
spine.

Another pause, and then a dial tone. Erin shoved the phone
back into the cradle, then, her hands shaking, dialed 1471 to call
the number back. She let it ring twenty times before replacing the
phone. Her landline was old-fashioned and didn't have caller ID.
She thought of calling the operator to find out where the call origi-
nated but wasn't sure that was even possible. And what if it was just
a wrong number or a simple crank call? It wouldn't do to panic over
nothing, she told herself.

She stooped to lay some kindling in the grate. The nights were growing colder now, and the thick stone walls of her cottage held in the morning chill. She stuffed a crumpled newspaper under the kindling. Lighting a match and holding it to the paper, she watched as the blue flames rose, licking eagerly at the kindling, blossoming yellow and then bright orange.

The cottage felt cheerier as the heat from the fire spread; the throbbing in her head subsided as she put the kettle on for tea. Coffee was too harsh for her stomach, but a good strong cup of Yorkshire tea would do nicely.

Outside, a crow huddled on the nearest branch of the beech tree, shoulders hunched, and gave a hollow caw that was swallowed up by the misty rain creeping over the moors. Winton Pettibone had once told her the tree was older than her house; she wondered if it was true. She also thought about a remark he had made to the effect that whoever had killed Sylvia was targeting her alone and not other members of the society. She agreed with him, but there was a sense of unease among the members, a feeling that they too could be in danger.

She dangled a tea bag into her favorite mug, creamy ivory with a ring of pale-pink hearts, a present from her mother. Pouring in the hot water, she watched as the copper swirls seeped into the clear liquid, turning it red. She settled onto the antique sofa with the chintz upholstery—a relic from earlier times, cheery and hopeful, like her mother. Erin remembered the day her mother picked it out. They were prowling charity shops in Oxford, and she had pounced on it the minute they entered the Oxfam shop on Broad Street.

"There it is!" she cried, her enthusiasm catching the attention of strangers. "Just what I've been looking for!" People looked up from what they were doing and smiled, stiff British matrons in brown tweed skirts and sensible shoes beaming at the sight of her mother waxing eloquent over the virtues of a chintz sofa. It was impossible to be glum when Gwyneth Coleridge was around.

Within thirty minutes she had haggled the price down a third, cajoled them into free delivery, and somehow made it seem like she was doing *them* a favor. Erin left the store filled with awe at her mother's effortless charm—whatever she wanted, she seemed to get. Defeat was not in her vocabulary.

Except, of course, when it came to the cancer. It had spread quickly, implacable and relentless, greedily gobbling up her body's healthy cells. The end, when it came, was ugly and sudden, leaving Erin and her father stunned and reeling with the unfairness of it all.

The phone rang again, and she trembled as she picked it up, hoping it was her father.

"Hello, pumpkin," he said.

"Hello," she said, relief flooding her veins. "How are things Southside?" Since moving north, she had taken to calling Oxford "Southside."

"Foggy and rainy," he said, his voice strangely subdued. "You?"

"The same," she said, looking out the window at the beech tree. Abandoned by the crow, its branches shivered in the misty drizzle.

"Pathetic fallacy," he said glumly. "Even Nature is somber today."

His remark brought an unwelcome realization. It must be the anniversary of her mother's death. Erin purposely avoided remembering the exact date she had died—seeing no point in such morbid anniversaries—but her father never missed it, and always called her on that day.

"Are you all right?" he asked.

"Fine, thanks." She decided not to mention the mysterious phone call.

"Are you hungover?"

"Why do you say that?"

"You always drink too much at funerals."

The last—and only—time she had overindulged was her mother's funeral. She didn't like to think about it.

"There's a tradition here, apparently, to lay on a massive spread of food and drink. I overdid both."

"I'm worried about you. There's a murderer loose."

"They were after Sylvia, not me."

"Why don't you come down to Oxford for a few days?"

"That's tempting, but I'm advising the police on the case." Not strictly true, perhaps, but close enough.

"You're keen on him—the detective, I mean."

"Why on earth would you say that?"

"A father knows these things."

"Shouldn't you be writing your sermon?" she said, looking at the clock.

"I'm taking the day off. Reverend Masters is taking over for me."

"Lucky you, playing hooky," she said lightly, knowing full well why he'd taken time off but wanting to steer away from the subject.

"If you caught a train, you could be here in time to go with me to see her."

"I'm not supposed to leave town," she lied. She was trying to move on with her life and wanted her father to do the same.

"Surely the police wouldn't mind you slipping away to visit your frail old da."

"That hardly describes you."

"I'm turning into a geezer. Yesterday I had to pluck my nose hairs."

"I'll come soon—I promise," she said. "And I'll bring tweezers."

She gazed out the window at the moors, covered in white mist.

The fog had thickened so much she couldn't see very far—it was like the landscape was wrapped in gauze. No telling what dangers lurked outside the snug walls of her cottage.

"Please be careful."

"I will. Good-bye—thanks for calling."

"Bye, pumpkin."

She hung up and wandered back into the kitchen. She didn't like disappointing her father. Not for the first time, she thought about how different she was from her mother. People always wanted things from Gwyneth Coleridge, and she thrived on it; it seemed to feed something deep inside her. Or maybe that was a mask—maybe all that energy and charm hid a secretly solitary nature she was too proud to acknowledge.

Erin hurried to her writing desk, pulled out her poetry notebook, and scribbled down a few brief lines.

WHAT WE ARE ASHAMED OF, WE OFTEN HIDE WITH EXCESS PRIDE.

She wondered if that was true of her mother—whether Gwyneth Gates Coleridge, in her brief and fiery life, had been caught up in a monstrous lie. Taking up her pen, Erin scribbled another line. TRUTHS WE HIDE ARE OFTEN WORSE THAN LIES WE SPREAD WITH PRIDE.

She wasn't entirely sure what all of this meant, or even if it applied to her mother, but one thing remained clear: in the village of Kirkbymoorside, hidden truths and outright lies served to mask the identity of a murderer.

Chapter Nineteen

∾

By lunchtime the fog and rain were lifting, so Erin put up the CLOSED sign and packed a water bottle, a thermos of tea, an energy bar, and a tin of biscuits into her backpack. She stuffed a waterproof rain poncho in the outer pocket just in case—online radar showed a line of showers still hovering over the area. Pulling on her hiking boots over a pair of heavy socks, she climbed into the car and slogged down the muddy driveway.

She needed to clear her thoughts, and a long ramble across the moors was the best medicine. But first she had a stop to make. Turning left out of the drive, she headed toward Owen Hardacker's house.

She found Owen mending the stone wall lining his property, bareheaded, his thinning gray hair standing up in wisps in the brisk wind rolling across the fields. A flock of grazing sheep paused briefly to look up at Erin. As she pulled up alongside him, he turned, squinting, and shielded his eyes against the light. The fog had given way to the kind of backlit glare that was more blinding than bright sunlight. She stepped out of the car, holding out his hat.

"Wondered where it got to," he said, taking it. He turned it over in his hands, as if studying it. "Where'd ye find it?"

She told him, and he nodded, frowning.

"Any idea how it got there?" she asked.

"Aye. Carolyn threw it out t'car."

"Why would she do that?"

"Because she were angry at me," he said, picking up a large stone and laying it on top of the wall. "We'd been fightin'."

"Really?" said Erin. "It's none of my business, obviously, but—"

"It were about her . . . problem."

"You mean her addiction?"

He stared at her. "That obvious, is it?"

"Not to everyone, I think."

"She don' like it when I bring it up, but I can't stand seein' her destroying herself."

"How long has it been going on?"

"She lost her job 'bout six months ago, so at least that long."

"Was that the reason she was fired?"

"I dunno, lass." He sighed deeply. "She won' talk to me 'bout it."

"You think she might talk to someone else?"

"You, y'mean?"

"Possibly."

"She likes you. Just don' mention it t'anyone, all right?"

"I won't—I promise."

"Cheers—and thanks fer th' hat."

"Take care," Erin said, and started back to her car, but then turned around. "Look, don't take this the wrong way, but you didn't—"

"Kill Sylvia? Good lord, woman, I didn' hate her that much."

His voice was sincere, but the glare was in Erin's eyes, and she couldn't see his face. "Sorry," she said. "I had to ask."

As she drove the little car down the winding roads leading to the moors, she couldn't escape the feeling that Owen Hardacker was hiding something. For all his gruff North Country ways, there was something evasive about him. But who was he protecting—himself or Carolyn? She wondered what Elizabeth Bennet would do. Get to the bottom of things, she supposed, which is exactly what Erin intended to do. But even Elizabeth Bennet was capable of misjudging people, an error Erin hoped to avoid. Owen seemed to be exactly what he presented himself as—a hardworking, gruff, honest Yorkshireman. But was he?

She headed north, toward the North York Moors National Park. Clouds gathered over darkening hills, chased by the wind as it rolled over the fields. After pulling up at one of the trailhead car parks, Erin struck out over the moors. She wasn't going to let the weather spoil her walk—if you did that in Yorkshire, you'd never go out.

She had walked less than two miles when the sky began to spit a fine mist of rain. Increasing her pace, she spied a figure coming toward her across the moors. Though a quarter of a mile separated them, she recognized his gait. Hands in his pockets, his wind-blown, wheat-blond hair forming a halo around his head, DI Hemming strode rapidly toward her, covering the distance between them so quickly she didn't have time to compose her thoughts.

"Fancy meeting you here," he said, only slightly out of breath, though the hills were rugged and steep. Instead of his usual jacket and tie, he wore a brown cardigan over a black turtleneck, and woolen knee breeches tucked into green Wellies. The way the black sweater set off his yellow hair made her catch her breath a little.

"Who's the stalker now?" she said.

He gave a wry smile. "What do you say we call it a draw?"

"Are you playing hooky today?"

"I get some of my best ideas roaming the countryside," he said, flashing a smile as the sun made a last-ditch attempt to poke through the rain clouds, glinting off the gold in his hair. Out here, he seemed more relaxed and open, even younger than the stern-faced detective he had appeared to be while on the job.

"Not the best day for it, perhaps," she said, drawing her jacket closer as a gust of wind hit them.

"I prefer cloudy days."

Me too—oh, me too, she thought.

"What brings you out to roam the moors?"

"I get my best ideas mucking about out here as well."

"What sort of ideas?"

"For my poetry," she said, before she could stop herself. She barely knew him—why was she telling him things she kept from her closest friends?

"You take after your august ancestor, then."

"Hardly. I lack his talent."

"False modesty?" he said, cocking his head to one side. She couldn't help notice how well shaped it was, with a high, noble forehead and prominent cheekbones.

"'Nothing is more deceitful than the appearance of humility. It is often only carelessness of opinion, and sometimes an indirect boast.'"

"Was Jane Austen talking about you when she said that?"

"What I lack in talent I try to make up for in fervor."

"As for me," he said, "what is it Darcy says? 'I lack the talent of conversing easily with . . .' How does it go?"

"'With those I have never seen before,'" she finished for him. "So you have added Jane Austen to your reading list?"

"Since being on this case, yes."

"And what have you learned?"

"That 'we do not suffer by accident,'" he said as a distant rumble of thunder shook the air. "We're in for it now," he added as they watched a jagged bolt of lightning jut across the northern sky. "We're miles from shelter."

"There's a stone hut about half a mile that way," she said, pointing to the direction she had just come from.

"'Lead on, Spirit.'"

"I'm sorry, you're only allowed to quote Austen," she said, as her toe caught a protruding root and she fell forward. Before she knew what was happening, his arms were around her, cushioning her fall. She felt his hands grip her shoulders, the firm fingers long and strong, as she inhaled the smell of him, a piny, woodsy aroma, like smoldering fireplace logs. Feeling the blood drain from her head, she dared not look at him. "Thank you," she said. Extricating herself from his grasp, she drew into herself like a cat.

"The ground here can be treacherous," he said as thunder sounded, closer this time, followed by another streak of lightning. Wind whipped across the bare ground, slashing at their faces, nipping their ankles like an angry dog.

"There it is," she said, pointing to a distant stone structure as fat raindrops toppled from the sky. "I'll race you!"

"Do you think that's a good idea?" he called after her as she dashed off across the moors. "You might fall again!"

But with the wind whistling hard and high in her ears, she could not hear him.

Chapter Twenty

~

Peter Hemming stumbled along the muddy dirt path as Erin Coleridge sprang ahead of him like a deer. He cursed himself for not wearing better shoes—the tread on his Wellies wasn't up to the challenge of rain-slickened moorland. Gritting his teeth, he took longer strides, which only made him slip and lose his footing. He hated being bested by a woman, and hated admitting it to himself even more.

And *this* woman, in particular . . . his feelings about her warred with logic, experience, and duty; every sensible instinct told him it was a bad idea, yet an even deeper instinct urged him on.

She reached the stone hut first. As he approached, she turned around and laughed, rain dripping from her nose and blonde eye lashes. He noticed she wasn't wearing her glasses.

"You look a fright, as my mother would say," she said.

"Whereas you look fresh as a daisy," he replied, panting as they pushed open the rotting door, stepping into the crumbling ruins of what was probably once a crofter's cottage. Of the three rooms, overgrown with vegetation, only the front one had the remnants of a roof, crude wooden slats attached to the front of the building. They perched on a pile of stones that had separated from the building's ancient walls.

"I must look like a drowned rat," she said, wiping off excess rainwater from the stones before sitting down.

"It suits you."

She looked away, and they sat for a moment listening to the rise and fall of wind as the storm swelled and receded, like waves on the shore. The *rat-a-tat-tat* of raindrops on the wooden slats was deafening, like a gathering of mad drummers on the roof.

"What did Constable McCrary say to you last night?" she asked. "I saw you conversing in the hall."

He stared at her, shaking his head. "You never quit, do you?"

"Persistence is one of my more annoying traits."

"With your interest in crime, why not join the force?"

"I don't know if I could deal with the reality of it. And I'm sure there's a lot more tedium than we see on television."

"Quite right. Paperwork doesn't make scintillating drama."

"I have my share of drudgery owning a bookstore."

"But you're a writer—isn't that all glamor?"

"Oh, yes, all caviar and cake. With the odd champagne brunch thrown in for good measure. Oh, that reminds me!" Digging a soggy plastic bag from her backpack, she pulled out a packet of ginger biscuits. "Biscuit?"

"My good luck, running into a Girl Guide," he said, taking one.

"I never venture onto the moors without sustenance."

He wolfed it down in one swallow. "That went down a treat."

"Have another. They're small," she said, taking her thermos from the other pocket. "Tea?"

"Ta very much."

"By the way, I don't know if it's important, but I got an odd phone call on my landline yesterday."

"What was it?"

"When I answered, all I could hear was breathing, and then they hung up."

"Did you call back?"

"Yes, but it just rang and rang."

"Do you get many crank calls?"

"I've never had one before."

"If it happens again, let me know and we'll trace it on your phone records."

"Okay, thanks."

She shivered a little, and it took all his willpower not to put his arms around her. "Would you like my jacket?"

"I'm fine, thanks. Would you like another biscuit?"

"Two's my limit."

"I'll save the rest, in case we get stranded again," she said, tucking them back into her coat pocket.

"It's like a scene from Austen, us meeting on the moors like this," he said.

Picking up a handful of pebbles, she tossed them against the stone wall opposite them one by one. "It's occurred to me that Elizabeth and Darcy might not have been so happy ever after. They share the same flaws—they're both proud and stubborn. That could spell disaster in the long run."

"Isn't that heresy?"

"I know that's the traditional ending of a romance, but I think romance is often a corrosive and misleading lie."

"Strong words from a member of the Jane Austen Society."

"Love doesn't always change and improve people," she said. "Sometimes it ruins them."

"And sometimes you just outgrow each other."

"'Happiness in marriage is entirely a matter of chance,'" she said, finishing off the last of her biscuit.

Hemming looked at her shining face, the translucent skin pink and white, like the interior of a seashell. His mobile rang.

"DI Hemming," he said, feeling equal parts disappointment and relief.

"Sir?" The line was bad, and he could barely hear Jarral.

"Yes, Sergeant," he said, shielding the phone from the rain leaking in from the waterlogged roof boards.

"You'd better come to down to the station." His voice crackled in and out, the line full of static.

"What's the matter?"

There was a pause, and he could hear Jarral talking with someone else in the room. Constable McCrary came on the line.

"There's been an incident," the Scotsman said.

"What happened?"

"It's Winton Pettibone. Someone attacked him."

"Is he all right?" Hemming said.

An enormous clap of thunder shook the heavens, and the line went dead.

Chapter Twenty-One

～

They emerged from the hut to find the rain slacking off, but the wind had picked up. It sounded like a freight train rushing across the moors, increasing in speed and volume as it hurtled toward them. The wind made Erin's eyes water, nearly sucking the breath right out of her, but she wanted to laugh from joy as she stood in front of the crumbling stone ruins with the vast, grand sweep of Yorkshire before her. She loved this landscape like no other, and it made her giddy.

She immediately felt guilty. Winton—poor Winton! She hoped he was all right.

"Do you want to call them back?" she asked Hemming.

"No, I just need to get back to town."

"Where is your car parked?" she shouted, straining to be heard over the din.

"Over there," he said, pointing across the moors in the opposite direction from her car.

"How far?"

"About a mile," he shouted, staggering back as a blast of wind nearly knocked them both off their feet.

"Can you give me a lift? Mine's over two miles in the other direction."

"All right—we have to move, though!"

The wind was blowing straight at them, so the mile hike to his car felt more like five. They arrived, panting and exhausted, still damp from the rain. Erin wanted nothing more than a long, deep bath, but she had something else in mind. Climbing into his old Citroën, she admired the car's interior, with its red leather seats and broad steering wheel with the single spoke.

"This car has great character," she said as she buckled her seat belt.

"Tell that to Sergeant Jarral," he said, shaking the rain from his hair. "He thinks it's a pile of junk."

"No appreciation for quality," she said as he pulled out into the deserted street. Roads in North Yorkshire were rarely crowded, and this time of year, with a storm hovering over them, it would be possible to get all the way to town without seeing another car.

When they reached her car, she turned to him. "Do you mind waiting just to make sure it starts? I've been having some trouble, and I'm afraid it's the alternator."

"Of course," he said as she jumped out and climbed into her Sunbeam. Looking back at him, she saw he was trying to make a call on his mobile. She sat in the driver's seat for a couple of minutes, then got out and went back to his car.

"It's dead."

"Is the engine turning over at all?"

She shook her head. "I'm just getting a clicking sound."

"There's no time to troubleshoot it. I'll drive you to town, and you can sort it later."

"Right," she agreed, sliding in beside him. Erin felt a little guilty about her deception, but mostly she felt exhilarated. Now she just had to launch the second part of her plan.

"I managed to get through to Constable McCrary," he said. "Mr. Pettibone is all right. Shaken up, but not seriously injured, it seems."

"Oh, good."

She looked out the window as the moorland gave way to farm fields, little cottages nestled in vales, and running brooks snaking through the countryside.

"My place is in the other direction," she said, trying to sound casual and unrehearsed. "Why don't you just—"

"Take you to the station house?"

"Well, it *would* be more—"

"Convenient?"

"Of course, if you want to drive all the way to—"

He gave her a sideways glance. "There's nothing wrong with your car, is there?"

"It's an old car, and—" she said, flushing, but he cut her off with another look. They drove for a while in silence; then he spoke.

"Look, I admire your persistence, but you can't just worm your way into a police investigation."

"I'm not—"

"I'll let you come inside, but you must promise to behave yourself," he said as they pulled up in front of the station.

"Cross my heart and hope to die."

He turned off the engine. "Don't say that. Not now, with all that's happened."

"All right," she agreed. It was plain from the way he looked at her that she wasn't just a nuisance—he wanted to keep her safe, not because it was his job, but because it mattered to him.

She hopped out of the car as if she were on springs. "Come on," she said, "Let's go in. I promise I'll be good."

Chapter Twenty-Two

 ❧

They arrived to find Winton Pettibone seated in the main room, flanked by Constable McCrary and Sergeant Jarral. Winton looked frightened—he pressed an icepack to the back of his head, which pushed his wig forward at a rakish angle, so he appeared to have a Beatles-style haircut.

"Mr. Pettibone says he was attacked outside his home and knocked unconscious," McCrary said as they entered the spacious room, with its bowed ceilings and faux Greek columns. "Sergeant Jarral is taking his statement."

"Did he see his assailant?" asked Hemming.

"Negative." McCrary frowned when he saw Erin. "What's she doin' here?" he asked, his mustache twitching.

"Her car wouldn't start, so I offered her a ride."

The Scotsman opened his mouth as if about to say something, but appeared to think better of it.

"Would you wait in there, please?" Hemming said, pointing to a conference room at the back of the station house.

"Of course," said Erin. She walked slowly through the main room, taking in the details. Half a dozen desks were scattered about the room, all unoccupied except the one where Winton sat with his entourage of policemen. A copy and fax machine lined the far wall; next to it was a coffee and tea station with a water cooler, as well as a small refrigerator and some wire shelving with snacks.

Opening the door to the conference room, she saw a corkboard festooned with snapshots of the local members of the Jane Austen Society. In the center, connected to the other photos, was a picture of Sylvia, smiling into the camera. She looked so carefree and innocent, so unlike the Sylvia she knew that Erin was struck with a pang of regret. She would never know the happy, sweet-faced woman in the photograph. People couldn't be summed up so easily, she thought, reduced to the handful of traits others used to define them. She was reminded of a line by one of her favorite American poets, Walt Whitman: "I contain multitudes."

Studying the board, she mused that there certainly were a multitude of viable suspects. Familiar faces looked back at her as if daring her to find the murderer in them. She studied them one by one, musing on what unknown darkness might lie deep within their soul.

Beneath each name were scribbled notes: under hers, for example, BOOKSTORE OWNER and PRESENT AT MEETING. ARRIVED IN TOWN TWO YEARS AGO. It was odd to read that—sometimes she felt as if she had always lived in the thatched cottage along the stream.

She continued to study the text beneath each photo. Under Farnsworth's picture was written LOCAL CAT LADY. ECCENTRIC. ARGUED WITH VICTIM NIGHT BEFORE. SERVED TEA TO VICTIM. KNOWN TO DISLIKE VICTIM. Was that true? Erin wondered. Did Farnsworth really dislike Sylvia, or did she just take exception to her controlling nature? She had never come out and actually said she didn't like Sylvia—in fact, Erin had the impression she rather admired her.

Beneath James Marlowe's photo was written LOCAL BUTCHER. LEFT THE MEETING EARLY. Surprised, Erin read the words again. *Left the meeting early.* But Polly had said her father hadn't arrived home until late. As she was pondering this discrepancy, she heard the door open behind her.

She turned to see Detective Hemming.

"Ready to go?" he said. "You all right?"

"Fine," she said, shivering. "Just a little chilled."

"Sorry, I should have offered you tea."

"There's tea at my place."

"What about your car?"

"I'll pick it up tomorrow—Farnsworth can drive me," she said, putting on her coat.

Winton Pettibone was still in the front room, talking with Constable Harris, a dark-haired, long-faced policeman she had seen around town.

"Anything else you remember?" asked Harris, making notes on a legal pad.

"There is one thing," said Winton. "I don't know if it's important, but there was a lingering smell of lilacs."

Harris stopped writing. "Lilacs?"

"Like a perfume?" asked Hemming.

"I don't know. I remember noticing it when I came to."

Erin's stomach contracted. Farnsworth wore lilac perfume. She looked at Hemming, but saw no sign of recognition. Then she remembered he suffered from allergies, which might affect his sense of smell.

"Do you want me to escort you home?" he asked Winton.

"I appreciate the offer," Winton said in his curiously flat way. "But I'll be all right. I should be going—you know how Pru worries."

"We'll walk out with you," said Erin, wishing she could have a moment alone to question him. She resolved to remedy that as soon as possible.

Chapter Twenty-Three

As they drove through the darkened countryside, Erin was burning to pepper the detective with questions but kept silent for the first couple of miles, thoughts swimming through her head. Was it possible Farnsworth had attacked Winton, and if so, why? Or was someone trying to frame her? Maybe Winton had mistaken another scent for the smell of lilacs, or misremembered the attack altogether—blows to the head could disrupt memory.

When they arrived at her cottage, she turned to Hemming.

"How about that tea?"

He hesitated, his profile sharp against the light from the front door lamppost. "Thanks," he said. "I could do with some."

The house was cold and damp as they made their way through the bookstore to her living quarters in the back. "I'll light a fire," she said, after turning on some lights. Even with all the lamps in the room lit, the room felt dark and clammy.

"Why don't I do that while you put the kettle on?"

"Great," she said, going into the kitchen. Her red electric kettle gleamed beneath the bright track lights in the kitchen—one thing Erin hated was a poorly lit kitchen. *A clean, well-lighted place*, she thought. It was the title of a short story by an American author she admired, Ernest Hemingway. Its themes of loneliness and despair had stayed with her long after she read it. Existentialism wasn't really her thing, but she liked his spare writing style and unflinching honesty. The Jane Austen crowd had more conservative taste, but Erin enjoyed all kinds of writers—a good trait for a bookstore owner, she supposed.

When she returned to the living room with the tea tray, the fire was blazing and the detective was standing at her piano, looking at the open album of sheet music on the stand.

"You play Bach?" he said.

"I try," she said, putting down the tray.

"Would you play some for me?"

"Well, I don't know—"

"Just one, while the tea is steeping?"

"All right," she said, sitting at the piano. "Anything in particular?"

"I never could resist the 'Prelude in C Minor'—that is, if you're up to it," he said, sitting in the overstuffed armchair next to the fire.

"I can stumble through it," she said, impressed he was able to identify it by name.

Her hands were stiff, and she started the piece at an unrealistically brisk tempo, so she had trouble keeping up, making several mistakes in places she usually knew well. But it wasn't as bad as it might have been; she played with passion and more concentration than she anticipated. Afterward, he applauded.

"Well done! I'm so envious of people with talent like that."

"I have no talent, just dogged determination," she said, rising from the bench.

"It's all about discipline in the end, isn't it? The willingness to overcome obstacles?"

"Who do you think attacked Winton?" she asked, pouring the tea.

"I really can't say."

"Shall I tell you what I think?"

"Can I stop you?"

"It wasn't the same person who poisoned Sylvia."

"Why not?"

"Different personality types. Poisoners are nonconfrontational, sneaky, and cunning. They're methodical, meticulous planners."

"But—"

"The attack on Winton was none of those things. It was poorly planned, badly executed, and failed to accomplish its goal."

"Which was—?"

"Presumably Winton's death. Otherwise, why attack him at all?"

He finished his tea and put the cup down. "How did you get involved with the Austen Society?"

"As the local bookstore owner, it seemed natural to join," she said, refilling his cup. "Maybe even necessary."

"Your taste seems to lie more in another direction," he said, indicating the bookcase of forensic books.

"Oh, that reminds me. I'm missing a book on poisoning—not from my private collection, but the one I keep in the store."

"Any idea who might have taken it?"

"No, but I thought I should tell you."

"I'm glad you did," he said, getting up to throw another log on the fire. It was odd, but that small gesture struck her as intimate and revealing. It was her fireplace, but he was treating it almost as if it were his own. She liked how that made her feel—as though he was slipping so naturally into an easy domesticity. And yet there was still something remote about him, a wariness she took as a challenge.

"I should be going," he said, draining the last of his cup. "Thanks for the tea."

"Thanks for the lift." Following him through the darkened shop, she turned on the outside light and opened the door.

"We will find the person who did this," he said, fishing his car keys from his pocket.

"I hope you do," she said, holding the door open for him, the light falling on his wheat-colored hair and broad, slightly stooped shoulders. He paused, and she imagined his lips on hers—soft, warm, slightly salty, perhaps. He leaned toward her, and she could feel her mouth relaxing, wanting to taste him, to inhale his woodsy smell. She half closed her eyes, waiting, willing him to want her too.

The clock in the living room struck, breaking the spell.

He gave a little cough and tipped his hat. "Thanks again."

She watched as he walked away, moving out of the pool of light cast by the lamp, getting into his car without looking back. She waited for the sound of the engine turning over before closing the door. Locking it behind her, she returned to her empty, silent house.

Chapter Twenty-Four

That night Erin tossed and turned, listening to the wind blow dry leaves against her windowpanes. She finally fell into a deep sleep and dreamed about having tea with Farnsworth. When her friend offered her sugar, Erin was horrified to see the box was labelled ARSENIC. She awoke in a sweat just before dawn.

Drawing the covers up to her chin, Erin stared out the window overlooking the stream behind the house. The sight of the graceful willow tree bending over the brook raised her spirits, and she reminded herself that her job was to clear her friend's name.

Pulling on her knee-length boots over a pair of black denim jeans, she brewed a cup of coffee and drank it standing up. Throwing on her checked polar fleece riding jacket, she picked up the phone to call Farnsworth, when she saw a gleam of metal outside the window. Her green Sunbeam sat in the driveway, a note pinned under the windshield wiper. She grabbed her car keys and went outside. Plucking the note from the windshield, she read it.

Thought you might like your car back. Luckily, Sergeant Jarral knows how to hotwire any car. I'll send you my bill later.
—P. Hemming

Tucking the note into her pocket, she climbed into the car and drove to the Beckers' house. She waited until Detective Hemming's car was a good distance from the house before pulling into the driveway. She parked in front of the house and went up the tidy walk to knock on the front door. When Suzanne Becker answered, Erin thought she looked relieved at seeing it was her instead of the police.

"I brought you some posies," Erin said. It was well known Suzanne loved flowers, and as everyone's gardens were beginning to die, Erin had selected a fall bouquet from the local shop.

Suzanne smiled sadly. "*Sehr schön.* Would you like to come in?"

Erin followed her into the immaculate house, waiting in the living room while Suzanne put the flowers in water.

"They are so beautiful," she said, entering with a cut-crystal vase, which she put on the glass coffee table. "Please, sit down." Everything about Suzanne was sharp and fragile, like cut crystal, Erin thought, as she settled onto the spotless white sofa.

"The police were just here for the second time," Suzanne said, fussing with the flowers. "I am so—*verzweifelt*—distressed. I think they suspect me."

"It's pretty stressful," Erin agreed, "having them digging around."

"Yes," Suzanne said. "And I'm afraid I lied to them."

"About what?"

Reaching into the pocket of her exercise jacket, she extracted a cigarette and lit it with trembling hands. "You must promise you won't tell anyone."

"All right."

"That night . . . I may have seen my husband leaving the alley."

"And you didn't tell the police?"

"No. I saw someone—I can't be sure it was Kurt, but it could have been him, darting around the corner just as I came out." She took a deep drag of the cigarette. "Please don't tell my husband about the smoking. He hates it."

"Where is he?"

"He usually goes to Sainsbury's on Sunday."

"Who else could have been in the alley?"

"I'm really not sure. Someone tall, I think." She took another drag from her cigarette, the smoke curling around her dyed blonde hair. "I don't think Kurt is capable of murdering someone—do you?"

"I don't want to scare you, but it's often surprising who is capable of murder."

"*Mein Gott*," Suzanne said, her voice unsteady. "If I thought Kurt had—I mean, I could never share his bed."

Erin looked out the window at the leaves skittering across the Beckers' little back garden, with its stone bird feeder and white trellis, a few disheveled pink blossoms still clinging to the rose vine twisting around it. Maybe she had more knowledge than was healthy, but Erin owed Suzanne the truth.

Stubbing out her cigarette, Suzanne fussed with the flowers in their crystal vase, plucking and rearranging them. "People don't blame me for her death, do they?"

"Why do you think that?"

"Because I am the—what is the phrase—'woman scorned.'"

"A lot of people seem to think it's related to what's going on in the society."

Suzanne sighed. "It's good of you to visit me. I appreciate it."

"Thank you for talking with me," said Erin, rising from the sofa.

"I must apologize for not offering you something—tea, and so on. I am quite disarranged."

"We're all a little unsettled."

Erin had started toward the front door when she heard a car door open and slam closed. Kurt Becker's voice came from just outside the front door. He sounded agitated.

"*Nein, ich weiss es nicht, wirklich!*" Becker was evidently speaking into his mobile. "*Aber warum? Du hast keine Ahnung!*"

She locked eyes with Suzanne, who shook her head and put a finger to her lips.

A pause, and then he said, "*Es ist nicht mein Schuld!*" Another pause. "*Tun Sie, was Sie wollen.*"

There was the sound of the front door opening, and Kurt Becker appeared in the doorway. When he saw Erin, he gave an unconvincing smile.

"Hello," he said, glancing at Suzanne.

"I was just leaving," Erin said.

"There's no need—"

"She really was going," said Suzanne.

"Good seeing you," Erin said.

"Thanks for coming," Suzanne said, walking her to the door.

Erin sat in her car for a few moments before leaving. Her German was decent, and she replayed Kurt's phone conversation in her mind. *Du hast kein Ahnung*—"You have no idea." But the phrase that stuck out the most was *Es ist nicht mein Schuld*—"It's not my fault." What exactly wasn't his fault? She had made a promise she would no doubt regret and eavesdropped on a conversation she wasn't meant to hear. What this would all come to, she couldn't possibly predict, she thought as she started the engine and drove in the direction of Farnsworth's house. She had promised to come over for Sunday roast, and there was a bottle of Pinot Noir in her trunk for the occasion.

She glanced over her shoulder before driving away and could see the Beckers through the living room window. They seemed to be having an intense conversation. She longed to hear what they were saying, whether in English or German. Sighing, she pulled out of the driveway, contenting herself with the thought of rare roast beef and a glass of Pinot Noir.

Chapter Twenty-Five

First thing Monday morning, Erin paid a visit to Marlowe's Meats, the butcher shop Polly's father owned.

The store was on the ground floor of a two-story stone building near the middle of town, where Market Place became Piercy End, at the intersection of Howe End. A pristine coat of white paint covered the exterior of the store, with its large picture window, MARLOWE'S MEATS stenciled on it in nineteenth-century gold lettering. Nestled between a Boots pharmacy and a beauty salon, the shop was ideally located near the public car park and bus stop.

Erin stepped inside the immaculate interior, the tinkling bell over the door announcing their entrance. The shop was spotless—counters gleamed, the polished glass of the display cases glistened. Rows of sausages snuggled up against perfectly trimmed lamp chops, pork loins, and beef steaks; another case contained a mouth-watering selection of meat pies and smoked fish. Shelves lining the side wall sported an array of sauces, jams and jellies; a chalkboard on the back wall listed the locally sourced specials: Bramley applesauce, poacher's chutney, farmhouse pickles.

James Marlowe entered from a door leading to a back room, wiping his hands on a starched white napkin.

"Hello, Erin. Nice to see you."

He wore a long apron, freshly pressed, white except for a few red stains in the middle, over a crisp blue-and-white-striped shirt. With his freckled face and thinning sandy hair parted on the side, he could have been a shopkeeper from two hundred years earlier.

"What can I get you?"

"I've actually come to talk to you about the night Sylvia was killed."

"Oh?" Marlowe said, picking up a knife with a black handle and a long, shiny blade. "Why's that?"

"I just wanted to clear up something you told the police. That is, if you don't mind."

"Erin the amateur sleuth, eh?" he said with a smile. "Mind if I work while we chat?"

"Of course not."

"With two children to look after, this is as relaxed as my day gets, I'm afraid," he said, sharpening the knife on a leather strap.

"So when did you leave the meeting?"

"Right before the tea break."

"Polly said you didn't get home until hours later."

"Oh?" he said, carefully slicing fat from a leg of lamb laid out on the blond wood butcher block behind the counter. The block was thick, over a foot deep, its uneven surface sunken in the middle, nicked and scarred from decades of knife blades.

"So," Erin said carefully, not wanting to sound confrontational, "I was just wondering where you went."

He laid the knife down and wiped his forehead. Though the shop was very cool, beads of sweat gathered on his face. Erin heard the squeal of brakes as a car slowed down to make the turn onto Howe End.

"I was at Chen's," he said finally.

"You mean Jimmy Chen?"

"Yes." Jimmy Chen was the owner of Chen's Palace, a popular

Chinese restaurant in town. He knew everyone in Kirkbymoorside by name, and everyone knew him.

"What were you doing there?"

"He was the host this month . . ." He looked away, grinding his teeth.

"The host for what?"

"There's a roving high-stakes poker game in Kirkbymoorside. It meets once a month, and the players take turns hosting. This month was Jimmy's turn."

"How long has this been going on?"

"Ever since I've lived here."

"So you could produce alibi witnesses, if it came to that?"

"As you might imagine, the regulars would prefer to keep a low profile."

"I understand," she said. There was a lot more going on in this sleepy market town than she realized. "I suppose you see Jonathan Alder there sometimes." The look on his face told her she had struck pay dirt. "Never mind," she said. "I won't ask you about it anymore. I only care about the murder."

He shook his head. "It's all so tragic. Sylvia's heart was in the right place—she just wanted to bring sanity and order to the society."

"Do you think her death was definitely society related?"

Marlowe laid the long, white strips of fat carefully on the butcher block, stacking them on top of each other. "Don't you?"

"I don't know."

"Do the police suspect *me*?"

"It seems a little odd that you left early, since you were on the tea committee, and they were short-handed."

"Yes, but I heard Farnsworth stepped in." He scooped up the lamb fat and formed it into a thick white ball.

"Suet?" Erin said, looking at it.

"I stud it with seeds and sell it to my customers with bird feeders. The plovers and finches really go for it."

"I remember my mother used to feed the birds suet."

"When you have mouths to feed, you learn the value of thrift. Our society is far too wasteful."

"So you left before Sylvia got her tea?"

"Yes. I knew I had to leave, so I stood in the back of the room to have a better shot at the front of the queue. I grabbed a quick cup and left. Sylvia was up at the lectern, so she would have been served after I was gone."

"Did anyone see you get in your car and drive away?"

A frown crossed his freckled face. "I couldn't say. It was dark out, and most everyone was in the church, I'm afraid." His complexion turned even paler. "The cops didn't say anything to you about me, did they?"

"No."

The butcher took a deep breath and rubbed his forehead wearily. "Fate hasn't been entirely kind to us. The children need a mother. But people in town have been lovely, especially you. I really appreciate the way you've taken Polly under your wing. I think Polly wishes I'd marry you," he added with a little smile.

"I'm very fond of her. They're both great kids."

"They get that from their mother," Marlowe replied as the bell over the door tinkled cheerfully, and Detective Hemming and Sergeant Jarral entered the store.

"Well, thanks very much for your time," Erin said hastily, turning to leave as the policemen walked toward them.

"I see you found your car," Hemming remarked.

"Oh, yes, ta very much. I'm glad Sergeant Jarral is using his superpowers for good instead of evil." Giving them a quick smile, she darted out of the store and into the street.

Chapter Twenty-Six

～

Erin arrived late to yoga class Monday afternoon and stumbled as she bent to unroll her mat in the back of the room. She hated being late. Her favorite spot in the far-right corner was taken, so she had to settle for a spot near the door. Joining the rest of the class sitting cross-legged on their mats, she tried to use her breath to calm her mind.

In the front of the room sat the teacher, Kira Robinson, a slim Anglo-Indian woman with the taut body and unlined face of a devoted yogi. She sat in a perfect lotus position, feet tucked over each other, limber as a cat. Erin frowned as her hips protested the pose; she would never be that flexible, no matter how many yoga classes she took. Years of running had seen to that, the pavement pounding already taking a toll on her joints.

"Pay attention to your breath," Kira said in a soothing voice. "Don't try to control it, just observe. In, out, in, out."

The smell of rubber mats and sweat mixed with the faint aroma of lavender from the burning candle behind the teacher. The flame flickered and blinked in the breeze coming from the ill-fitting window sash.

"In, out, in, out. Breathe in using your diaphragm, taking air all the way down into your belly. Hold it for a moment."

Erin closed her eyes, savoring the stillness of the room. The only sound was the wind whistling through the building's ancient eaves, punctuated by the occasional cawing from the family of crows who lived in the gnarled oak tree overlooking the graveyard.

"I invite you to chant the universal sound of om three times," said Kira.

Erin took a deep breath, letting it release slowly as she joined the rest of the class in the chant. There were a couple of men in class, their voices deepening the resonance of the collective sound.

Ooooomm.

When she'd first begun practicing yoga, Erin had thought the chanting was silly, but now she looked forward to it. The sound of many voices caressed the air in the room, soft as feathers.

Ooooomm.

She deepened her breath, the vibrations soothing her nerve fibers, surrounding her like a blanket.

Ooooomm.

After the chanting, Kira led them through a gentle flow, starting with floor poses before moving on to sun salutations. As she moved into her first Downward Dog, Erin caught a glimpse of curly black hair in the front row. Though nearsighted without her glasses, Erin was pretty sure it was Jonathan Alder. Those curls were unmistakable. What was he doing here? An unwelcome tingle emanated from her lower spine, and sweat dotted her forehead as she held the pose. Her yoga was a time for meditation, a sacred hour away from worldly things like sexual attraction. In class she was the Goddess Diana, pure and chaste, interested only in the hunt for enlightenment.

They moved through the vinyasa to plank pose, the top of a push-up, arms extended, back straight. She could no longer see Jonathan.

"And hold it . . . a little longer," Kira said.

Erin groaned as her arms began to shake and a few drops of sweat spattered the mat.

"Almost done," Kira crooned. She was getting on Erin's nerves, with that Earth Goddess voice, so full of her own virtue, so damn centered and calm.

"Three more seconds."

Erin began to pant.

"And move through your flow to upward dog."

Erin let out a rush of air from her lungs as she sank gratefully to the floor, pausing for a moment before sliding into upward dog. She could see Jonathan up in front, head thrown back, curls splayed across his shoulders. She felt the unwelcome tingle again, and took a deep breath before moving back into downward dog.

Steady on, old girl. The phrase her father used to say to her mother suddenly popped into her head, although she hadn't thought about it in years. Hardly an "old girl," her mother, dying before the bloom of youth had fled her cheeks.

"Let's work on some balancing poses now," Kira cooed serenely. "We'll start with tree pose."

Erin gritted her teeth. She was lousy at tree—not because her balance was bad, but because her joints were stiff, so she had trouble sliding her foot very far up the standing leg.

"Hands in prayer pose or over your head," Kira continued, effortlessly tucking the heel of her foot into her crotch.

Erin grimly willed her foot to go higher. To her dismay, Jonathan was very adept at the pose, balancing easily on one leg, hands over his head. *Show-off,* Erin thought, angry at herself for caring. She tried to avoid comparing herself to the other students, to not judge herself or others. That was the yogi way, and it was liberating—but today she failed to live up to the ideal, and it made her grumpy.

They moved through warrior three and half moon, which Erin was very good at. It was satisfying to see Jonathan fail to lift his leg nearly as high as hers. Kira finished the class with a couple of bridge pose back bends, and finally inversions. A few people were advanced enough to do headstands, but Erin was content doing her usual shoulder stand. She noted that Jonathan did not attempt a headstand.

After the final *Oooom*, Erin bowed to the instructor and rose, gathering up her mat. As she stood in line waiting to put her mat in the big straw basket in the back of the room, she saw Rosita Selario, Sylvia Pemberthy's housecleaner. Rosita was a good customer of the Readers Quarry, always in search of the latest cookbook. She was talking to a small, older woman with a long, lustrous black braid.

"She told me she was about to break it off with him, and he wasn't happy about it," said Rosita. She was a lanky Latina woman with a fashion model's figure, smooth brown skin, and long, sharp fingernails. Erin had no idea how she did housecleaning with those nails.

The other woman shook her head. "I don't like that man—there's something not right about him."

"So did she break up with him before she was—?"

Rosita leaned down to put her mat in the basket. "*Querido Dios,* I don't know."

"Did you tell the police?" asked the other woman.

"No."

"They didn't interview you?"

"Not yet," Rosita said.

Her friend unraveled her long black braid as the two waited in line to return their foam blocks to a second basket. "You should go to them. Might help catch the killer."

"I have a policy with the *policía*. They don't bother me, I don't bother them."

The other woman said something in Spanish Erin couldn't make out.

The two women walked toward the exit, speaking in hushed tones, their heads close. As Erin put her mat in the basket, her hair barrette came loose and clattered to the floor. She looked up to see Jonathan holding it out to her.

"I think you dropped this," he said, a friendly smile on his absurdly handsome face.

"Oh, cheers," she said breezily.

"I didn't know you were a yogi."

"I usually come to the earlier class."

"Got stuck late at the office, eh?"

"'Life seems but a quick succession of—'"

"'Busy nothings,'" he finished for her.

"Well played," she said, taking her mat to the bin in the back of the room.

"Sometimes this class is the only thing that keeps me sane," he said, following her. "After all day with the kids, you need something like this to clear the mind."

"Uh-huh," she said, busying herself tidying the mats in the bin.

"Fancy a coffee?"

"It's getting late, and I have to—"

"A pint, then?"

There was no dodging it.

"Why not?" she said.

Chapter Twenty-Seven

~

Like most English villages, Kirkbymoorside was not lacking in pubs. They decided on the George and Dragon—it was historic and homey, with hearty, unpretentious food. When they arrived, there was a fire in the grate and only a few other customers, so they settled in front of the fire. It was a raw, blustery night, and Erin was suddenly glad for the warmth and companionship as she sank into one of the armchairs.

"What'll it be?" Jonathan said, rubbing his hands to get out the chill. "What would Jane Austen order? A Reverend Tom Collins?"

"A Claret Cup, I think," she said, smiling.

"Living dangerously, eh?" he said, cocking his head to one side. "Do they even do that here?"

"I doubt it, but they should do a Pimm's Cup, if you ask nicely."

"Be back before you can say Georgian Romance," he said, going to the bar.

Erin looked around the room, warm with the glow of firelight, and she could smell pine needles and nutmeg, as if they were already gearing up for Christmas, when it was barely October.

Her phone buzzed—it was her father. She hesitated before answering.

"Hello, Dad."

"What are you up to on this blustery evening?" Since her mother's death, her father had become obsessed with weather, even joining a Facebook group for like-minded people. He had several sophisticated weather apps on his phone and computer and was contemplating setting up a small weather station in his study.

"Just come from yoga class."

"How very commendable. Are you fortifying yourself with nettle juice or something equally virtuous and repugnant?"

"Actually, I'm having a drink in the George and Dragon."

"What a relief. I was beginning to wonder if you were my daughter after all."

"I have your bad eyesight and short temper."

"You inherited all your mother's virtues and all my flaws."

"Not quite. I don't have your suspicious nature."

"What about your interest in crime?"

She told him about meeting Hemming on the moors, and about Winton being attacked.

"I was thinking about that phone call you got over the weekend. Have you thought of asking the police to tap your phone?"

"They might need more reason than a nuisance call. Sorry, Dad, I have to go," she said, spying Jonathan approaching with their drinks.

"Tell him I said hello."

"Who?"

"Whoever you're with. Bye for now, and please be careful."

"I will."

"One Pimm's Cup and one pint of pale ale," Jonathan said, placing the drinks on the table. Hers was decorated with an orange slice, a piece of apple, and a mint sprig.

"That was my father," she said, tucking her phone into her jacket pocket, annoyed with herself for feeling she had to explain. Was she afraid he'd be jealous? But this wasn't a *date*—was it?

"Checking up on you?" he said, smiling as he slid into his seat.

"Actually, he was checking up on the progress of the investigation into Sylvia's death."

Was it her imagination, or did he wince at her response? She thought she saw a shadow pass over his face, but couldn't be sure in the dim light of the pub.

"Chin chin," said Jonathan, lifting his glass.

"Cheers," she said, raising hers.

The drink was more delicious than she had anticipated—the aroma of fresh mint mixed with spices and citrus flavors, the terse dryness of the gin. She resisted the urge to gulp it down all at once.

"I'd better get some water," she said. "Didn't realize how thirsty I was."

"I can get it."

"My turn. You want some?"

"Why not? Yoga is thirsty business," he said, with that lopsided grin. And did he will that lock of hair to fall over one eye?

"Right," she said, heading for the bar.

Sitting alone at a table on the other side of the room, nursing a pint, was Sergeant Jarral. He was writing something in a notebook, a look of concentration on his symmetrical, well-formed features. She stood watching him for a moment, about to turn away, when he saw her. He gave her a warm smile and waved. Taking it as an invitation, she approached him.

"How's the case going?"

"Slowly. And now the boss is out of action for a while."

She frowned and cocked her head to the side. "Why?"

"Came down with a nasty bug of some kind. Apparently he got caught out on the moors in that rainstorm."

"Is he very sick?"

"He's flat on his back in bed, so I'd say pretty sick, yeah."

"Sorry to hear that." She had an urge to go to him. She imagined turning up with homemade soup, soothing his feverish forehead with a cool cloth . . .

"Listen," she said, "I don't know if this is relevant or not, but I overheard something tonight."

She told him what Rosita Selario had said in yoga class. Jarral nodded, listening carefully. "We haven't interviewed her yet, but she's definitely on the list. Thanks for the tip."

"No worries." Clutching the glass of water, Erin headed back to her table. When she returned, Jonathan's smile looked a bit forced.

"I saw you chatting with one of our resident sleuths."

"Trying to pick his brain a little," she said offhandedly.

"Learn anything juicy?"

"You know how they are—can't talk about an ongoing investigation, blah, blah, blah."

"Right," he said with a little chuckle, but it rang hollow. His hands fidgeted nervously with his drink, and his eyes darted across the room to where the sergeant sat.

"I did hear a rumor the other day, though it wasn't from the cops," she said.

"Oh? What was it?"

"I heard you and Sylvia were having quite the chat behind the barn at the fete last summer."

He frowned. "Who told you that?"

"I'm not at liberty to say."

"It was nothing salacious," he said, taking a long swallow of his drink.

"If you say so."

"The cops don't think Sylvia and I—"

"Oh, no, I don't think so."

"If I were going to get salacious with someone, it wouldn't be Sylvia," he said, looking down at his drink.

"Oh?" she said, her skin tingling a little.

"Are you . . . seeing anyone at the moment?" he asked, still not looking at her.

"Not at the moment."

He nodded, and in the dim light, she thought she saw him blush.

"Sorry," he said, laughing nervously. "I'm absolute rubbish at this."

"Half the women in town would find that hard to believe."

"You're not half the women in town."

"I find it hard to believe as well."

"Seeing is believing," he said, pushing a lock of hair from his forehead. "You know, all this talk of equality—which I'm all for, obviously—and yet the man's still expected to make the first move. Not really fair, if you ask me."

"I agree," said Erin. Leaning forward, she kissed him on the lips. "There," she said. "Is that better?"

"Much better. You are a socially progressive young woman, Ms. Coleridge."

"Don't tell my father. He would be horrified."

"I won't dream of it," he said, leaning toward her.

"More social progressivity?"

"Yes, please."

They kissed again. His lips tasted faintly of cherries, and were just soft enough, yielding without complete surrender, which made her want more. But they were in a public place, and Erin didn't really approve of excessive displays of affection in public—or PDA, as her father called it.

"Any more of that and we'll both turn into radicals," he said, and she laughed.

They sipped their drinks, and for a moment he seemed lost in his own thoughts.

"I can't believe it's less than two weeks until the bonfire," she said, to break the spell.

"I've been hearing so much about it since I arrived. I can't wait to see it."

"Where did you live before here?"

"Oh, here and there—I've moved around a lot."

"Where did you grow up?"

"Uh, the West Country—Devon," he said, avoiding her gaze.

"Funny—you don't have a West Country accent."

"This town is my home now."

"Speaking of which, I heard something a bit scandalous yesterday."

"What was it?" he asked, leaning into her. She could smell his aftershave, a sharp, piny odor.

"I heard that there's a monthly poker game in town. High stakes, very hush-hush and all that."

"Really? Who told you that?"

"I promised I wouldn't tell," she said. "It was one of the regulars."

"Just goes to show you never know about people, eh?" he said, downing the rest of his drink. "Care for another round?"

"Let me get this one."

"Absolutely not—my treat," he said, brushing his fingertips lightly across her cheek. It was an intimate gesture, perhaps even more than the kissing, she thought.

As she watched him head for the bar, Erin decided that charming, personable Jonathan Alder was hiding something. And even if she was a little bit in love with him, she was very eager to find out what it was.

Chapter Twenty-Eight

❧

"Hiding something? What on earth could it be, I wonder?" Farnsworth said as she poured hot water into the cone filter over a blue-and-white coffee mug.

Sitting at the kitchen table in her friend's farmhouse Tuesday morning, Erin inhaled the aroma of Arabica beans as the hot water coaxed out their flavor, filling the room with the dark, spicy scent.

"Obviously there's the gambling," Erin said. "But I have a feeling there's more. He seemed interested in me, but he was very uncomfortable about it."

"He would be, if he has a gambling problem," Farnsworth said, swirling the water over the ground coffee as she poured.

Though she had watched Farnsworth make coffee dozens of times, Erin had never quite figured out how to replicate the magic of her legendary brew. Erin made decent coffee, but Farnsworth had something—a knack, a mysterious je ne sais quoi.

"You should open a café," she said as Farnsworth handed her the steaming mug.

"And call it what—the Cat Lady Café?"

"Great idea! People could come for the coffee and to pet the cats. There are places like that in the States. They're quite popular."

"I can't imagine anyone in this town coming to a place I own."

"Now you're just fishing for compliments. Your coffee is brilliant, and you know it. What's your secret?"

"One thing I do is to make each cup individually."

"But there must be more—what is it?"

"One must maintain an aura of mystery, even around one's friends," Farnsworth said, brewing herself a cup.

"Did Austen say that?"

"No, but perhaps she should have."

"You know what we should do?" said Erin.

"Make up fake Austen quotes and watch Prudence try to figure out how she missed them?"

"I was going to say we should look up Jonathan online and see what we can find on him."

"You don't let up, do you?" said Farnsworth. Lumbering to the table with her coffee, she eased herself onto the chair opposite Erin. A woman of generous girth, Farnsworth never seemed the least bit self-conscious about it—if anything, she dressed to emphasize her size. She wore an electric-blue dress and matching scarf, her graying hair swept up in a simple chignon, highlighting her classically pretty face, strong cheekbones, and full mouth. Younger and thinner, Erin thought, she must have been a stunner.

"Almond biscotti?" Farnsworth said, holding out a chipped blue china plate.

"Cheers," Erin said, plucking one from the plate. Farnsworth's tableware looked old, like family heirlooms, expensive bone china yellowing at the edges.

"Now then, what about young Jonathan?" Farnsworth said as a sleek orange tabby leapt onto her lap. "Let's have it, pet—mind you don't leave anything out."

Erin recounted her evening at the pub, leaving out the kissing.

"It does sound like our young Bingley may have something unsavory in his past," Farnsworth mused, sipping her coffee while petting the young tabby with her free hand. The cat closed its eyes and stretched itself sinuously across her lap. "Mind you, no one knows anything about him. He's the original man of mystery."

"True—he just shows up here six months ago, lands a job at the middle school, and shows up at society meetings."

"But surely he must have provided work references to get the job."

"Those can be faked."

Farnsworth swept a few biscotti crumbs onto the floor, drawing the attention of several felines, who sniffed at them and turned away, tails twitching. "Even these days, with the Internet and all?"

"I know of several instances where people lied about their backgrounds and got away with it for a long time."

"And what about those money problems?"

"Maybe he's running from creditors. But I think he's gambling."

"There could be an innocent explanation. Alfred Hitchcock's father locked him in a jail cell to teach him respect for the law, leaving him with a lifelong fear of policemen." Farnsworth was a fount of information, well read in many different areas.

"Jonathan definitely has a secret of some kind."

"You can find out more about him now that he's taken a shine to you, pet," Farnsworth said with a sly smile.

"Maybe he knows about my interest in crime and is trying to enlist me as an ally."

"Wouldn't *that* be intriguing?" Farnsworth said, absently scratching her cat's ears. "Especially if he's guilty. But then you mustn't accept any food or drink from him."

"Too late for that—he bought me a drink last night."

"I suppose it's ridiculous to poison someone when there's only the two of you—it would be too easy to trace. Still," she said, frowning, "I don't like to think of you alone with him."

"I don't suppose any of the other ladies in town do either."

"I'm afraid he's proving to be more Mr. Wickham than Mr. Bingley," Farnsworth replied, lifting the orange cat from her lap, replacing it with a sweet-faced little gray tabby. "I have to rotate them," she explained. "Mustn't play favorites, you know."

"Sort of like children," Erin said.

"But not nearly as irritating."

"How is your son, by the way?"

Farnsworth wrinkled her perfectly shaped nose. "Why did you have to spoil a conversation by bringing up Philip?"

"On the outs again?"

"Regular as clockwork, these spats of ours. Usually involving politics, but this time it's a woman." She sighed. "Where did I go wrong?"

"Maybe it's just a rebellious phase."

"He's thirty-two, for Christ's sake!"

"Who's the woman?"

"Some news floozy. Writes a column for one of those Murdoch rags." She shuddered. "I never will understand how I managed to spawn a conservative."

"Maybe it's genetic, from his father."

Farnsworth gave a short laugh—a percussive burst of air, like a tire blowing out. "Dastardly Dick? Could be. He had the soul of a Tory."

Erin smiled. Farnsworth managed to play both sides of the coin, maintaining her status as Woman Scorned while making fun of her cheating husband. Erin also suspected she played up her eccentricities. It was difficult to stand out as peculiar in a rural English village, where oddballs were common as fruit flies.

"Let's not talk about Philip anymore," Farnsworth said, opening a drawer of the massive oak armoire containing much of her china, as well as electronics, cat supplies, and general bric-a-brac.

Erin never knew how she managed to find anything in it, but she seemed to have memorized the contents. "Here," she said, pulling out a dusty laptop.

"Right—let's do some research into Mr. Jonathan Alder," said Erin.

"Is that wicked of us?"

"Just wicked enough, I should think. If he's hiding something, now's the time to find out."

Farnsworth blew a cloud of dust from the cover before opening the laptop. "Here," she said, plugging it in. "Why don't you have a go—you're better at this than I am."

"Right," Erin said as the screen flickered to life. "Let's start with a good old-fashioned Google search, shall we?"

Her efforts were rewarded with several images, links to social media sites, professional business profiles, and so on, but none of them matched Jonathan.

"Curiouser and curiouser," said Farnsworth, a pair of reading glasses perched on her nose. She leaned in, cat hair billowing gently from her clothing.

"Some people don't have an online profile," Erin said. "This doesn't necessarily prove anything."

"Does Jonathan strike you as the social media type?"

"Hard to say . . . let me try something else."

"Do you think our copper friends will be Googling all of us?"

"I imagine they're too busy conducting interviews," Erin said, her fingers flying over the keyboard.

"Where'd you learn to type like that?" Farnsworth asked.

"I used to help my dad out in the parish office. He wasn't much of a typist, so I did a fair amount of his correspondence."

"Didn't he have people for that?"

"Yeah, but after my mother died we sort of needed each other's company, I suppose. Here we go," she said, as a site came up on the screen.

Farnsworth squinted through her glasses. "'Professional Profiles in Education.' What's that?"

"It's a relatively new networking site where teachers and administrators can post their résumés," Erin said, scrolling through the list of names. "Ackerman, Adams, Anderson—nothing on him here."

"How did you know about this site?"

"Polly wanted to show me her teacher's picture on it. Let me try something else," she said, typing ALDER and ARREST into the search box. Underneath, the Google prompt read, DID YOU MEAN: ALDER- SHOTT ARREST.

"Hmm," Erin murmured. "Maybe I do." When she typed that, a number of hits appeared. Erin hit the IMAGES tab, and a row of pictures appeared.

"Good heavens," Farnsworth said, leaning over her shoulder. There, on the top of the screen, was a mug shot of a man who bore a strong resemblance to Jonathan Alder. Scrolling down to view text documents, Erin clicked on a link to the Manchester *Guardian*.

The date was May 4, 2015, and the front-page caption read HEADMASTER ARRESTED FOR WIFE'S MURDER. Beneath it, the same scowling face stared out from the police mug shot. The curly hair was disheveled, the hooded eyes burning with rage, but there was no mistaking the familial resemblance: the same strong jaw, high cheekbones, same blue eyes. She looked at the screen, imagining a younger version of the face staring back at her. A shiver rippled through her when she realized that Jonathan Alder looked almost exactly as his father would have at the same age. Erin's eyes moved down to the opening paragraph. ON SUNDAY, POLICE MADE AN ARREST IN THE MURDER OF FLAVIA ALDERSHOTT, A TEACHER AT BRIMLEY MIDDLE SCHOOL. MRS. ALDERSHOTT WAS STRANGLED IN

HER BEDROOM SOMETIME SATURDAY EVENING, AND ALL EVIDENCE POINTS TO HER HUSBAND, HEADMASTER WILLIAM ALDERSHOTT. THE COUPLE'S SON JONATHAN COULD NOT BE REACHED FOR COMMENT.

"Good heavens," Farnsworth said softly. "So Jonathan's not a criminal—his father is."

"I remember that case," Erin said. "He was convicted and sentenced to life in prison."

"That's probably why Jonathan changed his name. And maybe it explains why he was so nervous around you."

"Afraid he might be like his father, you mean?"

"Exactly." Farnsworth slid her reading glasses from her nose and sat heavily next to Erin. There was sweat on her forehead, though the room was chilly. "Are you going to tell anyone?"

"That would be a violation of his privacy, and I don't see how it relates to the case."

"Unless murder runs in the family."

"Different MO, different circumstances."

"Still," Farnsworth said, "like father—"

"Genetics is not predetermination," she said, thinking about the feel of his lips on hers, the warmth of his breath, and his fingertips on her cheek.

"You are sweet on him, aren't you?"

"That has nothing to do with it," Erin replied, but she didn't entirely believe her own words.

Chapter Twenty-Nine

❧

After leaving Farnsworth's a little after noon, Erin drove straight to the George and Dragon. After checking in with Sally, who was serving lunch in the pub, she went upstairs to Room 207 and knocked on the door.

She listened for an answer, but there was none, so she turned to leave, but decided to knock one more time. This time a sleepy, muffled voice called out.

"Who's there?"

"It's me," she said. "Erin Coleridge."

"Just a minute." There was the sound of bare feet on the floor, then a closet door opening, accompanied by muttering, and finally the door opened to reveal a very disheveled Detective Hemming. His blond hair was uncombed, he had a day's growth of wispy beard, and his feet were bare. A plaid bathrobe was fastened around his waist, over a pair of blue-striped pajamas.

"I brought you soup," she said, holding out a container of chicken noodle soup Sally had given her.

"How did you know I was sick?"

"News travels fast around here, in case you hadn't noticed."

"Very kind of you," he said. "I would invite you in, but I might be contagious."

"How high is your fever?"

"I don't know," he said, holding on to the door frame to steady himself.

"Let's find out," she said, pulling a white digital thermometer from her pocket.

He smiled weakly. "You don't miss any tricks, do you?"

"Open up." He complied, and she slid it into his mouth. There was something unexpectedly intimate about the gesture. Did nurses and doctors feel this with their patients, she wondered, or did it become routine for them?

The thermometer beeped, indicating there was a reading. Carefully extracting it, she read the numbers on the display.

"It's thirty-eight point eight C," she said.

"Is that bad?"

"It's very high. Come along—let's get you back to bed."

"But—"

"No arguing," she said, slipping into the room, a little surprised at her take-charge manner.

He obeyed meekly, allowing her to fluff the pillows and smooth the blankets after crawling back into bed. In truth, he didn't look like he was able to stand upright much longer.

"There now," she said. "That's better. Are you allergic to any medication?"

"I don't think so."

"Here's some aspirin for the fever."

"But—"

"Take it. Now, how about some soup?"

"I'm not really hungry."

"Have you eaten today?"

"Mostly I've been sleeping."

"It's important to eat."

"In a little while," he said, closing his eyes. She thought he had fallen asleep, but then he spoke. "Did you think I might spill facts about the case in my weakened state?" His eyes were still closed, but a little smile played on his lips.

"I didn't come here to take advantage of your illness. Though if your fever gets any higher, you might become delirious."

She was interrupted by the sound of Bach's "Toccata and Fugue in D Minor." At first she wondered where the organ was, then realized it was a mobile phone ringtone, coming from the pocket of his jacket, hanging in the closet.

"Shall I get it?" she asked.

"Yes, please."

She handed it to him.

"Yes, sir," he said, sitting up against the headboard. "No, sir. Yes, sir. I'll find out and get back to you. Yes, quite all right, thank you, sir. Right. Good-bye, sir." Handing the phone back to Erin, he slid back beneath the covers.

"Your boss in York?" she asked.

"DCI Witherspoon."

"What did he want?"

"He wanted to know—ah, you almost caught me," he said, wagging a finger at her, but his voice was weak and his eyelids drooped.

"How about some soup?"

"Later. Right now I need to rest."

"I'm going to leave this here," Erin said, setting the soup on the bedside table. "Mind you eat some."

"I will, after I . . . have a little . . . nap," he said, closing his eyes again.

"I'll call later to see how you're feeling," she said, tiptoeing from the room. Closing the door behind her, she walked back down the hall, the ancient floorboards creaking beneath her feet.

As she walked through the lobby, she saw Sergeant Jarral in the pub having lunch.

"Hello there," he said with his usual cheery smile as she approached his table. "Care to join me?"

"I don't want to interrupt your lunch."

"Not at all—have a seat."

She did, ordering a ginger beer from the waiter.

"How is he?" Jarral asked when she told him she had come from Detective Hemming's room.

"A bit delirious, I'm afraid. He had trouble understanding what DCI Witherspoon was talking about on the phone."

"Really?"

"I overheard a bit of it myself. He was calling about—" She paused, pretending to be distracted by something floating in her ginger beer.

"He wanted us to look into that lorry accident in Dublin."

"You mean Farnsworth's husband?"

"Yeah," Jarral said through a mouthful of mashed potatoes and mushy peas. "He's not convinced it's an accident."

"I don't understand. What's that got to do with—"

"The boss got it into his head that if she offed her husband, she might be capable of—well, you know," he said, looking almost apologetic.

"That's completely insane," Erin said. This news made her furious, and any guilt she felt about lying to the sergeant evaporated.

Jarral shrugged. "I don't know much more myself."

She wondered what DCI Witherspoon had discovered about the death of Farnsworth's husband as she climbed into the Sunbeam. She loved the car, with its creamy leather interior and bucket seats, her one foolish extravagance. *Everyone has a weak spot*, she thought as she listened to the low purr of the engine before driving out of the car park. The killer too had a weak spot; she just had to figure out what it was.

But first she had to talk to Farnsworth. She dialed the number, but her friend's voice mail picked up at once. That could mean she was on the other line. Multiple redials brought no results, so Erin turned her car in the direction of Farnsworth's house.

Chapter Thirty

~

"What could I possibly have to do with the accident that killed my husband?" Farnsworth said. "I was nowhere near Dublin!"

"Apparently the chief inspector in York has got it into his head," said Erin.

They were seated at the kitchen table, surrounded by her friend's usually comforting clutter. It didn't feel very reassuring today, though, as they tried to sort through the strange turn of events.

"He was an alcoholic, for God's sake!" Farnsworth said. Her usually mellifluous voice had a shrill edge. "I saw him nearly get run over a couple of times myself."

"They'll soon find it's all rubbish."

"How on earth did they get this into their heads?" Farnsworth said, as a plump tabby jumped onto her lap.

"I think someone put them onto it."

"Who would do that?" she said, stroking the cat.

"Someone who wanted to divert attention from themselves."

Farnsworth's eyes widened. "The real killer, you mean?"

"Exactly."

Erin refused her friend's offer of tea—she needed time alone to think about how to ferret out the source of the rumor. When she arrived home, it was just after two, so she decided to open the bookstore for the rest of the afternoon. She didn't normally open on a Tuesday, but it was cheerier inside the cottage with all the lights on and a fire blazing in the grate.

She put on a recording of Glen Gould playing Bach fugues and lay down on the couch to think. Practically everyone in town knew about the lorry accident that had killed Farnsworth's husband, but only one person had the motive to suggest she had anything to do with it.

She almost didn't hear the bell over the front door when it tinkled an hour later. Wandering through the shelves, she came upon James Marlowe in the forensics section of the store. In his hands was a book she had acquired recently, *Deadly Concoctions: The Uses and Misuses of Poison Throughout History.*

"Hello," he said in a friendly voice, though he looked startled to see her. Wearing a crisp yellow shirt buttoned at the neck, no tie, and a gray flannel jacket, he looked very smart. She wondered if it was for her sake.

"Hi," she said. "I didn't expect to see you away from your shop at this hour."

"Leaving it in the questionably capable hands of Angus," he said, smiling. "He's got to learn to deal with the public if he means to be a butcher."

"Angus?"

"Angus McGregor, my new shop assistant—local lad, knows his meat, but a bit awkward with customers. So I took the sink-or-swim approach, figuring he's better without me breathing down his neck all the time."

"Where are James Chester and Polly?"

"Down with a stomach bug, I'm afraid."

She looked at the book in his hands. "Are you afraid they—"

"Oh, good heavens, no!" he said, laughing, though it sounded a bit forced. "Polly's got it into her head she's going to help you solve this crime, you know, so I promised I'd bring her a book."

"What makes her think I'm intent on solving it?"

"It's no secret—everyone in town knows what you're doing."

"And what is that?"

"Well, I mean, you're investigating on your own, aren't you?"

Erin liked James Marlowe, but she didn't entirely trust him and wasn't about to spill all her secrets.

"I was poking around a bit, but not so much anymore," she lied. "The police seem to have it under control."

"Really? Because that's not the impression I'm getting at all."

"I did hear a rumor they were looking into the death of Farnsworth's husband," she said, watching his reaction.

He frowned. "What on earth has that got to do with anything?"

Either he was a good liar or he really knew nothing. "I have no idea," she said. "Now, then, about this book for Polly—how about something for James Chester as well? I'll give you a family discount."

He looked as if he was about to say something, then thought better of it. "What do you suggest?"

"What's he into these days?"

"He's mad for superheroes. Transformers, X-Men, Spiderman—you name it."

"I have just the thing," she said, poking through the graphic novels and comics shelf. Though Erin hadn't read a comic since she was twelve, she remembered how much she had loved browsing through the shops in Oxford to find the latest issue of *Green Lantern* or *Superman*. "Here's a recent graphic novel involving a number of superheroes fighting together. He might like that. Tell you what—I'll throw it in for free."

"You don't need to do that."

"It's my pleasure."

"You're too generous," Marlowe said, looking distracted. Erin had the feeling he just wanted to finish the transaction and leave as soon as possible.

"Give them my best," she said, slipping the books into a paper bag. "I'm just glad to see children who read instead of playing video games all day."

"Video games are strictly verboten in our house," he said, handing her a twenty-pound note. "Keep it, please—you've done enough for us."

"Ta very much," she said, putting it in the cash drawer.

"Well, I'll be off, then," he said, tipping his cap.

Erin waited until the sound of his car engine disappeared down the driveway, then returned to the back of the house. She had a lingering feeling she had interrupted him in the middle of something—the expression on his face was like a little boy caught with his hand in the cookie jar. Had he been trying to read the book without being seen?

Pulling the *Collected Works of Samuel Taylor Coleridge* from the shelf, Erin settled down on the couch with the book. She turned to the opening lines of "Christabel."

> Tis the middle of night by the castle clock,
> And the owls have awakened the crowing cock;
> Tu—whit! Tu—whoo!
> And hark, again! the crowing cock,
> How drowsily it crew.

Outside, she heard the piercing screech of the barn owl, and a shiver stole down her spine. Pulling the burgundy afghan around her, she settled deeper into the couch, burying herself in the opium-fueled dreams of Samuel Taylor Coleridge. Lulled by the crackle of kindling and wind whistling in the eaves, Erin didn't realize she had dozed off until the harsh ring of her landline shot her abruptly into consciousness. Ears tingling, she staggered from the couch to snatch the receiver off the hook.

It was Farnsworth.

"Are you ready to go the meeting?"

"Meeting?"

"The Events Committee, pet. Did you forget?"

"That's tonight?"

"It is Tuesday, isn't it?"

"Yes."

"Wickham! Stop bothering Lydia, will you? Scat! Sorry," she said into the phone. "He's such a naughty boy. Keeps trying to mate with Lydia."

"Sounds like you named your cats appropriately."

"One does what one can," Farnsworth said, in a perfect imitation of the Queen. "Shall I pick you up in half an hour?"

"All right," Erin said, hanging up. She was disappointed at not having the evening to herself, but the meeting could be a chance to snoop around and glean more information.

Farnsworth arrived right on time, and soon they were zipping down the tree-lined road leading to town. Farnsworth liked to drive very fast, and Erin held on to the edge of her seat as her friend whipped around the turn to Castlegate.

After listening to Erin's account of Marlowe's visit, Farnsworth said, "If he wanted information on poison, why not just go online?"

"Maybe he was afraid his computer would be seized by the police. They can look at your web browsing history."

"Aren't there ways to erase that?"

"You can reformat the hard drive, but that would raise suspicion. And it's amazing what forensic computer experts can dig up. What's this meeting about again?" Erin said as they drove through the center of town, lights on in all the windows as darkness embraced the moorland.

"It's to formulate a plan on how to keep everyone safe with a murderer in town—allegedly."

"Why allegedly?"

"Personally, I think Prudence is consolidating her power base. There's bound to be an election after this is all over, and she's had her eye on the presidency for a long time."

"Does she have any opposition, now that Sylvia's gone?"

"That remains to be seen," Farnsworth said as they pulled into the car park on Church Street, just behind the handsome Norman building, with its sturdy yellow stones and square turrets.

Erin shivered as they entered through the sweeping archway in the front of the church. The chances were very good that somewhere within the ancient walls a murderer was planning their next move.

Chapter Thirty-One

The meeting was just getting under way when Erin and Farnsworth joined the half dozen people in the upstairs meeting room. When Reverend Motley had suggested they gather in the conference room next to the parish office, everyone had jumped at the chance. It was elegant and comfortable, with wrought ironwork on the tall arched windows, a thick, creamy Persian carpet, and deep burgundy wallpaper. It smelled of eucalyptus and communion wine (actually tawny port—Farnsworth joked that it helped keep congregation numbers up.)

Seated around the polished rectangular table were the reverend, Prudence Pettibone, Hetty Miller, Owen and Carolyn Hardacker, and Jonathan Alder. Jonathan gave Erin a sunny smile as she took a seat opposite him. He wore a baby-blue Oxford shirt that brought out his eyes, his curly hair just unruly enough, and the sight of him made her stomach go a little hollow.

"Did we miss anything?" Farnsworth asked, sinking into the chair next to Erin.

"The question on the floor is what we can do to keep our members safe," Reverend Motley replied sanctimoniously. He could make a simple statement sound like a sermon—there was something unbearably pompous about the way he inclined his head, or interlaced his fingers over his protruding stomach.

"How can we possibly keep anyone safe?" Carolyn asked.

"I agree with Carolyn," said Prudence, sniffling. "That's on the police, not us."

"Obviously they failed," said Hetty. "So the question remains—what can *we* do?"

"For starters, I'm not drinking anything served by the tea committee," Farnsworth said.

"Can we get *serious* about this, please?" said Carolyn.

Farnsworth leaned back in her chair. "I'm dead serious, pet."

"Ms. Appleby's suggestion is good, especially if you broaden it," said Jonathan. "We should all be careful eating food if we don't know its origins."

"Obviously," Hetty said irritably. "But what *else* can we do?"

Owen turned to Erin. "You're the crime expert."

"Yes, what do *you* think?" Pru said eagerly. "Will the poisoner strike again?"

"It depends on the motive behind the crime," Erin said.

"You mean it could be a one-off," said Jonathan.

"Right. It's impossible to answer without knowing why Sylvia was targeted."

"But," Reverend Motley said, "do we freeze membership until this whole thing is sorted?"

"Are people banging on doors to get in?" asked Farnsworth.

"We've had quite a few inquiries recently," Prudence replied.

"Good lord," said Owen, scratching his head. "That's perverse."

"Maybe this is a chance to increase membership," Erin suggested.

"If we can ever agree on how much to charge," Farnsworth added. She was right—the question of membership dues was a key struggle between the Old and New Guards.

"Why on earth would anyone want to join now," Carolyn said, "knowing they could be the next victim?"

"You know what they say," Farnsworth said, opening her ubiquitous thermos. "There's no such thing as bad publicity."

"What's in there?" asked Hetty, eyeing the thermos greedily. "Tea?"

"Darjeeling," said Farnsworth. "Special mountain blend."

Hetty licked her lips. "Ooo, could I possibly have just a little?"

"Aren't you afraid it might be poisoned?" Prudence said.

"Not if she's drinking it herself," Hetty shot back.

"Maybe she's built up an immunity," Jonathan suggested. "It's possible to do that, isn't it?" he asked Erin.

"Well—" she began, but Farnsworth cut her off.

"Or maybe we were all in on it—a massive plot, like *Murder on the Orient Express*."

"I can't believe you're joking about this!" Carolyn cried, her eyes brimming with tears. "Sylvia is *dead*—it's horrid to make fun of it. It's just horrid!"

"Everyone in this room wants t'find who killed Sylvia, love," Owen said in a soothing voice.

"For all I know, one of you *did* kill Sylvia!" Carolyn said, her voice rising to hysteria. Rising abruptly from her seat, she stormed out of the room. Owen got up without a word and went after her.

"Well!" Hetty said when they had gone. "I didn't see *that* coming."

"I have a feeling there's something more going on with her," said Jonathan.

"'Very seldom does complete truth belong to any human disclosure,'" the reverend opined. He took a breath to continue, but Prudence interrupted.

"'Seldom can it happen that something is not a little disguised, or a little mistaken,'" she finished for him.

Erin and Farnsworth exchanged a glance. Pru's desire to be the source of all Jane Austen quotes really was too much.

"Are you suggesting Carolyn isn't telling everything she knows about Sylvia?" Hetty asked, frowning. The room was warm and her lipstick was beginning to smear, giving her a lopsided look.

"I think that's what they're saying, pet," said Farnsworth.

"But why would she hide anything from us?" said Hetty. "Unless, of course, she—" She stopped midsentence.

Reverend Motley heaved a deep sigh, the purpose of which was to get everyone's attention. "The secrets of the human heart are ever perplexing to us mortals," he said sententiously. "Only the Almighty knows and sees all, and His wisdom surpasses our feeble attempts to understand the Mystery that is Life." He pointed heavenward with a flourish, resettling his hands over his bulging belly. His hands were delicate, pink and plump, like a child's hands. In fact, there was something eunuchlike about his entire person, from his bald head with its ring of fine, curly hair to his soft, round body and shiny, unlined face. Piety oozed like sweat from his pores.

"Why don't we just issue a statement telling everyone to be careful?" Farnsworth said impatiently. "And that we'll give updates on the case as they become available."

"Good idea," said Jonathan. "We can send out a group email. What do you think?" he asked Erin.

"Very sensible," she agreed.

"As for updating people on the case, you have your ways of getting information, don't you?" Hetty said with a sly smile.

"Well, I wouldn't say that—" Erin said, but to her relief, Pru cut her off.

"I'll compose a memorandum!" she said eagerly. "I can send it out to all the members."

"Why don't you encourage anyone with information to come forward?" Erin suggested.

"Don't you think anyone who knew something would have already done that?" Hetty said, her eyes flitting around the room.

"Not necessarily," said Erin. "Sometimes people need to be encouraged."

"Virtue should be its own reward," the Reverend said, frowning.

"It doesn't always work that way, pet," said Farnsworth, rising from her chair. "Are we done here? I have hungry mouths to feed."

"We might as well wrap it up," said Jonathan. "I guess the Hardackers aren't coming back."

"And you have to get up early for school," Hetty added, winking at him.

"I do indeed," he said, rising. He followed Erin as she headed for the door. "So have you become the police confidante?" he asked, giving her his trademark smile.

"If I have, it's news to me."

"No new developments in the case?"

"Not that I know of," she said, thinking she probably wouldn't tell him if there were. She liked Jonathan, but she was beginning to wonder if his interest in her was merely an attempt to get closer to the investigation.

Across the room, Reverend Motley was chatting up Hetty—or was it the other way around? She was leaning against the antique sideboard, with its curly maple carving and burnished finish. It was a handsome piece—maybe she had chosen it as a backdrop on purpose, thinking it would show her off to advantage.

She threw her head back to laugh at something the Reverend said, opening her mouth so wide Erin could see the dark fillings in her molars. She had to hand it to Hetty—she might be sex-crazed and obsessed with men, but at least she went after them with gusto. It reminded Erin of her mother's energetic embrace of life, an appetite so fierce that in the end it devoured her.

She and Jonathan followed Farnsworth out of the church into the cold night air. A carpet of glittering white stars shone overhead. Erin turned back to Jonathan. "Tell you what: if I learn anything of interest from the coppers, you'll be the first to know."

She wasn't sure if she meant it, or why she'd even said it, but he broke out in a smile so wide she hoped she could make good on her promise. At this point, though, finding Sylvia's killer seemed as remote as the distant stars high overhead in the cold, dark sky.

Chapter Thirty-Two

"So . . . investigation . . . progressing?" DCI Witherspoon's voice was tinny and faint over the landline, like he was in a metal container underwater. The line crackled and spat. So much for technology, Hemming thought as he strained to hear.

"Can't quite hear you, sir," he said, locking eyes with Sergeant Jarral, who was making short work of a jelly doughnut. They were in the back room of the station house on Wednesday morning, waiting for Chief Constable McCrary to return from dealing with an incident involving a drunk motorcyclist.

Hemming rubbed his forehead wearily. Though his fever was down somewhat, he felt awful. He had dragged himself from bed and down to the police station—this case wasn't going to solve itself.

"I SAID, HOW IS THE INVESTIGATION GOING—"

Wincing, Hemming held the receiver away from his ear. "Coming across loud and clear now, sir," he said, rolling his eyes at Jarral, who was gobbling up the rest of his doughnut.

"What's going on down there?" said the chief. "Is there some kind of interference on the line?"

"It seems to be gone now."

"I have lads in Dublin looking into the lorry accident. Meanwhile, I'd like a progress report on the investigation from your end."

"Yes, sir. I'll send it along ASAP."

"You all right? You don't sound well."

"Just a little congestion, sir."

"You look bloody awful," Jarral muttered.

Hemming glared at him.

The sergeant shrugged. "Sorry, but you do."

"What's that?" said Witherspoon.

"Sergeant Jarral said something. Sorry, sir."

"Be sure to send me that update."

"Yes, sir," Hemming said, and rang off.

He looked out the picture window into the main room, where Constable Harris sat quietly in front of a computer screen, his smooth black hair shiny in the pale-green glow.

"Cybercrime's the future, sir," Jarral said, brushing powdered sugar off his shirt. "That's where the big money is."

"Perhaps, but murder will always be up close and personal."

"Sir?"

"Yes, Sergeant?"

"It's probably not my place, but—"

"Out with it," Hemming said. His head pounded, his mouth was dry, and he wanted nothing more than to crawl back in bed.

"Well, sir, Ms. Coleridge is not yet officially eliminated from our list of suspects."

"That's right," he answered warily, knowing where this was headed.

"I was just wondering if it might be best to—"

"To what, Sergeant?" He knew perfectly well what Jarral was getting at but wanted to make him say it.

"Well, sir, maybe not socialize with anyone who's still on the list of potential suspects."

"Is that what you think I was doing—socializing?"

"Well, sir, I saw her coming out of your room last night—"

"I ran into her on the moors, completely by chance, and when she heard I was ill, she dropped off some soup for me. That's the extent of it."

"Yes, sir—sorry, sir," Jarral said sheepishly.

"Look," Hemming said, taking pity on him, "I don't want you to think you can't be frank with me. But I assure you there's nothing untoward or unprofessional going on between us," he said, knowing it wasn't entirely true.

"Yes, sir," the sergeant said, but he still wouldn't make eye contact.

A wave of dizziness swept over the detective, and he leaned on the desk to steady himself.

"You all right, sir?"

"I'll be all right."

"Shouldn't you be in bed, sir?"

"The investigation isn't going to wait," he said, putting on his coat. "Sorry we couldn't stay to see the chief constable," Hemming said to Constable Harris as they went through the main room.

"Any message for him, sir?" he asked, looking up from the computer, his basset hound face serious. His voice was as dolorous as his face, with a slight Welsh lilt.

"Just that we'll keep him updated."

"I'll tell him. Are you going to the bonfire next week, sir?"

"What bonfire?"

"Did you not know? We have a village fete every year, rain or shine, the Friday before Halloween—or All Hallows' Eve, as some folks round here like to call it."

"There are posters all over town about it, sir," said Jarral.

"When the chief constable returns, tell him I think we should maintain a sturdy police presence at the fete—assuming we haven't caught our killer by then."

"Indeed I will, sir," Harris replied, turning his attention back to his computer.

When they left the station house, the wind had picked up again and was blowing anything not moored down—leaves, sticks, discarded fish-and-chips wrappers—all whirling around in funnels, like miniature tornadoes. Hemming supposed that accounted for the bad phone reception.

"What's the weather forecast?" he asked as they climbed into the car.

"Checking, sir," Jarral replied. He had several weather apps on his phone—not unusual on an island where weather was a national obsession. "Looks dicey, sir," he said, squinting at the phone. "Winds rising steadily, with gale force expected by tonight."

As they drove, dry leaves rushing past the car as if in a hurry to be somewhere, Hemming thought about huddling in the ruins on the moor, sharing a thermos of tea with Erin Coleridge, as the leaves scattered around him like lost souls.

Chapter Thirty-Three

By ten o'clock on Wednesday evening, the candles had burned low around Farnsworth Appleby's dinner table. Seated around the oblong oak table were Erin, Prudence, and Hetty. The four friends met for dinner once a month, taking turns hosting. Sometimes they added other people to their little party—if Hetty was dating anyone, he might come along, and of course Winton was always there when Pru hosted. Erin's father had joined them once or twice, as had Farnsworth's sister, who lived in York. Her son Philip had even shown up once and spent the evening arguing with his mother, pointing out her flaws.

There had been some talk about skipping this month, but Pru had insisted the ritual would be comforting. Looking at her friends' faces, flushed with wine and Yorkshire lamb, Pru was glad she had prevailed—she felt safe, sheltered, secure.

"Well, that was a *splendid* dinner," Hetty Miller said, wiping her mouth delicately and placing her napkin neatly beside her plate. Prudence never ceased to be amazed that, even after a full meal, her friend's lipstick remained magically in place, as though tattooed to her face.

"You hardly ate a thing," Farnsworth said, frowning at Hetty's unfinished plate.

"How do you think she stays so thin?" Prudence said, pouring the last of the Malbec into her glass. She had downed a bit more than her share, but after all, she had brought it, and it wasn't a cheap bottle. She'd splurged because Winton wasn't there—if he'd been looking over her shoulder, she would never have spent so much. Sighing with contentment, she leaned back in her chair, enjoying Farnsworth's dining room in the soft glow of candlelight. Winton hated candles, so she was never allowed to use them at home. He insisted they might cause a fire that could burn down his beloved cottage. Though she thought his fears were exaggerated, she had learned over the years that capitulation was easier than arguing.

"I have to watch what I eat," Hetty said, "because I'm seeing someone."

"How exciting!" Farnsworth said. "Who is it?"

Hetty lowered her eyes modestly, but the triumph in her voice was unmistakable. "Reverend Motley."

Pru's jaw dropped. She couldn't imagine anyone wanting to date the vicar, let alone brag about it.

"Of course, he's an older man," Hetty said, and Pru nearly spit her mouthful of wine across the table. *Older man!* Who did she think she was kidding? Hetty was at least ten years older than the reverend. Prudence looked at Erin and Farnsworth to see how they were taking it, but their expressions betrayed no hint of mockery.

"That's wonderful," said Erin.

"Yes," Prudence agreed, forcing herself to smile. "You must keep us updated on how it's going."

"We're going to a movie over the weekend," Hetty said smugly. "I'll give you a blow-by-blow."

"I look forward to it, pet," Farnsworth said, but Pru thought there was a hint of sarcasm in her voice.

"Thank you again for a wonderful meal," Hetty told Farnsworth.

"Yes," said Erin. "That rosemary from your garden was brilliant with the lamb."

"It feels a little strange, enjoying ourselves, with all that's happening," Farnsworth mused. "Poor Sylvia and all."

"It's important to maintain some semblance of normalcy in times like these," Pru declared firmly.

"I thought we'd skip the sweets for dessert," Farnsworth said, lumbering to the table with a basket of fruit and a plate of cheese. Plaintive meowing came from behind the parlor door—at Hetty's insistence, the cats were locked out of the dining room during these meetings. She claimed to have allergies, but Prudence thought she just didn't want cat hair on her expensive clothes.

Prudence thought of Winton at home, probably feeling sleepy by now, putting on his striped flannel pajamas before drinking a warm glass of milk with just a touch of honey. Such a creature of habit, and she felt lucky to have him, but she relied on her friends for stimulation and excitement—not that much was to be had in a town like Kirkbymoorside. Lately, of course, there had been nothing *but* excitement, with Sylvia's death and its aftermath. It was as if the whole town had gone crazy.

"The one I feel sorry for is Suzanne Becker," Farnsworth said.

"Such a pretty woman," said Erin, plucking a glistening red grape from the bunch in the basket.

"If you like skeletons," Hetty said dismissively, sniffing an orange.

Prudence smiled to herself. Hetty was incorrigibly vain and competitive around any women she perceived as a threat to her self-image as Belle of the Ball. Prudence had no illusions about herself and knew she was anything but glamorous—one reason she and Hetty got on well, she supposed. Still, she noted with satisfaction, she was the one with the faithful husband, while Hetty cycled through men like a gambling addict picking winners at a racetrack—and with approximately the same odds.

"I heard she was a nurse in Germany," said Hetty. "I think that makes her *terribly* suspicious."

"Why?" said Pru, helping herself to a chunk of Stilton.

"Nurses make good poisoners," Erin said. "The classic Angels of Death."

"Oh, yes, that's true," said Prudence, though she had no idea what Erin was talking about. Erin was obsessed with crime and had all kinds of gruesome knowledge.

"I heard she was fired under murky circumstances," said Farnsworth.

"That's it, then!" Hetty declared. "She poisoned Sylvia out of jealousy. It makes total sense."

"Things are not always what they seem," Erin remarked. "There are plenty of cases where the most obvious suspect turns out to be innocent."

"But what could be simpler?" said Hetty, nibbling on the orange. She reminded Pru of a rabbit, with her tiny little bites. She had big, rodentlike teeth, too, prominent beneath her brightly painted lips. "She killed her husband's mistress."

"Then why not poison him too?" said Prudence, draining the last of her wine.

"Maybe she was too afraid to try," suggested Farnsworth.

"Afraid?" Pru said.

"Kurt Becker has been intimidating his wife for years," Farnsworth said.

Pru's eyes widened. "Physical abuse?"

"Psychological, mostly, though I wouldn't put it past him."

Hetty shook her head. "What a cad."

Farnsworth shrugged. "He's a man. They're all brutes."

"Now, Farnsworth," said Erin, "you know I hate it when you generalize—"

"*Fine,*" she said, rolling her eyes. "Not *all* of them."

"Just most of them," said Hetty.

"Not my Winton," Pru declared proudly, feeling the rosy glow from the Malbec.

"We all agree, he's a treasure," Hetty snapped. Pru felt a little shiver of pleasure at her friend's jealousy. With all her airs and pretense, Hetty Miller would be lucky to snag someone like Winton.

"What's all this about the police thinking you're behind the death of Dastardly Dick?" Hetty asked Farnworth.

Pru's ears pricked up. "I didn't hear anything about that," she said, looking back and forth from Erin to Farnsworth.

"It's total rubbish, of course," Hetty continued. "I hope you've convinced them of that," she told Erin.

"I'm doing my best," she replied. "Apparently it's coming out of the head brass in York."

"What about Kurt Becker?" said Hetty. "What hold does he have over his wife?"

Farnsworth picked a plum from the basket of fruit. "He's probably convinced her that she needs him because she's too weak to survive on her own."

"And she believes him?"

"'It isn't what we say or think that defines us, but what we do,'" Prudence declared. Quoting Jane Austen was a way of asserting her presence when she felt left behind in a conversation. To her disappointment, no one remarked upon it, or even seemed to notice. "That's from *Sense and Sensibility*," she added lamely.

"Suzanne Becker probably married young," said Farnsworth. "Big mistake. Don't you go and do that," she warned Erin.

Erin rolled her eyes. "It's a bit late for that."

"You're young still," Hetty said.

Erin smiled. "Thank you for saying so."

For some reason, Pru noted, Hetty never seemed jealous of Erin Coleridge, even though she was young and attractive. Perhaps it was because the bookstore owner seemed to go out of her way to downplay her charms, slouching around in yoga pants and dowdy sandals, with no makeup, her hair piled on top of her head willy-nilly.

"'Happiness in marriage is entirely a matter of chance,'" Farnsworth said, which irked Prudence, who considered herself the queen of Austen quotes.

"You can say that again," said Hetty. "My second husband—"

"It's time we were off," said Prudence. When Hetty started enumerating her exes, it was time to hit the road. "Thank you for a lovely evening," she said to Farnsworth. She was still a bit toddly from the wine, but they had come in her car, and she trusted Hetty to drive even less.

"My pleasure," Farnsworth said. "You were right—this was a good idea, and I'm glad we did it."

"Come along, Hetty," Pru said, as they slung on their coats—Hetty's was a creamy peach wool designer jacket, while her own was a dun-colored castoff, tattered at the sleeves and collar. Sometimes she wondered what it would be like to care about her appearance as much as Hetty did, but the thought of trying that hard was exhausting. Throwing open the front door, she took a deep breath of cold air to fortify herself.

To her dismay, her car refused to start. In spite of Hetty's insistence to the contrary, Prudence knew she hadn't left the lights on. When she went back inside, Erin suggested she take her car.

"But you have to get home," Pru protested.

"Farnsworth will drive me," Erin said, pressing the keys into her hand.

In the end, she accepted the offer—after all, she and Hetty lived in one direction, Erin in the other. After quick hugs and farewells, they stepped back out into the night.

* * *

As they listened to the sound of Pru's car driving off, Erin turned to Farnsworth.

"Let me help you tidy up."

"That's an offer I can't refuse," Farnsworth said, carrying wine glasses into the kitchen. "That was a decent bottle of plonk. Pru must have bought it when Winton wasn't looking."

"Shall I blow out the candles?"

"Leave them for a bit. I don't usually bother with them when I'm alone, so I want to enjoy them," she said, opening the parlor door. Half a dozen cats dashed into the room, sniffing the air, stretching toward the kitchen counter to poke their noses at the remnants of the meal. A blue-eyed seal-point Siamese wrapped around Farnsworth's shins, purring loudly. "There's a good little girl, Jane," she cooed.

"Get down, Darcy!" Farnsworth yelled as an athletic black-and-white tom leapt at the stack of dishes in the sink. "Come along," she said, bending to place a couple of the dirty plates on the floor. The cats responded by rushing to gobble up the scraps, crouching as they licked the remnants from the creamy porcelain.

"Farnsworth?" Erin said, wrapping the cheeses in cellophane and putting them in the fridge.

"Yes, pet?"

"You don't really hate all men, do you?"

"I suppose not." Farnsworth plucked a spear of celery from her salad plate and chewed on it dutifully. She sighed. "But I do hate celery."

Erin leaned over to brush stray crumbs off the tablecloth into her open palm. A few escaped, hitting the floor, where they were pounced upon by half a dozen felines. She laughed. "Your cats will eat anything."

"True dat, as the kids say nowadays."

"Why, Miss Appleby, you astonish me," Erin said, slipping into her posh "Austen voice." "I had no idea you kept up with the vernacular of the hoi polloi."

Farnsworth flipped a tea towel over her shoulder. "Indeed, Miss Coleridge, there are a great many facets of my character that may reveal themselves through careful study."

"I have no doubt that is so. Your revelation of hidden qualities hints at more depth than I had hitherto dared suspect," Erin said, filling the sink with hot soapy water.

"I have always maintained that the ability to surprise one's intimates is important in sustaining any friendship—would you not concur?"

"Indeed, it would be churlish not to, under the circumstances," Erin replied, plunging the sterling silver cutlery into the water.

"I am gratified we have come to an agreeable conclusion," Farnsworth remarked, wiping the kitchen counters with a blue sponge.

"I hope in the future I can persuade you to alter your opinion of the male species," said Erin, rinsing the cutlery before placing it in the dish drainer.

"If anyone is capable of such a feat, no doubt you are high upon that list."

They were interrupted by a frantic knocking at the door.

Opening it, Erin was startled to see Hetty Miller, barefoot and bedraggled, her elegant jacket smeared with mud.

"We had . . . an accident," she panted, dazed and out of breath. "Please, call for help!"

"Where's Pru? Is she all right?" Erin said, helping her inside as Farnsworth hastily dialed 999 on her landline.

"She—she's—" Hetty said, and then she fainted.

Chapter Thirty-Four

◡

"Hetty, wake up!" Farnsworth said, slapping her face rather harder than necessary, Erin thought. Luckily, they had caught Hetty as she fell, lowering her gently to the floor. They propped her against the china cupboard, legs splayed out on the uneven paving stones of the kitchen floor. Most people who owned old houses in the area had remodeled, but either through inertia or a taste for authenticity, Farnsworth had done little to alter the farmhouse's original appearance.

Hetty looked out of place in the rustic room, with her expensive clothing and makeup—though now she was a sorry sight, smeared with mud and traces of blood, which worried Erin.

"Hetty!" Farnsworth said, shaking her. "*Where* is Prudence?"

"Pru . . ." Hetty said groggily, opening her eyes. "She was run off the road . . ."

"Where? *Where* did it happen?"

"At the bend in the road . . . before the golf club," Hetty murmured. She sounded drunk.

"On Kirkby Lane?" Farnsworth prompted her.

"Yes . . . went into the ditch. Couldn't find my mobile . . . so came here."

"Look for the car on Kirkby Lane near the golf club," Erin said to the emergency operator on the phone. It wasn't far—less than a quarter of a mile from Farnsworth's house.

"I'll relay that information now," the dispatcher said.

"Then tell them to come here afterward," Erin said, giving them Farnsworth's address.

"Do you have an emergency there as well?" the woman asked.

"We have an injured person," Farnsworth said, holding a glass of water up to Hetty's lips, "but please come when you can."

Hetty soon rallied and, with some assistance, tottered over to the parlor sofa.

"Was Prudence conscious?" Erin said, helping her ease onto the couch.

"I don't think so. She wouldn't answer me."

"Was she bleeding?"

"I didn't see any blood."

"What happened?" said Farnsworth. "You said she was run off the road?"

"A car came up from behind," Hetty said. "It started to pass, then swerved toward us."

"On purpose?" said Erin.

"I don't know," Hetty said, brushing bits of dried mud off her soiled coat. "It all happened so fast."

"Did you get a look at the other car?" Farnsworth interrupted as the sound of rapidly approaching sirens pierced the night.

"No," Hetty said. "By the time I knew what was happening, they were gone."

"What kind of person leaves an accident?" said Farnsworth.

Erin frowned. "A guilty one."

"Poor Prudence—I hope she's all right. We should go to her," Hetty said, rising unsteadily from the couch.

"They're already there," Erin said. The sirens had stopped, so the rescuers must have arrived at the site of the accident.

"But—I want to be there," Hetty protested, trying again to stand.

"*You* stay *put*," Farnsworth commanded.

Hetty grabbed one of the cats, a wispy little calico, and began stroking it fervidly. "Ohhh," she wailed softly. "Poor Prudence. She's the best friend I ever had." The cat looked startled at first, but soon decided it was onto a good thing and rubbed up against her, stiff-legged, purring loudly. "Oh, kitty," she said, hugging it impulsively. "You know how I feel, don't you?"

"That's Lydia," Farnsworth said. "She's a flighty little thing."

"Like the Jane Austen character?" Hetty said. "Elizabeth Bennet's youngest sister?"

"Yes. She's a little vixen. It seemed appropriate."

"Well, *I* think she's adorable!" Hetty moaned, clasping the cat tighter in her arms. It was then Erin realized Hetty was in shock.

"Lie down!" she commanded.

"What?" said Hetty.

"Lie. Down. *Now*," Erin said, taking the cat from her arms.

"Why does she have to do that?" asked Farnsworth as Erin helped Hetty lower herself back onto the cushions.

"She's in shock," Erin said, taking her wrist and feeling for the pulse. It was a little rapid, but nothing alarming. "Does your skin feel clammy? Are you dizzy, nauseous?"

"I don't—think so," Hetty said, looking alarmed. Her mascara was smudged beneath her eyes in wide black rings; she looked like a demented pirate.

A loud rapping at the front door signaled the arrival of the emergency crew. Erin hurried to answer it, while Farnsworth kept her eye on Hetty.

"Thank you for arriving so quickly," Erin said to the burly EMT as he brushed past her, carrying a first-aid kit.

"George Atkins, Fire and Emergency Squad," he said briskly. "Where is the injured person?"

"In here," Erin said, leading him to the parlor, where Farnsworth sat holding Hetty's hand. "I think she's in shock."

George Atkins was built like a brick oven, thick and solid, with a graying crew cut and a bullet-shaped head. Erin had seen him around the village, at the butcher's or buying fish and chips, and hadn't remarked upon him much at the time, but now was grateful for his presence. His businesslike attitude inspired confidence.

"She was in the same accident?" he said, kneeling in front of Hetty.

"She was a passenger in the car," Farnsworth replied.

Relief flooding Erin's veins as she watched him monitor Hetty's pulse before examining her eyes.

"Are you looking to see if the pupils are dilated?" she asked, remembering details of the first-aid course she'd taken in Oxford.

"They look fine," he replied. "Her pulse is a little fast, but nothing to worry about. Any nausea or vomiting? Dizziness?" he asked Hetty.

"I—I fainted earlier, but I'm all right now."

"You're coming with us," he said. "Can you walk?"

"Yes."

"Can you help me with her?" he asked Erin.

"Of course," she said, taking Hetty's other arm as they helped her slowly to her feet.

"Normally we'd use the gurney, but it's occupied," he said as they guided her through the hall to the kitchen.

"P-Prudence?" Hetty said. "Is she all right?"

"She'll be fine. Broken arm, looks like a simple fracture. Maybe a slight concussion, some bruising—we'll take you both in for observation."

"She's awake?"

He frowned. "She didn't tell us she lost consciousness."

"She didn't answer me when I tried to talk to her."

"Well, she's talking plenty now," he said, holding the front door open so they could escort Hetty out of the house. Farnsworth trailed behind, carrying Hetty's muddy jacket.

The ambulance sat in Farnsworth's driveway, lights still spinning, throwing its multicolored reflection at the cloud bank that had settled over the village like a miniature aurora borealis. Swinging open the vehicle's back doors, George Atkins revealed a young female EMT sitting next to a gurney containing a very animated Prudence Pettibone.

"I want to tell my friends I'm all right," Pru was insisting as the doors were flung open. "Ah, there you—it's about time!" she said, not missing a beat. "Hetty, dear, you look terrible," she said as the EMTs helped Hetty into the back of the ambulance.

"You don't look so brilliant yourself," Hetty muttered at she took a seat next to her friend. "Oh, I was so worried about you!" she cried suddenly, bursting into tears and flinging herself upon Prudence, who looked embarrassed by the emotional display.

"Steady on," she said, patting Hetty's cheek. "It takes more than a fender bender to bump off this old bird."

Erin and Farnsworth laughed with relief, but Hetty just cried harder. "What would I do without you? It's not funny!" she said, glaring at Erin and Farnsworth.

"We're laughing from relief, silly," Farnsworth explained.

"Time to get a move on," George Atkins said as his colleague strapped Hetty into her seat.

"Mind if we follow behind you?" asked Farnsworth.

"You know where the hospital is?" he answered, sliding into the driver's seat.

"Maiden Greve Lane?"

"Right. Why don't you just meet us there?"

"Very well," Farnsworth said, sounding put out. She didn't fluster easily, but Erin could see all the hubbub was beginning to get to her.

"Shall I drive your car?" she suggested.

"Yes, please," said Farnsworth. "Let me get my coat."

Chapter Thirty-Five

～

Twenty minutes later they were seated in the A&E waiting room, sipping vending machine hot chocolate, while Prudence and Hetty were treated by medical personnel. It was a little before midnight, and the waiting room was empty except for Erin and Farnsworth.

Suddenly the doors burst open and Winton Pettibone came flying through, wearing an oilskin coat over blue-striped pajamas and Wellies. His head was bare except for his unkempt toupee, which resembled a molting muskrat.

"Where is she?" he cried, rushing over to Erin and Farnsworth. "Is she alive?"

"She's being treated," Erin said. "She's going to be fine."

"Oh, oh, oh," he moaned, shuffling in his thick boots toward the double doors leading to the treatment area, where he was intercepted by the receptionist, a slim Indian woman with glossy black hair and thick glasses.

"Excuse me, sir, but no going in until you are signed in," she said firmly.

"B-but I'm her husband," he pleaded, his eyes wild.

"If you would please just sign in, we will be helping you," she said, thrusting a clipboard in front of him.

"Oh, oh, oh," he moaned again, clutching the clipboard with his left hand while scratching out a signature with his right. "There," he said, pushing it back at her. "Can I please go in now?"

"Of course, sir," she said, pushing a button behind her desk to release the doors.

"Oh, oh, oh," he continued to moan. Erin thought she heard him say "It's all my fault" as he disappeared into the bowels of the A&E.

"Well, *that* was dramatic," Farnsworth declared, arching an eyebrow. "Say what you like about Winton Pettibone, but he does love his wife."

"Did you hear what he said just now?"

"What?"

"'It's all my fault.' Why would he say that?"

"Maybe he felt he should have picked Pru up after the party. She does have a tendency to imbibe a bit freely at these things."

"You think maybe her story about the other car is exaggerated?"

Farnsworth shook her head. "Hard to say. Could be."

"Did you think Winton looks thinner?" Erin mused, sipping her chocolate, now long cold.

"It's hard to tell under a sou'wester and Wellies. Why?"

"Just an observation."

"When do you think we should go in?" Farnsworth asked, draining the last of her chocolate.

"Should we give him a few minutes alone with her?"

"I suppose so." Farnsworth sighed and looked around the room, with its whitewashed walls, beige tile floor, and insipid paintings on the walls. They looked to Erin like cheap Norman Rockwell imitations, with the same flat colors and obvious story lines. In one, a girl in a pink flowered dress played with a smiling puppy on a lime-green lawn, a discarded birthday card in the foreground indicating the dog was a birthday present. In another, a kindly bespectacled doctor affixed a bandage to a cut on a little boy's knee. The little fellow was struggling manfully with his emotions, remnants of tears still clinging to his cheeks as he clutched a red lollipop, the universal consolation prize of childhood medical visits.

The snack machine whirred quietly in the far corner, an oasis of comfort in the dismal surroundings. "I hate hospitals," Farnsworth remarked.

"I'm not keen on them myself."

"Have you spent much time—oh, of course you have. Your mother. I'm sorry."

"Nothing to be sorry about. It wasn't your fault."

"It must have been horrible."

"I don't remember much of it."

"But it wasn't that long ago—?"

"I suppose a shrink would say I'm burying the memories."

"You didn't have any counseling?"

"Never had the time," she lied. "Well, Mrs. Appleby, shall we apply ourselves to our mission of mercy and comfort our injured companions?"

"I cannot conceive of anything to prevent that eventuality."

"Then let us venture forth with good humor and fortitude."

They rose stiffly, the agreeable effects of the Malbec having worn off, replaced by a dry mouth and niggling headache. Having signed in earlier, they followed the receptionist's directions and turned left once they entered the treatment area, past equipment and trays of medical supplies, as monitors purred and beeped in the background. A few young residents padded past them on rubber-soled shoes, their foreheads shiny, hair pulled back or hastily combed, dressed in unflattering green scrubs of thin, papery cotton.

"It's not like this on hospital shows on the telly," Farnsworth remarked.

"No," said Erin. "Medical work is really demanding."

Pulling back the white curtain as instructed, they found Hetty and Prudence reclining on gurneys, side by side. Hetty still wore street clothes, while Pru was clothed in a white cotton hospital gown with tiny yellow daisies. A snowy white bandage wound around Hetty's forehead; Erin thought she looked rather dashing, like a wounded warrior. Pru's right arm was in a cast, held in place by a sling around her shoulder. Winton was nowhere in sight.

"Why, hel-loo, you two!" Prudence sang out gaily.

Erin followed Hetty's gaze to a vial of pills on the metal table between them. The label read Hydrocodone Bitartrate and Acetaminophen Tablets, USP 7.5 mg/300 mg. Erin nodded— Vicodin, no doubt the reason for Pru's elevated mood.

"How *are* you?" Farnsworth said, plopping onto the plastic orange chair next to Pru's gurney.

"Lucky to be alive," Pru replied dramatically.

"It wasn't *that* bad an accident," Hetty said.

"I have a broken arm, contusions, and a strained tendon on my right leg."

"Aren't you clever with the fancy medical jargon," Hetty said.

"I'm so sorry about your car," Pru told Erin. "I know it's vintage and all that."

"No worries—it's insured. Hetty said you were run off the road."

Pru nodded. "Came from behind to pass us, then swerved, and before I knew it we were in the ditch."

"Did you get a look at the other car?" asked Farnsworth.

"No."

"Anything at all you can remember?" Erin said.

"Light colored, maybe—it's so hard to say, though. It was so dark and I was trying not to get us both killed."

"And you succeeded," Hetty said, tearing up a little.

"I'm just glad you weren't hurt worse," said Erin, looking at her broken arm.

Pru nodded. "Good job I'm left-handed."

"And you, pet?" Farnsworth asked Hetty. "Do you have a concussion?"

"Very likely," she replied, touching her bandaged forehead.

"They said it was impossible to tell for sure without an X-ray," said Prudence. "But they thought it was *un*likely."

Erin smiled—the two were back to form, competing over who had the worst injuries. She was reminded of one of her favorite Monty Python sketches, in which four men with heavy Yorkshire accents competed for who had the most impoverished childhood, inevitably resulting in absurdities. After one man claimed he lived in a drain pipe, his companion replied, "You were lucky to have drainpipe. We lived int' cardboard box at side of the road."

Erin thought such masochistic fantasies were one of the odder aspects of the British character, but she didn't think Prudence or Hetty would appreciate the observation, so she said nothing.

"How long are they keeping you here?" Farnsworth asked.

"They said we can go. Winton's just gone to the loo," said Pru. "Then he'll go to fetch the car."

"Erin, would you be a dear and get me some water?" Hetty said. "I'm parched."

"Of course," she said, ducking through the curtain back into the corridor. About to turn the corner en route to the waiting room, she heard low voices. Recognizing one as Winton's, she stopped to listen.

"I think we should try combining gemcitabine with cisplatin and see how that goes." The voice was assertive, authoritative—a doctor's voice.

"And if that doesn't work?" said Winton. Even with his rigid vocal inflections, Erin could tell he was frightened.

"Let's just take it one step at a time, eh?"

"You're the doctor."

"I know how difficult this is, but hang in there, all right?" he said, and then Erin heard retreating footsteps.

She inhaled deeply, realizing she had been holding her breath. Now she knew why Winton was looking thin. Erin recognized the drugs the doctor had mentioned, knew them as well as she knew her own phone number. They were used to treat pancreatic cancer, the disease that had killed her mother.

And now it was going to kill Winton Pettibone.

Chapter Thirty-Six

~

Erin stood in the empty corridor, trying to digest what she had just heard. The knowledge left her stunned—obviously Winton hadn't told Prudence. If he had, Pru would be devastated and talking of little else. She leaned against the wall as a wave of dizziness swept over her, the tile cool and soothing against her skin. How much time did he have left, and how would she manage to hide this from Prudence?

Questions swirled through her head as she located the nurses' station, where she was given a yellow plastic pitcher of water along with four small plastic cups. She walked back, looking over her shoulder, afraid she would run into Winton and blurt out something. But there was no sign of him, either in the hallway or at Pru's bedside—the three women were just as she had left them.

"Thank you, dearie," Hetty said as Erin handed her a cup of water, then poured one for each of them.

"Chin chin," said Farnsworth, raising her cup.

"I wish it was Malbec," Pru said wistfully.

Erin drank hers in one gulp, suddenly very thirsty. She quickly downed another, but her mouth was still dry.

"Did you see Winton?" Pru asked.

"No," she said, which was technically not a lie.

"He was just going to fetch the car. I wonder what's taking so long."

As if in answer to her question, the curtain opened and Winton appeared. "Sorry," he said in his stiff, formal way. "I got a bit lost, then had a chat with a doctor."

"About what?" asked Hetty, applying lipstick, holding a compact mirror close to her face. She was extremely nearsighted but too vain to wear glasses.

"Nothing very exciting," Winton said. He was a better liar than Erin would have given him credit for. "I had a couple of minor medical questions. How are you feeling, Prudy?"

"Better now that you're here," she said, beaming like a schoolgirl. Erin felt a pang as she watched the couple, the spark still strong between them. How much longer could he hide his diagnosis from his wife?

"The car's just outside. Would you like a lift?" he asked Hetty.

"I'll be fine," she muttered, pushing her lower lip forward like a sulky child.

"Don't be daft," said Prudence. "Of course we'll take you."

"If you insist," Hetty said.

Erin wondered what bee was in her bonnet, but Hetty's moods were legendary. Once she'd gone for a week without speaking to anyone. It was something about a crab sandwich—Erin had forgotten the details.

"It's been a long night," said Farnsworth.

"I expect you all feel a bit bedraggled," said Winton. He was trying to be solicitous, but his words left an awkward pause in the air.

"I know *I* am," Erin said too heartily, avoiding eye contact with him.

"Well, I for one am looking forward to a hot bath," Hetty declared, snapping shut her compact. Erin wondered who the makeup was for—did she hope to meet some dreamy doctor on her way out of the hospital?

The staff insisted Prudence and Hetty make their exit in wheelchairs—something to do with insurance, according to the night-shift nurse. Prudence enjoyed the attention, but it put Hetty in an even fouler mood. Standing outside the front entrance watching Winton drive off slowly with the two women safely stowed in the car, Erin was relieved to see the last of them for a while.

"Shall we go?" said Farnsworth.

Erin shivered as the night air wrapped around them like a cloak, a crown of stars glittering overhead, cold as diamonds. She looked back at the hospital, its glowing windows warm and beckoning.

"Yes," she said. "Shall I drive?"

"I'm all right now," Farnsworth said.

They drove for a while in silence. Then, as they turned off Barugh Lane, Farnsworth said, "Do you really think people in town are biased against the Beckers?"

"Why do you ask?"

"I was just thinking about what Suzanne said to you."

"I have heard one or two people grumble about how 'German' they are."

"And just how German *are* they, allegedly?" said Farnsworth.

"Oh, you know—punctual, neat, humorless; that kind of thing."

"That could describe half the people in Kirkbymoorside."

"Stereotypes can be recycled to include so many groups."

"True enough," Farnsworth agreed. "The Scots are supposed to be stingy, but so are the Dutch and the French—"

"Not to mention the Jews."

"My mother was part Jewish, and she could be outrageously extravagant."

"I didn't know you were part Jewish."

"I strive to maintain an aura of mystery," Farnsworth said, turning into Erin's driveway.

As she pulled up to the house, Erin blurted out, "Winton Pettibone has cancer. I think it's pancreatic."

Farnsworth's jaw actually dropped. "*What?*"

"I thought he looked thinner."

"I remember you saying that, but how—"

"I overheard a conversation with a doctor in the hospital. I recognized the drugs they were talking about."

"How did you—?"

"My mother. She died of the same thing."

"Does Prudence know?"

"I'm pretty sure he's hiding it from her."

"Good lord."

They sat for a moment, their breath fogging the windows. Outside, an owl hooted softly from the sycamore tree.

"You can't tell anyone I told you this."

Farnsworth unbuckled her seat belt. "Poor Prudence. What will she do without him?"

"What any of us do when we lose people we love," Erin said. "We muddle on."

Her friend sighed deeply. "I know it sounds daft, but sometimes I miss Dastardly Dick."

"Really?"

"We had some good times. And I try to think only of the past as its remembrance gives me pleasure."

"That may have worked for Elizabeth Bennet, but is it realistic? I can't seem to manage it."

"But you're so much like Elizabeth."

"You flatter me."

"You're independent and loyal, and determined—"

"You really must stop, or my head will be too big to fit through my front door."

Farnsworth laid a hand on her arm. "The coppers don't seriously think I offed poor Dick, do they?"

"They'll find out soon enough that's rubbish."

"Snoop around and let me know, would you, pet?"

"Of course."

Farnsworth yawned. "I'd better go. I'm sure the furries are wondering what's become of me. Darcy will be waiting up for me."

"Lucky you."

"You'd have a real Darcy waiting for you if you weren't so standoffish, pet."

"I have more important things on my mind."

"Like solving murders, you mean?"

"Exactly," Erin said. She felt a little guilty about neglecting to tell Farnsworth about kissing Jonathan Alder, not to mention her crush on Detective Hemming, but she knew if she did, she'd never hear the end of it.

"Blasted stupid thing," Farnsworth said, struggling to put her seat belt back on. Farnsworth was constantly at war with the physical world. Sometimes Erin thought it was all on purpose, since she did some things so well, like cooking and making coffee.

"Good night," said Erin. "Try and get some sleep."

"You as well, pet. Sorry about your car."

The Sunbeam was Erin's one extravagant possession, a gift from her father. She hoped her insurance would pay for the damage. She unlocked her door, Farnsworth waiting until she was safely inside before leaving. Erin turned on the outside light to signal all was well, the yellow glow illuminating her little front patio. A soft harvest moon had broken through the cloud cover and cast its pale light over the countryside.

She watched Farnsworth's tail lights disappear down the driveway, then went through the shop, past silent shelves of books illuminated by moonlight streaming through the windows. The living room smelled musty, and she thought of opening a window, but it was so late she wanted nothing more than a bath and bed.

As she slid into the hot water, Erin couldn't stop thinking about the accident. Who passed a car on a country road late at night? A sneaking dread worked its way into her consciousness. What if it hadn't been an accident at all—what if the driver had deliberately been trying to run Prudence off the road? But why? A sudden realization sliced her thoughts like a shard of glass, and she wondered why it hadn't occurred to her earlier. Whoever had run her car off the road wasn't after Prudence at all.

They were after her.

Chapter Thirty-Seven

The wall clock in the conference room in the back of the police station had just passed nine when Sergeant Rashid Jarral looked up to see Detective Hemming enter the room. His suit was rumpled, he had deep circles under his eyes, and his thick blond hair looked uncombed.

"Good morning, Sergeant," he said, sinking wearily into the nearest chair.

"You don't look well, sir."

"I've been better," he answered, taking notes out of his briefcase and spreading them on the table.

"My cousin has a herbal remedy—"

"Which I've no doubt is delightful," Hemming said, going over to the bulletin board. "But I'd like to focus on the case, if you don't mind."

"Yes, sir."

Crossing his arms, the detective studied the board, a photograph of a smiling Sylvia Pemberthy at its center. Other photographs fanned out in a circular pattern around her, connected by pieces of string, radiating out from Sylvia's picture like spokes on a wheel. Most of the people on the board were members of the Jane Austen Society: Owen and Carolyn Hardacker, Hetty Miller, Jonathan Alder, and so on.

"Rub-a-dub-dub, three men in a tub," Hemming murmured.

"Sir?"

"I was thinking about our suspects."

"Oh, yes—the butcher, the baker—"

"But no candlestick maker."

"Carolyn Hardacker makes candlesticks," Jarral said. "I saw some at her house."

"Does she, now?" Hemming said, stroking his chin, which looked unshaven. "If only we could narrow it down to the three of them."

Jarral cleared his throat. "This Jonathan Alder fellow is a bit mysterious, isn't he?"

"Yes. No one seems to know much about him."

"I can see why the ladies are so stuck on him. He is quite good-looking."

"A bit too much of the flowing locks and rosy cheeks, if you ask me."

There was a quiet knock on the conference room door. Jarral opened it to see Constable Harris, his helmet of black hair shiny under the fluorescent lights.

"There's a call for you, sir."

"Where?"

"Line one—the extension's right there," Harris said, pointing to the landline on the desk.

"Thank you, Constable," Hemming said, picking up the phone. "DI Hemming here."

"Do you know what you're in for?" The voice on the other end was muffled, raspy, as though the speaker was covering his mouth with a scarf as well as deliberately altering his tone—that is, if it was a man. It was hard to tell the speaker's gender.

"Can I help you?" Hemming said calmly, though he felt anything but calm.

"Do you know what you're in for?" the speaker repeated.

Hemming snapped his fingers at Jarral, pointing to a stack of paper near the printer. Jarral looked confused until Hemming mouthed the word *paper*. The sergeant grabbed a sheet and a pen and handed them to the detective, who scribbled the words TRACE THE CALL! Jarral nodded and dashed out to the front room, while Hemming returned his attention to the mysterious caller.

"Perhaps you can explain what you mean," he said into the receiver.

"Sylvia were a trollop," the speaker rasped.

"How so?"

"Ask Carolyn Hardacker, why don' ye?"

"What should I ask her?" Hemming said, but the line went dead. "Damn," he muttered, hanging up. "*Damn*."

Sergeant Jarral burst into the room. "Sorry, sir—we couldn't—"

"Never mind. Could you call the phone company and find out where the call was made from?"

"Yes, sir," he said, lifting the receiver of the landline.

"Don't use that—he might call back. Use your mobile."

"Not much of a signal here, sir."

"Try mine," Hemming said, fishing it out of his pocket. "You might get better reception out front."

As the sergeant headed through the station house, Hemming carefully wrote down exactly what the caller had said. DO YOU KNOW WHAT YOU'RE IN FOR? SYLVIA WERE A TROLLOP. ASK CAROLYN HARDACKER, WHY DON' YE? The wording and accent suggested someone local to Yorkshire, though someone with a decent ear could easily fake that.

A moment later Jarral returned, followed by Constable Harris. "It came from a pay phone located at the Malton Sainsbury's," said the sergeant.

"There's a bank of pay phones at the entrance to the store," said Harris. "If you like, I'll take you there."

"Someone needs to stay here in case there's another call. And no doubt he's already long gone."

"We can check the security footage," Jarral suggested.

"We will," said Hemming, putting on his coat. "Can you set it up so every call to the station is recorded?" he asked Harris.

"Of course, sir."

"And please contact us right away if he calls back?"

"Right you are, sir."

Just then the door to the station house opened and Erin Coleridge walked in. It was clear something was amiss. The usual bounce in her step was gone; worry lines creased her pale forehead.

"What's happened?" said Hemming.

She looked at Jarral, then back at him.

"I'm afraid someone may be trying to kill me."

Chapter Thirty-Eight

⁓

Detective Hemming listened carefully to Erin's explanation of the previous night's events, his face increasingly worried. When she finished, he glanced at Sergeant Jarral and, to her surprise, invited her to go with them to Malton.

"I'm not asking you to join the investigation. If Constable McCrary can spare the manpower, I'd like to give you police protection, but until then, I can keep an eye on you."

Erin's heart leapt at the idea of a ride along—not to mention the possibility of spending time with Detective Hemming. "Sure," she said, trying not to sound too enthusiastic.

Malton was over ten miles away, so there was little hope the caller would still be hanging around. He had obviously gone to some trouble to make the call where he wouldn't be recognized.

"Why not just use a burner phone if he didn't want to be identified?" Jarral said as they barreled down the Malton road in Hemming's Citroën. The car might be old, but it could move, Erin thought, as she watched the scenery from the back seat.

"It suggests someone with limited knowledge of technology— or someone trying to throw us off by giving that impression," said Hemming.

"He didn't use voice-altering software, sir?"

"It sounded like he was just holding a scarf or something over his mouth."

Erin leaned forward. "Could it have been a woman with a deep voice?"

"Possibly. It was muffled."

"People used to mistake my mother for a man over the phone all the time," Erin said.

"We should keep an open mind, sir," Jarral agreed.

Erin watched the houses and farm fields zipping by. After days of inclement weather, the air was warm and balmy for October, and she opened the window, enjoying the wind on her face.

When they arrived at the Malton Sainsbury's, Hemming parked the car and turned around to face Erin. "You can come in with us if you just observe, all right?"

"Of course," she said, trying to sound nonchalant.

As Hemming climbed out of the car, he gripped the door to steady himself, beads of sweat prickling his forehead.

"Are you all right?" she asked.

"I'm fine," he said, but he didn't look well.

"You shouldn't be out of bed, sir," Jarral remarked.

"I'm all right," the detective said, tidying his uncharacteristically unruly hair. Erin wondered what it would be like to run her own hand through that blond thicket.

As they crossed the car park, Jarral fell into step with Erin. "He's being bloody stubborn," he whispered. "Trying to play the hero."

"I can hear you," Hemming said. "And murder doesn't wait. Come along, Sergeant."

Jarral shook his head and quickened his stride. Erin had to stretch her legs to keep up with the two policemen. They found the single phone booth at the Malton Sainsbury's deserted, and none of the staff remembered seeing anyone use it.

"Sorry, sir, but it's busy today, y'see," said the manager at the customer service counter. "We get all the spillover from the town markets. Folks round here like to shop on Wednesdays." He was a small, round man with large, mild eyes behind thick lenses. Sweat gathered on his upper lip as he spoke, looking back and forth earnestly between the two policemen.

"May we see your CCTV footage?" Hemming asked.

The sweat intensified. "I'm 'fraid it's broke, sir."

"We could write you up for that, you know."

"Yes, sir—sorry, sir," he said, squirming in his rayon uniform. "It were workin' yesterday. Don' know what happened."

"If anyone remembers anything at all, no matter how trivial, please ask them to call me," Hemming said, handing him a card.

"Certainly, sir," he said, tucking the card into his breast pocket.

"Can we dust for prints, sir?" Jarral asked.

"I can't see Witherspoon sending up crime scene techs for that. Especially as we don't have any proof the call was made by the person who poisoned Sylvia. And they could have used gloves—not to mention that there are probably prints from dozens of people in that booth."

"Why make the call, sir, and risk getting caught?"

"Someone may have deliberately sent us on a wild-goose chase."

"Mind if I do something?" said Erin.

"What's that?" said Hemming.

"It'll only take a few seconds." As the two policemen watched, she went to the phone booth, closed the door, and lifted the receiver, sniffing at it. After a few moments, she replaced it and came out of the booth.

"What was that all about?" said the detective as they walked back to the car.

"Just sniffing around. Some people have a distinctive smell, and since I know everyone in the society, I thought I'd check it out."

"Any luck?" asked Jarral.

"I'm afraid not," Erin lied. The truth was that she had detected a very familiar scent, but she wasn't sure yet what to do about it. The phone booth had the distinctive aroma of lily-of-the-valley perfume, and she knew only one person who wore that fragrance.

Chapter Thirty-Nine

Erin spent most of the ride back staring out the window. The presence of the perfume was unsettling, but was it just coincidence? She needed to talk the police out of giving her protection—she couldn't possibly continue her sleuthing with a cop constantly tailing her.

When they arrived back at the police station, Detective Hemming asked her to come inside. "I'd like to know why you think the accident might have been deliberate," he said, shielding his eyes from the glare of sunlight. With the light directly on them, his eyes were pale turquoise, like pictures she had seen of the Caribbean Sea.

"I may have overreacted. I don't want to waste your time."

"It's our job to protect people."

Sergeant Jarral stepped in. "Did Mrs. Pettibone get a look at the other driver?"

Erin shook her head.

"Maybe we can find some paint transfer to identify the other car," Hemming suggested.

"But the other car never actually hit my car. You can talk to the patrolmen who took their statement."

The two men exchanged glances, and Hemming turned to Erin. "Can you think of anyone who might want to hurt you?"

"I think my imagination got the better of me. I'll be fine, really. Are there any updates on the investigation into the death of Farnsworth's husband?"

Hemming looked surprised. "What?" He glared at Sergeant Jarral, who hung his head.

"Sorry, sir."

The detective rubbed his eyes wearily. "What did you tell her?"

"Just that we were looking into the—"

Hemming turned to Erin. "Let me make two things clear. First of all, *I'm* not looking into Mr. Appleby's death—that's entirely on our boss in York, DCI Witherspoon. Secondly—"

"You wouldn't tell me if you did know."

"Correct," he said sternly, though she thought he was suppressing a smile. "Now let us take you home."

"I'm going to do a bit of shopping; then I'll call a cab."

"But—"

"Thanks for everything," she said, shaking his hand. It was warm and unexpectedly soft, though she could feel the strength in his fingers.

Erin walked resolutely in the direction of the shops, but when she was a few blocks from the police station, she called a cab and gave them Prudence Pettibone's address.

*　*　*

Prudence was at home nursing her broken arm—she seemed to be having a fine time, as Winton hovered over her with tea and biscuits. After plying Erin with homemade zucchini bread, he withdrew quietly into his woodshop, where, according to Pru, he was making a new set of kitchen drawers.

"He loves working with his hands," she said, sipping her tea, perched on a chaise in the sunroom at the back of the house, a lamb's-wool comforter draped over her. The lemony October sun stretched languidly across the room, creeping halfway up the side of the far wall. "He's taking such wonderful care of me during my recovery." She pronounced *recovery* as though it were synonymous with *deathbed*.

"I never heard Hetty say anything against Sylvia," Prudence said when Erin brought it up. "Do you have reason to suspect her?"

"No really," Erin lied. She didn't want Prudence running to warn Hetty, and besides, she didn't have any concrete evidence. It was entirely possible someone else wearing lily-of-the-valley perfume had used that phone booth. "I was thinking," she said to Prudence, "if you have any old minutes from past meetings, we might find a clue there."

"I have minutes from all the meetings," Prudence said proudly. "Ever since the first ones—long before your time."

"Could I have a look at them?"

"I don't see why not. Would you mind fetching my laptop from the study? It should be on the desk."

Erin went down the hall to the little study in the corner of the house. It was a model of organization, all the books and papers stacked in tidy rows on shelves Winton had made himself. The workmanship was good—solid and well crafted. She found the computer on the desk.

Erin returned to the sun porch and gave Prudence the computer.

"Let's see," Pru said, opening a folder titled JAS MINUTES. Scrolling through it, she pointed to a subfolder with the heading 2002. "That's our first year, when we had all the meetings in York, and Farnsworth was the club secretary."

"So these are her minutes?"

"Yes. We only had eight members that year, but we grew quickly."

"Who were they?"

"Let's see . . . apart from me and Sylvia, Farnsworth and her husband, there was—"

"Farnsworth's husband?"

"Oh, yes—it was later that year he ran off with the barmaid."
Prudence shook her head. "It's really too bad Sylvia and Farnsworth
never made up after that. They used to be such good friends."

"Really? I never knew that."

"Oh, yes, they were very close, but they had a terrible
falling-out."

"How was it related to Farnsworth's husband?"

"Sylvia knew about it, you see—the business with the barmaid.
And she never told Farnsworth. So of course when Dastardly Dick
ran off with that girl, Farnsworth blamed Sylvia for not telling her."

"I can see why she was upset, but—"

"Farnsworth really values loyalty."

"She never said anything to me about it."

"It's still a touchy subject."

"Do the police know?"

"I certainly didn't mention it."

"Someone might have told them."

"That was years ago," Prudence said, sipping her tea. "If Farnsworth had murderous feelings toward Sylvia, don't you think she'd
have acted on them earlier?"

"The human heart is a strange labyrinth of twists and turns."

"You should put that in one of your poems," said Prudence.
"That's quite good."

"I hear rumors that you're keen on putting your hat in the ring
for club president."

"Well, I don't know about that," Pru said, pouring more tea.

"I think you'd be quite a good candidate."

"Really?" Her whole body came to attention, like a bird dog on
a scent; her spine was stiffer and her eyes sparkled. Then she gave a

wry smile. "'I wish, as well as everybody else to be perfectly happy; but, like everybody else, it must be in my own way. Greatness will not make me so.'"

The idea of equating greatness with being president of the Jane Austen Society was so absurd, Erin nearly burst out laughing, but Pru wasn't being ironic. Swallowing her impulse, Erin said, "What's that from?"

"*Sense and Sensibility*. And yes, to be completely candid, I did fancy a go at the post, but now with poor Sylvia's death, I wonder if it would be the wisest thing."

"That's a good point," Erin said, thinking that if Prudence had poisoned Sylvia, her remark would be a logical attempt at a cover-up. "Mind if I take a copy of those minutes with me?"

"There are some spare memory sticks in the study. Top right desk drawer—go fetch one and we'll make a copy."

Erin found the thumb drive right where Pru said it was, and was about to leave when a photograph on the bookshelf caught her eye. It was of a much younger Prudence, her arm around an older woman with the same delicate, small-boned features and turned-up nose. Erin was struck by how pretty Prudence was at that age—time had not been kind to her. Her face had taken on a pinched aspect. Erin remembered overhearing Sylvia calling her "a constipated prune." She didn't imagine there was a time when Pru and Sylvia had ever gotten along—they were so different. And yet Hetty and Pru were pals, even though they were so different, and the friendship had its share of mutual sniping.

She returned to the sun porch to find Prudence sipping the last of her tea, her nose in a book she had recently purchased from Erin, *What Jane Austen Ate and Charles Dickens Knew*.

Pru looked up when she entered. "This is a fascinating book.

Everything was so ritualized in those days—everyone knew what the rules were and what was expected of them. I think I would have much preferred it."

"I know what you mean," Erin said, inserting the memory stick into the laptop. "Sometimes the price of freedom is uncertainty."

"Another bon mot. You're on a roll today."

Opening the files on the laptop, Erin selected the ones to copy. "That picture in the study—is that you with your mother?"

Pru's face went soft, and in that moment she resembled the pretty young woman in the photo. "Oh, yes—Winton took that when she was living with us. She died not long after."

"She looks so healthy in the photo."

"She came down with a terrible case of food poisoning. By the time we got to hospital, it was too late."

"I'm so sorry."

"Winton was devastated. He blamed himself—the car battery was dead, so there was a delay getting to hospital."

"It wasn't his fault."

"The poor old dear. A weakened immune system, the doctor said. How is your car?"

"It should be ready in a couple of days."

"Of course I'll pay for any repairs."

"Don't worry about it," Erin said, removing the thumb drive with the copied files.

"Nonsense—I insist."

"I'm just glad you weren't seriously injured."

"Tell you the truth, it's given me an excuse to take it easy. Winton has been a lamb, looking after my every need." She sighed. "I'm afraid I won't be up to going to the bonfire this year—but maybe I can convince him to go without me. He always loves it so."

"Thanks for the files," Erin said, getting up. "Can I get you anything?"

"There's one thing you could do, if you're willing."

"Of course."

"Get me a cutting from Caroline's latest orchid. She emailed me that she got a new *Phalaenopsis schilleriana* and promised me a cutting. When you have your car back, of course."

"I'll take my bike."

"There's no need—"

"It's a nice ride, only three miles each way. I'll go Saturday morning, on my way to the shops; then I'll drop it off afterward."

"If you're sure—"

"Absolutely. It's good exercise."

"Let me write it down for you," Pru said, scribbling on a piece of paper with her good left hand. "Sorry my writing is so bad. Can you read that?"

"It's fine," Erin said, slipping it into her pocket.

"It's an especially graceful variety," Prudence said, her eyes dreamy. "The blossoms are the loveliest pale lilac." When Pru talked about orchids, her face softened and her whole body relaxed.

"I'd like to have a quick word with Winton before I go. Do you think he'd mind?"

"I'm sure he'd be delighted. His woodshop is at the back of the house."

"Thanks," Erin said, winding through the narrow hallway leading to the back. The shop was a shedlike structure attached to the rear of the ancient cottage, done with such taste and skill that it perfectly matched the original in style.

"Oh, hello," Winton said when she entered the little room with its low, sloping ceiling. He held a hammer in his hand; on the worktable in front of him was a partially finished birdhouse. "It's for the finches," he explained. "Prudy loves their singing, and since she's laid up for a while, I thought she'd appreciate havin' them nearby."

"How lovely. She's is lucky to have you."

"I don' know 'bout that," he said, looking away.

"I wanted to see how you were getting on after being attacked the other day," Erin said. "It must have been terrifying."

"Oh, don' bother 'bout that. It weren't nothin'."

"Did you get a glimpse of your attacker?"

"'Fraid not—it all happened so fast, like."

"Did someone have a look at your head?"

"I didn' want t'cause any bother."

"May I see it?"

"I'd rather not, if y'don't mind."

"All right—I didn't mean to be intrusive."

"Aye, it's just that I'm kinda private that way, y'understand."

"Of course. I didn't mean to pry."

"Thanks so much for droppin' in on Prudy. It means the world to her."

"My pleasure."

After saying good-bye, Erin took another cab to her cottage. Winton offered to drive her, but she didn't want to put him out; he looked so happy with his woodworking. During the ride, she gazed out the window, wondering why Winton didn't want her examining his head injury. Was it just his vanity—did he really think he was fooling anyone with that dreadful wig?

By the time she returned, it was long after sunset, so she cut a few slices of roast beef from a joint in the fridge, made a sandwich, and sat down to study the meeting minutes. Before long, her eyes were drooping. Looking at the clock, she was surprised to see it was nearly eleven.

Too tired for a bath, she crawled into bed and was soon asleep. She dreamed of riding her bike through fields of orchids, pursued by a hulking lorry, lurching and belching smoke from its black tail pipes. The driver behind the wheel laughed at her, his face a mask of malice. She awoke just before dawn, shivering, and lay watching the sun rise before sinking gratefully back into the arms of oblivion.

Chapter Forty

~

Images of disquieting dreams had faded by the time Erin took a cup of coffee onto her patio the next day. She breathed in the morning air, sweet with the promise of fall. Inhaling deeply, she savored the crisp aroma of dead leaves and the soft peaty smell of damp soil. The faint whiff of burning wood carried by the wind recalled her family's first house in Oxford. She remembered sitting in front of the fireplace that first night, surrounded by crackling logs and her parents' love.

On days like this, she felt she could reach through the mist of time and touch the past, as though the air itself was permeable. Summer air was thick, sluggish, and she felt rooted in the present during the warmer months, but the fall brought deep longing, a seasonal nostalgia.

By noon only three customers had shown up, so after lunch Erin closed the shop, climbed on her bike, and rode to the Hardackers' house. Before long she was standing in front of the thick oak door of the farmhouse, listening for a response to her knock. The door was flung open to reveal Owen Hardacker, wearing blue overalls and his signature red-and-green tweed cap. She wondered if he slept in it.

"Can I help ye?" he said.

"Sorry to disturb you. Is Carolyn home?"

"Aye, but she's restin'. What d'ye need?"

"I told Prudence I'd drop by for an orchid cutting."

"Why can't she come by her own self?"

"She was in a car accident."

"Oh, aye, I heard 'bout that. She all right, then?"

"She's going to be fine, but she's got a broken arm, so I told her I'd bring it to her."

"Well aren't ye a good friend," he said, though she couldn't tell whether he was being sincere or sarcastic.

"Do you think I could just get it myself without disturbing Carolyn?"

"Aye, if you know what you're lookin' for."

Erin pulled the handwritten note from her jacket. "*Phalaenopsis schilleriana*. Can you help me find it?"

"Ye might as well come in an' have a look," he said, opening the door.

Erin followed him through the spacious living room, past the dining room, and through a metal door leading to the attached greenhouse. Inhaling the warm, musty aroma of potting soil, fertilizer, and blossoms, she was transported to her mother's greenhouse in Oxford. Though nowhere near as grand as this one, it was her mother's favorite place. She loved to dig in the soft earth, surrounded by her plants and flowers, emerging hours later with smudges of dirt on her smiling face.

"The orchids are over int' corner," Owen said, pointing to a partially shaded shelf with a stunning variety of plants in a spectacular array of passionate purples, creamy whites, delicate pinks, riotous reds. Looking at them, Erin could understand how people became obsessed with the elegant, finicky flowers—a devotion propelled by the challenge of caring for them. She longed to linger and admire the delicate blossoms, but she felt Owen's eyes on her, so she peered at the little plastic markers in the soil of each pot: DORITAENOPSIS, EPIDENDRUM, PAPHIOPEDILUM. The opulent flowers were so voluptuous and seductive she had trouble tearing herself away from them.

"Here it is," she said, as her eyes fell upon a graceful plant with lilac blossoms. The little plastic tab read PHALAENOPSIS SCHILLERI-ANA in careful, neat block letters. As she reached for it, she heard the hinges on the metal door creak and turned to see Carolyn standing at the entrance to the greenhouse.

Dressed in a long, flowing white nightgown, hair loose around her shoulders, her face devoid of makeup, she was like a beautiful apparition. Used to seeing her in full regalia, with jewelry and makeup and her hair swept up in its usual chignon, Erin couldn't help staring. She looked like a ghost.

"Why didn't you tell me we had visitors?" she said to Owen, who was clearly startled by her unexpected entrance. His attitude changed instantly from slightly surly to anxious and solicitous.

"It's all right, dear—it's all under control," he said soothingly, as one might to a child or a demented person.

"Hello, Erin," Carolyn said dreamily, drifting toward her. It was as if she was floating, her feet, bare beneath the diaphanous gown, hardly touching the ground. She peered at Erin earnestly, coming so close their faces nearly touched, yet it was as if Carolyn was looking through her. Though the greenhouse was flooded with light, her pupils were pinpricks, the emerald green irises enormous. Her smile was frozen, as though she had planted it there and forgotten about it. The orchids in their clay pots showed more life than her lovely, vacant face.

"You shouldn't be out of bed," Owen said nervously.

"I just came to get a cutting for Prudence," Erin explained.

"Ah, yes, *Phalaenopsis schilleriana*," Carolyn said, stroking its petals. "The moth orchid." Picking up a pair of garden shears, she carefully snipped off one of the stems near the base. "Such a lovely species," she said, handing it to Erin. "You're rather like a moth yourself, aren't you? Pretty little Erin, with hair of gold," she said, reaching out toward Erin's face as if to caress it.

Her husband stepped forward and grasped her by the wrist. "Come along," he said, "let's get you back upstairs, shall we?"

The sounds of an approaching car made them all turn toward the driveway. Through the glass windows of the greenhouse, Detective Hemming's blue Citroën could be seen pulling up in front of the house.

"What the hell do they want?" Owen muttered as Carolyn started for the door. "Come along, love," he said, panic in his voice, but she pulled away from him.

"It would be rude to leave the nice policemen waiting."

Erin had no idea what he would do if she weren't there to witness, but under the circumstances, he had little choice but to follow his wife out to the front foyer.

"You're really not dressed for visitors," he pleaded, but she ignored him, throwing the door open before the policemen had time to knock.

"Hello again," she said. "How nice of you to stop by."

Seeing Erin, Detective Hemming's face registered surprise.

"Hello, Ms. Coleridge," he said rather stiffly. He still looked pale, and his voice sounded weak.

Sergeant Jarral gave his usual sunny smile. "Fancy meeting you here," he said, entering the house as if he were attending a garden party.

"Ms. Coleridge is here t'get a cuttin'," Owen said. "From an orchid. My wife raises 'em, y'see."

"So I've heard," Detective Hemming said. "I hear you've quite the green thumb," he told Carolyn.

"You're tooo kind," she demurred, slurring her words. "I jusst muddle along—don't I, darling?"

"We really must get ye back to bed," Owen said. "My wife's not been well," he explained.

"If she has just a minute to answer a couple of questions, I'd appreciate it."

"I'm f-fi-ine, really," Carolyn said. "They came a-a-all the way out here; it would be a sh-shame to turn them away."

"If you insist on talkin' with police, at least be presentable," Owen muttered, throwing a light cotton jacket over her shoulders.

"Oh, get me my matching robe, won't you, darling?" she said, pinning a stray strand of hair in place.

Erin lingered near the door, reluctant to leave. Her gaze fell on a book sitting on a small table next to the coatrack—the copy of *The Poisoner's Handbook* from her shop. She recognized it as hers because of the slightly tattered upper right corner on the cover.

Carolyn's gaze followed hers, and their eyes met. Carolyn gave her a pleading look of such desperation that, against her better judgment, Erin said nothing.

Detective Hemming turned to Erin. "You'd better get that cutting in water. I'll walk you out."

Was he trying to get rid of her or finding an excuse to get her alone? Erin wondered as he followed her out onto the front stoop.

"How did you get here?" he asked.

"On my zero-carbon-footprint machine," she said, fetching her bike from the side of the house.

"I still think you should have protection."

"I'll be all right. I really didn't mean to alarm you."

As she mounted her bike, he laid a hand on her arm.

"Be careful—please."

"I will," she said, and pedaled down the long driveway. She tried to focus on her surroundings, but all she could see was the way the slanting sun reflected off his blue eyes, with their tawny lashes.

As she steered her bike around a bend, she thought about seeing her missing book, and the startled look on Owen Hardacker's face when his wife agreed to be interviewed. In that instant, she had two realizations. Owen wasn't covering for himself—he was trying to protect Carolyn, which could only mean one thing.

He believed she was a murderer.

Chapter Forty-One

~

Erin arrived to find Winton in his shop, sanding a table leg. He was so concentrated on his task he didn't see her at first, and gave a start at the sound of her voice.

"Sorry to disturb you," she said, "but no one answered my knock at the front door."

"Aye, Prudy is havin' a lie-down," he said, putting down his sandpaper. "Jus' go on in—she's on't sun porch."

"Thanks," said Erin. She hesitated a moment before leaving. She had an impulse to say something about his illness, but what? She had overheard his conversation with the doctor by accident. Seeing he was already engaged in his woodworking task, she turned and crept out of the shed.

She found Prudence reclining on her chaise on the sun porch, reading glasses perched on the tip of her nose, peering at an annotated copy of *Pride and Prejudice*.

"Don't you think it's tragic the way Charlotte settles for marrying Mr. Collins?" she said with a sigh, putting down her book.

"She's also very practical," said Erin. "Not that many avenues were open to genteel young ladies in those days."

"I know," Prudence answered, removing her glasses and rubbing her eyes. "It's still sad."

"How are you feeling?"

"Much better, thank you," Prudence said, stifling a yawn. "Winty has been such a dear."

"I brought you the cutting," Erin said, fishing it from her knapsack.

"You're a dear to do that for me. Beautiful," she said, caressing it as if it were a child. "Must get it in a proper vase. I've just the thing in the kitchen."

"It gave me a chance to snoop around a bit," Erin replied, following Pru into the kitchen.

"Would you fetch me that crystal vase from the high shelf?" she said, pointing to the top cupboard. "I suppose I identify with Charlotte Lucas," Prudence said as Erin stood on tiptoe to reach the vase. "That's probably why her fate strikes me as so tragic. Imagine spending your life with someone like Mr. Collins," she added with a shiver. "I was so lucky to have found my Winty."

Erin felt a pang of guilt at her words, but said nothing. She hated that she knew his secret and wished he would just get it over with and tell poor Prudence.

"Here it is," she said, handing her the vase.

"Perfect!" Pru said, taking it with her good hand. "I'll just get it in some water."

"Would you like me to—"

"No, dear—I need to learn how to function or I'll become totally dependent on poor Winty. And that wouldn't do, would it?"

"I suppose not," Erin agreed.

"Oh, that reminds me—I have some old handwritten notes from society meetings that haven't been transferred to digital yet. Most are from Sylvia, when she was secretary-treasurer. Now where did I put those?" she said, wandering into the hall. "Ah, here they are!" she said, handing Erin a small stack of papers. "There might be something useful there."

"Thanks," Erin said, stuffing them into her backpack.

"Would you like tea, dear?"

"Thanks, but I'd best be getting on," she said, zipping up the backpack.

Ten minutes later she was riding her bike furiously down the road, on her way to see Farnsworth. Fighting a wicked head wind a mile or so out of town, the whoosh of air loud in her ears, she didn't even hear the car that had been gaining on her steadily since she turned onto Park Lane. She caught a glint of metal to her right, and slowed down so it could pass. She didn't take any notice of what the car looked like or who was driving it, focusing on not going into the ditch on the side of the road.

But when it drove alongside her for a quarter mile without passing, she felt a sickening horror in the pit of her stomach as she realized the car had no intention of passing. She turned to look, but it was too late. She felt the sharp slap of metal against her right side, flying forward as she became unmoored from her bike. She felt her breath leave her body as she hit the ground and struggled for air, finally inhaling the deep smell of earth, her face pressed against the dirt and twigs in the ditch. She had the sensation of wanting to remain conscious but was unable to fight through the gray fog that settled over her prostrate body like a thick blanket.

Then she knew only silence.

Chapter Forty-Two

~

"Erin Coleridge has been in an accident."

Peter Hemming felt the air being sucked out of his lungs. Without thinking, he rose from his chair, and was hit by a wave of dizziness that made him grip the desk to steady himself from falling.

Sergeant Jarral's handsome face crinkled in concern. "You all right, sir?"

"Yes," he said, wiping a thin layer of sweat from his upper lip. The station house was quiet, but Jarral's words had shattered the air like the blast of a shotgun. "What happened?"

"She was knocked from her bike by a car. They didn't stick around, so McCrary's got patrols out looking for the driver."

"How is she?"

"She wouldn't go to hospital. Insisted on being taken to Mrs. Appleby's house, sir."

"When was all this?"

"McCrary just called while you were fetching your mobile at the George and Dragon."

Having left his mobile in his room that morning, Hemming had gone back to get it after dropping Jarral off at the station house.

"Where is she now?"

"She's over at Mrs. Appleby's, far as I know."

"Let's go," Hemming said, throwing on his coat.

"Sir?"

"Come along, Sergeant."

"You think it's related to the case?"

"It's our job to find out," he said, walking so briskly from the room Sergeant Jarral had to stretch his long legs to keep up.

The sergeant had barely buckled his seat belt when Hemming took off down the road, going from zero to forty within seconds.

"This thing has more pickup than I realized," Jarral said as they zoomed through town. An old man with a black Labrador on a leash glared at them as the detective pulled away from a traffic light, gunning the engine.

Jarral rolled down the window, letting in the lingering aroma of roast lamb from one of the houses along the road as they swept past hedgerows and farm fields. A sheep farmer in Wellies and an oil-cloth duster was working a couple of border collies on his herd, the dogs working smoothly to drive the sheep toward the barn, nipping at their heels to keep them in a tight bunch.

"My cousin has a couple of herding dogs," Jarral remarked as they pulled up behind a slow-moving lorry.

"Of course he does," Hemming said, trying to keep his blood pressure from climbing as they crawled along behind the lorry.

"She, actually—runs a B and B in Wexford, and got them off a local farmer. They were the runts of the litter, and she couldn't bear the idea of them being sent to the local shelter."

"What a range of morality we Homo sapiens display," Hemming said as they followed the lumbering lorry, its truck bed brimming over with harvested hay.

"How's that, sir?"

"Your sister—"

"Cousin, sir."

"Your cousin is so softhearted she takes in two dogs she doesn't need to save them from a few weeks of kennel life. Yet someone in this village thinks nothing of poisoning a fellow human. Oh, thank

God," he said as the lorry turned off the main road, the hay tipping precariously as it swung around the corner. A few wisps of straw fluttered into the air and landed on his windshield.

He turned on the wipers—a few swipes sent the errant strands flying, taken by the wind, their next destination a mystery. If only people were so easily disposed of—murderers, thieves, poisoners, he thought as he steered clear of a badger on the side of the road. He watched in the rearview mirror as the creature waddled across the pavement, its striped face reminding him of the black-and-white clothes prisoners used to wear. Now, of course, orange was the new black and white.

Pulling up at the back entrance to the ramshackle farmhouse, Hemming vaulted out of the car as Sergeant Jarral hurried after him. A mangled red bicycle leaned against the dilapidated garage, its rear wheel twisted. Hemming took a deep breath and knocked on the kitchen door.

A voice he recognized as Farnsworth Appleby's called out, "Coming!"

He waited impatiently, biting his lip, until the door was opened, Mrs. Appleby's impressive body filling most of the door frame. She wore a flowered silk kimono over black leggings.

"Hello, pet," she said. "I've been expecting you. Come in."

The two men filed into her spacious, cluttered kitchen while being sniffed at by half a dozen felines. An orange tabby rubbed against Hemming's ankles, and he sneezed violently.

"Now, Wickham, behave," Farnsworth said, picking up the cat. "Can't you see the nice detective is allergic to you?" The animal purred loudly in her arms and attempted to lick her face.

"Where is she?" Hemming asked, looking around.

"If you mean Erin," Farnsworth said firmly, "she's resting."

"Can I speak to her?"

Farnsworth put the cat down, and it immediately made a bee-line for Hemming. "He likes you," she said. "And no, you can't talk to her at the moment."

"It's all right—I'm awake."

They all turned to see Erin Coleridge standing at the door separating the kitchen from the rest of the house. Dressed in pajamas several sizes too large, she looked pale and shaken. Her left arm was in a sling and a white bandage was wound around her forehead, a little blood seeping through. Hemming's knees went a little weak.

"Why aren't you in hospital?" he said sternly.

"I don't like them."

"I'm a registered nurse," Farnsworth said. "Or at least I was one in my previous life."

"So you patched her up?" Jarral asked.

"I did, though I warned her about the dangers of concussion and urged her to seek professional care."

"But she wouldn't?"

"I was just wasting my breath, pet. She'll do what she likes, and that did not include seeing a doctor."

"Who did this?" Hemming asked Erin. "Did you get a look at the car?"

"No," she said, sitting gingerly on the nearest chair.

"Should you be up, pet?" Farnsworth asked.

"I'm all right."

"You don't look all right," Hemming said, frowning. "Is there anything you can tell us about the car that hit you?"

"It came from behind. Next thing I knew, I was in a ditch."

"Who found you?" Jarral said.

"Winton Pettibone. He was returning from the shops, and he stopped to help me."

"He tried to take her to hospital, but she insisted on coming here," Farnsworth said.

"That's it—from now on, you're under police protection," said Hemming.

Erin frowned. "But—"

"It's not up for debate."

"Do you have the manpower for that, pet?" asked Farnsworth.

"I'll bring in men from York if I have to."

"Poisoners aren't confrontational," Erin pointed out. "So this wasn't necessarily the same person."

"I'd say it was a pretty cowardly act," Hemming said. "Hitting you from behind like that. You know you have to stop investigating on your own, right?"

"He's right, pet," said Farnsworth. "You could become the next victim."

Erin didn't answer.

"I want you to check in with me every day," said Hemming, handing her a card. "Here's my mobile number. And please be careful!" He looked at Farnsworth. "Get her to a doctor, will you?"

"Right," she said. "Why don't I solve global warming while I'm at it?"

Back in the car, Jarral said, "Who do you think did it, sir?"

"I have a hunch," Hemming said, turning the key in the ignition. "Let's see what the professor was up to this morning."

A few minutes later they drove up to the handsome townhouse, with its multiple chimneys and crisp white stucco exterior. Parking the car in front, they approached the black-lacquered door with the brass lion's head knocker.

Several loud knocks brought no response, and they turned to leave when Hemming noticed the lid of the mailbox was ajar. A few envelopes and periodicals poked out at different angles—it was evident no one had picked up the mail for several days.

"Are you thinking what I'm thinking, sir?" Jarral said.

Hemming looked at the empty house, its windows dark and silent.

"It appears Professor Pemberthy has gone on the lam."

"He could also be the next victim, sir," Jarral said as they climbed back into the car.

"His car isn't here, though, suggesting he's flown the coop."

Either way, Hemming thought as they pulled away from the empty house, it wasn't good news.

"Where to now, sir?" said Jarral.

"Let's drop in on Mrs. Pettibone. We'll get to the bottom of this."

But the promise felt hollow as the bell high atop All Souls as it summoned believers to Saturday evening vespers. Peter Hemming did not believe in God—as he listened to the solemn, mournful sound, he realized he had little faith in anything at all.

Chapter Forty-Three

❦

Erin watched Farnsworth bustle about as cats wandered in and out of the room, playing with bits of string, cleaning themselves, investigating half-open drawers or lying in the sun streaming in through the windows.

"I'm going to make you a good strong cup of Yorkshire tea, then it's back to bed with you," Farnsworth said, putting out a plate of muffins.

"First I want to look through these minutes Pru gave me," Erin said, spreading the pages out on the kitchen table.

"What do you think you'll find?"

"I don't know, but I'm starting with the most recent ones."

"Don't wear yourself out, pet," Farnsworth said, filling the teakettle with fresh water. "That shoulder of yours had a nasty bang, and you need to give it a rest."

"'Nothing ever fatigues me, but doing what I do not like.'"

"Pouring through minutes is not my idea of a jolly time," Farnsworth said, as Erin's mobile rang.

Erin answered it, finding a very distraught Carolyn Hardacker on the line.

"I heard about the accident," Carolyn said. "Are you all right?"

"I'm fine, thanks. I was lucky."

"I owe you an explanation. I'm sorry about the book. Thank you for not mentioning it to the police."

"Why did you take it?"

"Take what?" Farnsworth said. "What did she take?" But Erin waved her off.

"I was afraid it would look suspicious, and you'd tell the police," said Carolyn.

"So you just took it?"

"I was going to give it back."

"Can you put her on speaker phone?" Farnsworth whispered. "Please?"

Erin shook her head. "But why did you need it in the first place?"

"I was afraid Owen . . . well, I thought maybe he did it."

"He didn't care about being society president that much, did he?"

"It's not that," Carolyn said, her voice shaking.

"Please, oh *please*, put it on speaker phone!" Farnsworth whined.

"What then?" said Erin as Farnsworth tried to grab the phone from her.

Carolyn lowered her voice, as though she didn't want someone else to hear. "It's because I was—involved—with Sylvia."

"Involved? You mean—"

"It was before her marriage. We were young and in love—or so I thought. But she met Jerome and moved on."

"So Owen knew about you and Sylvia?"

"Somehow he found out."

"When?"

"I'm not exactly sure, but when she was poisoned, I was afraid he thought we were—you know, back together."

"Were you?"

"No! God, no."

"Have you told the police?"

"Told them *what*?" Farnsworth said, miming pulling her hair out.

"No. I think they suspect him already."

"You can't hide information from them—it just looks worse when the truth comes out."

"When *what* comes out?" Farnsworth yelled. Erin covered the speaker.

"You won't tell them, will you?" said Carolyn.

"No, but you have to tell them about you and Sylvia. They're bound to find out."

"I have to go. Owen just came in. Good-bye," she said, ringing off before Erin could answer.

"All right," Farnsworth said. "Now you have to tell me *everything*."

"Before I do that, why didn't you tell me about you and Sylvia?"

"What about us?"

"Don't pretend, please. Just tell me the truth."

Farnsworth stopped what she was doing and heaved a sigh. "Fine," she said, wiping her hands on a kitchen towel. "As far as I was concerned, it's all water under the bridge."

"Obviously it's not, because you could barely stand her. And Pru said you used to be best friends."

"Prudence tends toward the melodramatic," she said, putting the full teapot on the table.

"It's true, then—her knowing of your husband's affair and not telling you?"

"It's more complicated than that. She was friends with the girl's family, and she told them, but she didn't tell me."

"Why not?"

"That's what I'd like to know, pet."

"Didn't you ask her?"

"I never had the chance. He was run over by the lorry the day after they eloped to Dublin."

"You could have asked her then."

"It seemed like a moot point," Farnsworth said, stirring the steaming pot. She poured out two cups and handed one to Erin. Seeing Erin's expression, she said, "Don't worry, pet—if I had wanted to kill Sylvia, I'd have done it back then."

"I don't know if I'm supposed to find that encouraging or not," she said, but couldn't help thinking of the phrase *Revenge is a dish best served cold.*

And, she mused, nothing was more cold-blooded than poison.

Chapter Forty-Four

Erin woke early Saturday morning, after sleeping nearly ten hours. After turning down Farnsworth's offer to stay the night, she had accepted a ride home. She wanted to sleep in her own bed, and in spite of Farnsworth's urging had no intention of subjecting herself to a hospital visit.

After putting up the shop's OPEN sign, she stood in the morning sun on her patio, a cup of fresh coffee in one hand, almond croissant in the other. She felt stiff but refreshed—her neck didn't hurt as much, and her sprained shoulder was sore but not nearly as painful as it had been. She took a sip of coffee and stretched, enjoying the pale autumn sun on her face, even though it was half hidden by a cloud bank.

She was about to bite into the croissant when the faint ring of her landline came from the cottage, and she hurried back in to answer it. It was Farnsworth.

"How are you feeling, pet?"

"Much better, thanks to your excellent nursing skills."

"I still think you should have gone to hospital."

"Do you want to come round and go through the minutes with me?"

"When?"

Hearing the sound of a car engine, Erin looked out the window to see Detective Hemming's blue Citroën rattling up the driveway.

"I have to go," she said. "Come by in an hour?"

"See you then, pet."

Ignoring the trickle of anticipation in her stomach, Erin plastered on a cheery smile and came out to meet them as the old car slid to a halt on the slick earth. Her driveway wasn't much more than a couple of tire tracks in the damp ground leading from the road to her cottage, but she liked it that way—and besides, putting in a proper driveway was expensive.

"Good morning," she said, shielding her eyes from the sun, which had popped out resolutely from behind the clouds.

Sergeant Jarral gave his usual cheery smile, while Detective Hemming studied her closely in a way that made her blush. He looked exhausted.

"Would you like some tea?" she asked, sitting in one of the cast-iron chairs.

"No, thanks—we'll only be a few minutes. How are you?"

"Much better, thanks. Please, have a seat," she said, and the detective eased himself into one of the chairs. He did not look well. Sergeant Jarral remained standing, notebook in hand.

"Did you go to hospital?" Hemming asked.

"No, I came home and slept."

"You don't like doing what you're told, do you?" he said, a trace of a smile around his rather inviting lips. Erin wondered what those lips would feel like against her own.

"I've had enough of hospitals."

"Still, you might have had a concussion."

"Did you come to upbraid me about my bad decisions?"

"Actually, we wanted to pick your brain about a couple of things," Jarral said.

"Glad to help in any way I can."

"What do you know about Jerome Pemberthy?" asked Hemming.

"Teaches history at the Uni in York. Bit of a wanker."

"Anything else—about his background, perhaps?"

"Like what?"

"Anything at all."

"I wasn't very close to the Pemberthys."

"Anyone else in town who might be?"

"Has something happened?" Erin said, studying their faces.

"We'd just like to have a word with Mr. Pemberthy, so if you should happen to see him—"

She looked at Sergeant Jarral, then back at Hemming. "He's missing, isn't he?"

"Not exactly," said Jarral, but the detective silenced him with a glance.

"It's not the sort of thing we're keen to spread around," Hemming said. "We'd appreciate your discretion."

"Are you afraid something's happened to him? Or is he on the lam?"

"Does he have family in Yorkshire, or anywhere else you know of?"

Erin frowned, racking her brain for any stray details about Jerome. "He doesn't really come in here much. Sylvia used to come. It's so strange thinking of her suddenly not here anymore." Erin pulled her cardigan close as a chill slid across the fields. "She wasn't my favorite person, but still . . . Do you get used to it?" she asked Hemming. "Death, I mean?"

"If I ever get used to it, I'll know it's time to quit."

"I wish I knew more about Jerome, I really do."

"We appreciate your time," Hemming said, rising stiffly. "If you're not going to go to hospital, at least stay put for the next day or two, will you?"

"I'll try," she said, thinking that was sufficiently vague to not constitute a promise.

"I hope to get a protective detail for you by tomorrow. Until then, promise me you'll be careful."

"I promise."

"And no more sleuthing," he added sternly. "I won't have your death on my conscience."

The look he gave her was such a beguiling mix of concern and protectiveness, it made her go a bit soft in the knees.

"Wait!" she said as they turned to leave. "I have just the thing for you—won't take a minute." Before he could protest, she popped into the house, returning moments later with a plastic baggie containing dried yellow flower blossoms.

"What is it?" he said, peering at it dubiously.

"Chamomile. You'll sleep like a baby."

"It really does work, sir," said Jarral. "My cousin—"

"Grows it?"

"I was going to say he swears by it."

"Thank you," Hemming told Erin, with a smile that made her throat swell.

"It really does relax you," she said.

"If Sergeant Jarral's cousin swears by it, I'm sure it will work."

The sergeant cocked his head, as if unsure whether or not Hemming was teasing him. "Shall I drive, sir?"

"Certainly not," Hemming said, winking at Erin. "You might start actually liking my car. And we can't have that, can we?"

"No, sir."

"Don't let him get to you, Sergeant," said Erin.

"Yes, Miss—I mean no, Miss," he said, with a glance at Hemming.

"Don't spoil my fun, Ms. Coleridge," the detective said, squeezing her elbow. Her skin felt hot beneath his fingers. "Of course you can drive, Sergeant."

"Right you are, sir."

She watched them drive off, arms crossed, her flesh still warm where his fingers had touched it. She lingered for a few more minutes, watching the sun slip behind the clouds as shadows deepened over the surrounding fields, then turned and went inside.

A dozen or so customers wandered in and out of the shop over the course of the day. One scholarly-looking gentleman bought a rare edition of Dickens that Erin had been lucky enough to snag from an estate sale. Even with the discount she offered him, the price would easily cover two months of mortgage payments.

Around four she heard the sound of Farnsworth's car chugging up her muddy driveway. After pondering long and hard about her friend's guilt or innocence, Erin had decided that, come what may, she would behave as though she could trust her. Every instinct told her Farnsworth was trustworthy, and if she was wrong, Erin decided, she deserved what she got.

"Hello," Farnsworth said, wiping her feet on the front mat. "What do you say to a cuppa, love?"

"Coming right up," Erin replied, going into the kitchen to put the kettle on.

When the phone rang, she wasn't surprised to hear her father's voice on the line and was relieved to hear him sounding much cheerier.

"How are things in the wilds of Yorkshire? Any promising leads?"

She told him everything, except being run off her bike, ending with the disappearance of Jerome Pemberthy.

"You know, that name rings a bell," he said. "I thought so the other night, but couldn't remember why. Then finally I realized we were at Eton together."

"You know him?"

"Not really—I was ahead of him by five years, a senior class man when he arrived."

"I'm surprised you remember the name."

"Well, he was rather infamous on campus."

"Really?" she said, her scalp tingling with anticipation. "Why?"

"It seems he ratted out another boy for cheating. The other lad was eventually expelled, but nobody really thought much of Pemberthy after that—considered him a bit of a tosser."

"Do you remember the other boy's name?"

"Let me think . . . had the same name as a famous playwright. I remember wondering if they were related. Shaw? Wilde? No, someone older . . ."

"Wycherley? Sheridan? Marlowe?"

"That's it—Marlowe! Can't remember the chap's first name, though . . ."

"Could it be James?"

"Maybe—can't say for sure."

The sharply ascending whistle of the kettle pierced the air, and Erin tucked the phone receiver between her ear and shoulder as she pulled two mugs from the cupboard. "Sorry, dad, but I've got company."

"Don't let me keep you—attend to your guests."

"Thanks for calling—that was really helpful."

"I'm glad. Erin?"

"Yes?" she said, warming the teapot.

"Be careful, will you?"

"I will."

"Love you," he added. That was unusual—she couldn't remember him ever saying that.

"Love you too," she said, and rang off.

There were no pastries in the pantry, but there was a fresh loaf of Portuguese bread—Farnsworth wouldn't approve of it being whole wheat, Erin thought, but she'd eat it. Farnsworth liked to rail against what she called "health-obsessed tofu-snorting ninnies" but would eat whatever was put in front of her.

"What did your father have to say?" Farnsworth asked as Erin laid out the tea on the tiled coffee table. Each tile was a painting of a different European city, all by the same artist. Her mother had collected a tile for each city she had been to—Rome, Brussels, Vienna, Prague—eventually buying a coffee table to display them on. She'd left it to Erin in her will, and Erin had brought it with her to Yorkshire.

When Erin told her about the Eton connection, Farnsworth clapped her hands like a child. "What a good motive for murder—vengeance! Just like Darcy and Wickham—simmering resentment against past wrongs, only in this case it turns deadly. James Marlowe kills Sylvia to get back at Jerome, making it look like her death is related to the conflict in the society."

"It's more Poe than Austen, don't you think?" Erin said, stirring the pot. "And why now, after all this time?"

Outside the cottage, a hawk cried sharply as it pounced on an unlucky field mouse who happened to be in the wrong place at the wrong time.

Chapter Forty-Five

～

"I'm glad you're here," Erin said, as the shadows deepened while they poured over Sylvia's handwritten notes at the kitchen table.

"'Friendship is certainly the finest balm for the pangs of disappointed love,'" said Farnsworth.

"Why do you say that?"

"Clearly you're smitten."

"I am *not*."

Farnsworth just looked at her and laughed. "You might as well wear a sign around your neck."

Erin ignored her, pretending to study the minutes.

"And he can't date a suspect, now, can he?" Farnsworth said.

"I'm not a suspect."

"We're all suspects until they find the killer."

"So let's get on with it," Erin said tightly, shuffling through the pile of papers spread out in front of them. So far there had been nothing promising, just pages of routine meeting minutes. DISCUSSED ANNUAL BUDGET. MEMBERS AGREED TO FIVE PERCENT DUES HIKE TO COVER COST OF FANCY DRESS BALL, and so on.

"Look at this," Farnsworth said, holding up a page with a phone number scribbled on the upper right corner. Erin recognized the area code as belonging to the city of York. Beneath it was a name: ANTONIA MORELLI. "Who's that, I wonder?"

"That's what Google is for," Erin said, opening a web browser on her computer. Typing in the name, she got several hits, one of which was a link to the University of York. "Bingo," she said, clicking on it. "Teaches in the languages department."

"Hmm," said Farnsworth, looking over her shoulder. "I wonder if she knows Jerome Pemberthy?"

"One way to find out," Erin said, reaching for her landline.

"You're *calling* her?"

Erin nodded. "Hello?" she said when a female voice answered. "Is this Antonia Morelli?"

"This is Antonia," the woman said in a thick Italian accent. "Who is this, please?"

"Sorry to bother you, but I was wondering if you know Jerome Pemberthy?"

There was a silence, and in that moment, Erin knew there was something between Antonia Morelli and Jerome Pemberthy. She made up a story about being a former student looking for him, and got off the phone.

"Well?" said Farnsworth.

"What are you doing on Monday?"

"Besides feeding cats? Nothing."

"Fancy a drive to York?"

There was a knock at the door. Erin jumped up to answer it and found Polly standing on her front doorstep. She wore red pedal pushers, long black socks, and a green polar fleece jacket, which set off her pale hair.

"What happened to you?" she said, seeing Erin's cuts and bruises.

"I fell off my bike."

"Want some help catching Sylvia's killer?"

"Who told you I was—"

Polly rolled her eyes, putting her whole body into the gesture so that she looked like a puppet being released from its strings. "The whole town knows, for Christ's sake!" When she was around Erin, she liked to use phrases her father would never let her get away with at home.

"The whole town, huh?" said Erin.

"Pretty much. I thought you could use an assistant."

"Come along, then," Erin said, opening the door.

Polly followed her past the shop, though the living room, and into the kitchen. Upon seeing Farnsworth, she looked disappointed. "Oh. You already have a helper."

"The more, the merrier," said Erin.

"Hello, Polly," said Farnsworth. "What a pleasant surprise. What brings you here on this lovely day?"

"I'm going to help Erin catch the killer."

"I see," Farnsworth said, with a glance at Erin. "Sort of a junior detective, eh?"

"Can I use your computer?" Polly asked.

"Why do you need a computer?" Farnsworth asked.

"You'll see. Is it online?"

"Yes," said Erin.

"Do you happen to know Sylvia's email address?"

"I have it on my contact list," said Erin, opening her Gmail account. "There it is."

Polly squinted at the screen. "LadycatherinedebourghIV."

"How appropriate," said Farnsworth with a snort. She did not care for computers, did not use email, and barely knew what a browser was.

"She was rather like Lady Catherine, wasn't she?" Erin mused.

"I don't suppose you know her password?" said Polly.

"No," said Erin.

"Not to worry," Polly said, her fingers flying over the keyboard.

"No good," she said, shaking her head. "So it's not her address . . . let's try something else. Do you happen to know her birthday?"

"As a matter of fact, I do," said Farnsworth. "October 11."

"And the year?"

"I'm afraid she never shared that with me. Sylvia was—well, let's just say she regarded a lady's age as a private matter."

"All right, let's see if we can work with that," said Polly. Head bent, she continued to type. "There! I'm in."

"You figured out her password that quickly?" said Erin.

Polly shrugged. "Most people are lazy and use something obvious, even though they know better. I tried a couple of different combinations before finding the right one: her birthday, minus the year, all lowercase letters."

"This can't be legal," said Erin.

Polly shrugged. "Whatever."

Erin looked at Farnsworth. "I don't think we should—I mean, it's a question of privacy, isn't it?"

"What privacy?" Polly said. "She's dead."

"She has a point, love," said Farnsworth.

"All right," Erin said. "Let's have a look."

Sylvia's inbox was cluttered with the usual spam messages, as well as emails relating to society business. Erin read through the ones sent just before her death, but nothing struck her as suspicious or unexpected.

After a few minutes, Polly said, "I'm hungry. May I have something to eat?"

"Help yourself," Erin said, without taking her eyes off the screen.

"Anything of interest?" Farnsworth asked Erin, as Polly busied herself in the kitchen, raiding Erin's fridge.

"Nothing so far."

"Try checking the Sent folder."

"Good idea," Erin said, scrolling through the list. One addressed to Jonathan Alder caught her eye. It was dated two days before Sylvia's death. She opened it. It was brief but telling.

DON'T WORRY—YOUR SECRET IS SAFE WITH ME.

"Look at this," she said to Farnsworth.

Peering over her shoulder, Farnsworth gave a low whistle. "Do you suppose she's referring to—"

"What else could it be?"

"Well, one thing is for certain," said Farnsworth. "His secret is safe with her now that she's dead."

Erin stared at the screen. *Your secret is safe with me.* In fact, she thought, nobody in the town of Kirkbymoorside was safe.

Chapter Forty-Six

Erin spent Sunday minding her shop, which was busier than it had been. She suspected Sylvia's murder was responsible—it had been a lead story on all the local news channels for days now. Several people asked her if she knew Sylvia, to which she replied that she did, but not well, which was technically the truth.

Monday morning her calls to Jerome Pemberthy's office at York University went immediately to voice mail. Her plan to have Farnsworth drive her to York to hunt down the mysterious Antonia Morelli changed when her garage called to say her car was ready. Farnsworth acted disappointed, but Erin thought she didn't really relish a trip to York. Parking could be next to impossible, and Farnsworth wasn't able to walk long distances—more than half a mile and she was pretty knackered.

Erin decided to pay a call to James Marlowe before heading down to York. Her neck was still stiff, but her shoulder was moving more easily—she brought her sling along just in case. What she hadn't told anyone about were the purple bruises along her collarbone and upper arms—probably from hitting the handlebars as she fell. Easing herself into the front seat, she was glad to be back in the little car. She had an impulse to put the top down, though she knew it was too cold to be comfortable.

James Marlowe's butcher shop was tidy as always, the jars of jams and pickles lined up like sentinels on spotless, gleaming white shelves. As Erin stepped into the store, the aroma of boiled potatoes and sautéed beef wafted through her nostrils. Marlowe was nowhere in sight, but at the tinkle of the bell over the door, he appeared from the back, wearing a snowy-white apron, a blue-and-white dishcloth in his hands.

"Hi, Erin," he said cheerfully. "What can I get you?"

"Do you have a couple of minutes to talk about Sylvia?"

His face darkened, but he recovered quickly and gave a wry chuckle. "Polly failed to convince you I'm not a cold-blooded killer, eh?"

"I just have a couple of questions you might help me clear up."

"Give me a moment, would you? It's Monday, so I'm making shepherd's pie."

"It smells good."

"Customers come in for it every week, so I must be doing something right."

"I'll have to give it a try."

"I'll just pop back and turn down the stove. Won't be a minute," Marlowe said, ducking behind a burgundy curtain separating the front of the store from the back. The clanking of pots and pans was followed by his reappearance, minus the apron.

"Now then, what can I do for you?"

"I understand you were at school with Jerome Pemberthy."

"Who told you that?"

"My father, actually. He attended Eton as well."

"Small world, eh?" the butcher said, but sweat beaded up beneath his crisp white collar.

"Rumor was that Pemberthy was instrumental in your being expelled."

Marlowe's mouth tightened, and he gave another, if less convincing, chuckle. "The only person 'instrumental' in my expulsion was myself. I can't lay the blame on anyone else."

"But he—" Erin began.

"He did report me, yes. But I got what I deserved."

"If it's not too personal, why did you—"

"I am—was—a compulsive people pleaser. I wanted good grades to make my parents proud of me. Ironically, it's the only time in my life I ever cheated, and I got caught. Serves me right."

"No hard feelings, then?"

"Jerome Pemberthy isn't my favorite person, but that's nothing to do with our school days."

"What does it have to do with, if you don't mind my asking?"

"The fact that he's a self-important prig and a bully."

"Was he like that at school?"

"People don't change." He pulled another spotless apron from a drawer in the tall white cabinet behind the counter and tied it around his waist. "That's a fantasy promulgated by the self-help industry and reality television."

"You sound cynical."

"Just realistic," he said, slapping a rack of lamb down on the butcher block. Wielding a polished cleaver, he brought it down with a *thwack* on the meat, cutting it in half with one well-aimed stroke. "And I wasn't the only one he ratted on, by the way. There were others."

"Do you know who they were?"

"It happened after I was gone—I heard about it afterward. But I'll tell you one thing: Jerome Pemberthy found the perfect profession for a narcissist. His massive ego gets all the stroking it needs there."

"York University, you mean?"

"As a 'learned professor,' he can cultivate the admiration of fresh young things who don't know any better." Picking up a thin, pointed knife, he began trimming fat from the meat with deft, practiced strokes.

"Are you saying he has affairs with his students?"

Marlowe gave a short, sharp laugh. "He wouldn't know what to do with a woman if his life depended on it. It's admiration he craves. Sex is too messy, too personal—not to mention too demanding. All that untidy emotion," he said, throwing a few strips of fat into a metal basket.

"So you don't hold a grudge against him?"

He put down his knife and leaned on the polished butcher block table. "Life's too short for that kind of nonsense. I've got two fabulous kids who lost their mother. Why would I risk depriving them of their father as well?"

Erin had to admit, looking into his earnest blue eyes, she had no good reason to doubt him. He sounded so sincere, and his feelings for his children seemed genuine. "They are lovely kids," she said.

"They like you too," he answered, taking up his knife and going back to his work.

The bell over the door tinkled, and Erin turned to see an elderly woman enter the store.

"Good morning, Mrs. Dobbins," Marlowe said with a friendly wave. "Be with you in a moment."

"Thanks so much for your time," said Erin. "I really appreciate it."

"Come by for shepherd's pie sometime—on the house."

"I will. Cheers."

The butcher wiped his hands on a clean white towel. "Until this person is apprehended, no one in this town is really safe."

As she got in her car to drive to York, a line from an Emily Dickinson poem popped into Erin's head.

The heart wants what it wants.

Sometimes, she thought, what the heart wanted was very, very evil.

Chapter Forty-Seven

The trip to York was less than thirty miles and usually took about an hour. Erin stopped at a roadside pub for fish and chips along the way. She was tempted to indulge in a pint but feared even one drink might put her over the legal limit, so she had a lemonade instead. Feeling more tired than usual, maybe because of her injuries, she topped it off with a double espresso.

Fortified, she set off for the historic city of York. Erin had walked the medieval wall surrounding the city many times, but the sight of it never failed to thrill her. She longed to browse the bookshops along Micklegate Street, but she was on a mission and there wasn't time. She could have bypassed downtown York entirely, since the university campus was built along a lake to the south of the city—technically the village of Heslington—but she wanted to see the city center.

As she drove through the narrow Micklegate Bar, the Normanesque tower looming over the street bearing its name, she gazed at the crosses carved out of the stone and imagined hordes of Normans rampaging a city that had already seen invasions by Romans and Danes. She took a slight detour to peer at her favorite spot in York, a medieval cobblestoned street known as The Shambles. It was a tourist draw, with its ancient timbered buildings, many of them in the old Tudor style. There didn't seem to be a single right angle in any of the houses, their crooked second stories hanging over the street as if about to topple onto the paving stones at any minute.

Continuing on, she reached Heslington, an attractive village of red brick buildings just south of the city. The history department was located on the larger western campus—Antonia Morelli's office was in a nondescript brick building opposite the cozy thatched cottage known as The Warren. Erin pulled into the public car park and checked her notes. According to the history department secretary, Professor Morelli's office hours were Mondays through Thursday from twelve to four PM, and it was just a few minutes before two, so hopefully she would be in. By showing up unannounced, Erin would catch Morelli off guard, hopefully giving her an advantage.

After walking up the flight of stairs to the faculty offices, Erin found Morelli's at the end of a bright corridor, the polished tile floor reflecting the sun streaming in through the ceiling skylights. Shielding her eyes, she read the placard on the door.

Angela Morelli
Medieval Studies
OFFICE HOURS 12–4 M/W

Taking a deep breath, she knocked on the door.

"Who is it, please?"

It was the same voice she had heard on the phone, low and liquid, with a pronounced Italian accent.

"Hi—I'm here about Professor Pemberthy."

"Do you have an appointment?"

"No."

"Just a minute."

Erin thought she heard Morelli talking to someone—it sounded like she was on the phone. High heels clicked against the floor, and the door opened to reveal a slim, dark-haired woman of about forty. Her face was long and leonine, with prominent lips, dark almond eyes, and a long, sweeping nose. She looked like the frieze of an Egyptian princess come to life.

"Professor Morelli? I'm Erin Coleridge."

"How can I help you?" she asked warily.

"May I come in?"

"I have a three o'clock meeting."

"This won't take long."

Without a word, Morelli walked back into her office, leaving the door open. Taking it as an invitation, Erin followed her inside. The office was sparsely but tastefully decorated—across from the narrow windows with latticed cross-hatching was a bookshelf containing history texts and Italian pottery. A creamy floral area rug with twining green vines sprouting tiny flowers covered the center of the small room; at one end was a small rust-colored sofa, and at the other end, Morelli's desk. Erin wondered how much of the decor was furnished by the college and how much was Morelli's.

The room gave the impression of a very organized, controlled person, reinforced by the woman herself. Dressed in a short gray dress, heels, and a crimson jacket, she was elegance personified. Her straight dark hair was pulled into a tight knot at the base of her long neck, her olive skin shone with moisturizer, and her understated makeup was perfectly applied, down to the coral-red lipstick. Erin was amazed by women who wore lipstick on a regular basis—on the few occasions she'd thought to apply it, it had seemed to rub off within minutes.

"What can I do for you?" Morelli said, sitting behind her desk and crossing her black stocking–clad legs. "Please, sit," she added, pointing to the crimson sofa.

"I understand you know Professor Pemberthy," Erin said after sinking onto the couch, which was lower than it looked, the springs creaking under her weight.

"He's my colleague, yes."

"I live in the same town as he and his wife."

"Poor woman—so tragic. We all feel terrible about it." Her manner suggested nothing of the kind; her voice carried all the emotion of someone reading a recipe for raisin scones. "What has that to do with me?"

"Actually, he's a suspect in his wife's murder—"

"Ridiculous. Jerome wouldn't harm a fly," she said, flinging her hand in the air as if chasing away the pesky insect.

"He seems to have vanished, which makes the police think he's guilty."

"Ha!" she said with disgust. "British detectives are even more stupid than Italian *polizia*."

"Can you help me find him?"

"I spoke with him on the phone just before you came in."

"Where is he?"

"How should I know?"

"Do you know whether he had life insurance on his wife?"

"Why would I know that?"

"Because you're his mistress."

Morelli's face hardened; then she laughed. "How quaint—*mistress*. Do you British really use that anymore?"

"What word would you use?"

She shrugged. "I'm his lover. Or at least I was. He's been distant since his wife's death."

"Do you think he did it?"

Morelli leaned back in her chair and crossed her thin arms. "Why should I answer any more of your questions?"

"If you don't, you may find yourself talking to a police detective instead."

"Are you working with them?"

"Yes," Erin lied. "I'm their civilian liaison." Being somewhat familiar with the complex, arcane elements of Italian law enforcement, she thought she might get away with such an outrageous claim.

Professor Morelli frowned. "What's that?"

"Shall I just pick up the phone and tell them you won't cooperate?"

"No—wait," she said, biting her lip. "Yes, he had an insurance policy on her, through the university."

"Do you know for what amount?"

"I got the impression it was substantial. But he didn't kill his wife."

"Do you know that for a fact?"

"I just don't believe Jerome is capable of such barbarism."

"Thank you, Professor Morelli—I appreciate your cooperation," Erin said, rising from the couch. "Oh, one more thing— do you know Carolyn Hardacker? She used to teach in the art department."

Morelli took out an emery board and filed the tip of one of her perfect nails. "Hardacker . . . is she a very pretty black woman?"

"Yes."

"I went to one of her openings. Very talented artist."

"Do you know why she left the university?"

"There were rumors it had to do with substance abuse. But please, don't quote me on that."

"I—we won't," Erin said. Walking the short distance to the door, she opened it to find Jerome Pemberthy standing there.

"What the hell are you doing here?" he demanded, scowling.

Erin's first impulse was to run. The fury in his eyes made her knees go weak, and she wasn't sure she could run even if she wanted to.

"I was just passing through," she said, but she could see that explanation wasn't going to fly. She began to back away slowly, but he seized her by the arm and pulled her inside, shutting the office door behind them.

Chapter Forty-Eight

After some effort, Erin managed to calm Jerome down, with some help from Antonia Morelli, who for some reason seemed to have taken her side.

"Of course you didn't do it!" she told him. "But just listen to her, why don't you?"

"It's bloody preposterous," he told Erin. "If you think the motive was money, you should be looking at that pompous pastor."

"Reverend Motley?"

"He had a hundred thousand reasons to kill Sylvia."

"What do you mean?"

"She left his church a hundred thousand pounds."

"How do you know that?" said Antonia.

"I just came from the reading of the will at our solicitor's."

"I didn't realize Sylvia was that religious," said Erin.

"She wasn't."

"That's rather strange, then, isn't it?"

"It's enough to pay for repairs to that damn carillon, plus a new wing named after her. That was one of the stipulations in the will."

Erin wondered what hold the reverend had over Sylvia. "The police have been trying to reach you," she told Jerome. "You might want to return their calls."

"Why should I do that?"

"Otherwise you look guilty, silly," Antonia said, lighting a cigarette.

"She's right," Erin said. "They think you're on the lam."

He snorted. "'On the *lam?*' Do they really think in thirties movie clichés?"

"What means this idiom?" Antonia said. "You escape by riding on a lamb?"

"It just means to run away," Erin explained.

"Oh," she said, taking a drag from her cigarette, the smoke escaping in long plumes from her crimson lips. Erin wondered if Jerome was going to say anything. Most public buildings were smoke-free these days.

"It's very bad, I know," Antonia said, seeing Erin's reaction. "But I'm Italian."

"Thank you both very much for your time," Erin said, taking that as her cue to leave. Jerome nodded curtly, but Antonia seemed sorry to see her go.

"Nice meeting you," she said. "Good luck with your investigation."

"Thanks," Erin said, closing the door behind her. She lingered in the hallway for a moment, hoping to overhear something useful, but the only sounds coming from the room were low murmurs and what sounded like kissing. Then the sofa springs creaked, and Erin tiptoed down the corridor, leaving the lovebirds to their afternoon shenanigans.

Once she was north of the city, Erin called Farnsworth on her mobile and told her everything she had learned.

"That's very interesting," Farnsworth said, "because I've been doing some digging, and the church is in some financial distress."

"How did you find that out?"

"Let's just say Polly has something to do with it."

Erin didn't like the idea of Polly being involved in the investigation—it wasn't safe. She would explain all that to Farnsworth and Polly upon her return, she thought as she pulled up in front of a roadside pub. She had forgotten to use the loo at the college and now was in some discomfort.

As she pulled into the car park, a lone hawk circled in the sky above, looking for prey. Shivering, she pulled her coat tighter around her as she ducked into the building, just as the sun was blotted out by a quickly moving cloud cover.

Chapter Forty-Nine

⌒

"Are you going to tell the police what you learned?" Farnsworth asked after Erin had finished answering all her questions about her sleuthing in York. She and Farnsworth were seated at the big kitchen table with Polly as the sun set in the western sky, throwing pink and gold fingers of light through the windows.

"If I do, they'll insist on tailing me."

"But clearly you're in danger!"

"I'll handle it."

"You are so *stubborn*!" Farnsworth said, as a plump yellow tabby made a beeline for a bag of crunchies she had left on the sideboard. Erin had arrived just after feeding time, and Farnsworth hadn't yet put away all the cat food.

"I'm with her," Polly said as Farnsworth snatched the bag away.

"No, Mrs. Bennet!" Farnsworth said. "She's such a greedy girl," she added as she stowed the bag safely in a high cabinet. "What do you mean?" she asked Polly.

"If she tells the coppers, they'll muzzle her completely."

"It's not as if she's a dog, dear," said Farnsworth.

"Polly's right," said Erin. "I have to be free to operate on my own. So I'll have to find a way to tell them anonymously."

"What's that mean?" asked Polly.

"It means they won't know it's coming from her," said Farnsworth.

"I can help you with that," said Polly.

"You've done quite enough already," said Erin. "I don't want to involve you any further."

"Oh, but it's so *fun*!" Polly made a face and crossed her arms.

"Now don't you go into one of your pouts," said Farnsworth.

"It's not *fair*!"

"Life isn't fair, pet."

"What's this about Sylvia giving money to the church?" Erin asked. "Sounds as if she's playing Lady Catherine to Reverend Motley's Mr. Collins."

"Yes, indeed, but the question is why?" said Farnsworth.

"Maybe she just wants to be remembered," Polly suggested. "You know, have her name on a building."

"But it might be something more sinister," said Erin. "I've got to be going," she added, looking out the window. "The sun has nearly set."

"Let me just follow you to make sure you get home safely," said Farnsworth.

"Absolutely not. Come along, Polly, I'll drop you off."

"All right."

"Call me when you get in," said Farnsworth.

"It's not—"

"*Call me*."

"All right," Erin said. "Come along, Polly."

Driving through the village, they could see the bonfire had been laid in the center of the town square. It loomed against the darkening sky, like the hump of a great beast, ominous and threatening.

"You going to the fete?" Erin asked Polly.

"Wouldn't miss it."

"James Chester too?"

"*If* he doesn't do something to get grounded."

Erin smiled. "It almost sounds as if you're hoping he will."

"I just don't want to have to look after him." It was too dark to see her face, but Erin imagined Polly rolling her eyes.

By the time she dropped the girl off and reached her house, dusk had deepened into twilight, a pale moon rising in the west. The cottage loomed ahead, its eaves dim against the silvery moon. Usually Erin left the light on over the entrance, but today she had forgotten—she was rattled, though she didn't want to admit it. Her shoulder was starting to ache, and she rubbed it as she pulled to the end of her driveway. She parked in front and turned off the car lights, suddenly wishing she weren't entering that dark house alone. Shadows flickered and danced across the facade of the cottage as she closed the car door behind her. Usually her home felt warm and welcoming, but tonight there was a chill in the air—she shivered at the sight of the empty windows.

She hesitated before unlocking the door. Pushing it open, she realized she had never noticed how loudly it squeaked. She stepped inside, inhaling the aroma of eucalyptus and apples. She kept an antique copper pitcher full of eucalyptus by the front door, but the cottage had smelled of apples since the first day she saw it—one of the many reasons she'd fallen in love with it. But it smelled musty tonight, and when she got to the living room, she opened a window, though it was a cold night.

She called Farnsworth.

"I think you're making a mistake being on your own, pet. You have a weapon?"

"The fireplace poker."

"Why don't you sleep with it next to your bed?"

"All right."

"Please check in first thing tomorrow."

"I will," she said. "Good night."

After ringing off, Erin went to turn off the light over the front door. A few late-season moths fluttered lazily around its dim glow, until they got so close they were burned to death, immolated by the very thing they sought so blindly.

Chapter Fifty

❧

"'The person, be it gentleman or lady, who has not pleasure in a good novel, must be intolerably stupid.'"

Prudence Pettibone's right arm might be in a cast, but her ardor for quoting Jane Austen remained undimmed. Reclining on Erin's lawn chaise lounge Tuesday afternoon, she held court like a duchess, draped in Erin's burgundy afghan. In a circle surrounding her like courtiers were Erin, Farnsworth, and Hetty. Perched on patio chairs, teacups balanced on their knees, they were here to discuss the impending society meeting that evening to choose a new president. The thermometer had climbed overnight, and faced with another spate of unseasonably warm weather, Farnsworth had declared they would have their impromptu meeting outside.

The discussion having turned from crime to crime novels, Prudence seized the opportunity to hijack the conversation, regaling her companions with tasty morsels of wisdom only she (via Jane Austen) could deliver. Since she had cast herself in the role of bravely suffering invalid, there was little anyone could do to stop her without seeming like an insensitive cad.

Hetty's elaborate ritual of sighing and fidgeting made little impact on Prudence, who continued to prattle on, no doubt buoyed by the painkillers she had been prescribed in hospital.

"Of course, having a near-death experience makes one appreciate all *sorts* of things, aside from the pleasures of literature," she continued, waving her teaspoon in the air as if conducting an invisible choir.

"What else does one appreciate?" Farnsworth asked, egging her on.

Failing to catch her ironic tone, Prudence leapt at the bait. "Oh, goodness, *so* much! The taste of jam and toast—this is *excellent*, by the way," she said to Erin, who had provided crusty rolls and fresh butter.

"The jam is mine," Hetty pointed out, a petulant expression on her lacquered face. Erin never stopped marveling at the fact that she had never seen Hetty in anything less than full "war paint," as her mother used to call it.

"The jam is very nice too," Prudence acquiesced.

"Elderberry," Hetty informed her.

"So it says on the jar," Pru shot back, no doubt irritated at having her monologue so rudely interrupted. "Of course," she continued grandly, "coming so close to dying does make one aware of dear departed loved ones."

"Like Sylvia, you mean?" Farnsworth said, a wicked gleam in her eye.

Prudence spared a moment to glare at her before continuing. "I was thinking of my dear mother, since you ask." A single tear gathered at the corner of her eye, miraculously balancing there, defying gravity. "But since you mention Sylvia, as a matter of fact, my poor mother died in a very similar way."

Erin held her own mother's death at arm's length, like an unwashed suit of clothes. Not really wanting to be part of Pru's maudlin remembrances, she sprang from her chair.

"More tea, anyone?"

"I'll have some," Hetty said, making no offer to help.

"My dear mother, God rest her soul, left this earth too early," Prudence lamented, with the tragic gestures of a grand diva.

Farnsworth caught Erin's eye and mouthed the word *Vicodin*. Erin escaped to the kitchen, ducking inside the front door of the cottage just as Pru's voice rose to a dramatic crescendo. Erin was uncomfortable with her knowledge of Winton's illness—obviously he hadn't yet told his wife. Thinking about it nudged Erin closer to carefully buried feelings about her mother, so she concentrated on making tea in her cozy kitchen.

She returned with the fresh pot just in time to see Polly Marlowe's red bicycle wobbling up her driveway, such as it was. The recent rains had turned the already muddy surface into a near swamp, and Polly's tires were nearly swallowed by the deep ruts. She narrowly avoided tumbling over as she pedaled through the layer of mud at the bottom.

"Good timing," Erin said as Polly dismounted and leaned her bike against the stone foundation of the tiny shed next to the house. "I've just made a fresh pot."

"Alarming driveway you have here," Polly said. "Can I help carry something?"

"Why don't you get yourself a cup—or a mug, if you prefer."

Polly disappeared into the cottage, returning moments later with a mug with WORLD'S BEST DAUGHTER stenciled on it in large black lettering.

"Hello, ladies," she said, plopping down in one of the spare chairs.

"Hello, Polly," said Farnsworth.

"Are you really?" said Prudence.

"Am I what?" Polly said.

"World's Best Daughter," Pru said, pointing to the mug.

Polly shrugged. "This is Erin's mug. I'm the World's Worst Daughter."

"I'm sure that's not true," Farnsworth said kindly, catching Erin's eye again. Erin shook her head—she didn't think it was appropriate to mention Pru's medicated state in front of a ten-year-old. Besides, she rather liked this version of Prudence, a little wild and unpredictable. Erin glanced at her, contentedly sipping tea, a black wool beret perched on her head at a rakish angle. The old Prudence would never wear a beret, much less so stylishly. Hetty wore a pinched expression, put out by the attention her friend was getting.

"Does it hurt much?" Polly asked, pointing to her arm in the cast.

"One mustn't complain," Prudence replied heroically, with a little sniffle.

"Who do you think you are, the bloody Queen?" Hetty muttered under her breath, loud enough for Erin to hear.

Prudence swung her head in Hetty's direction. "What?"

"Shouldn't we discuss the next society meeting?" Erin said quickly.

"Yes," Farnsworth agreed. "That's what we're here for."

"Who do you think is going to be in the running for president?" asked Hetty.

Prudence put down her teacup and yawned. "Winton thinks I should put my name in the hat."

Hetty stared at her. "*You?* You're kidding!"

Pru looked at her with a hurt expression. "I fail to see why that's so surprising."

"Aren't you afraid you'll be poisoned?" Polly said.

Prudence frowned. "Shouldn't you be in school?"

"Half day today on account of a teacher's meeting," Polly said, kicking her legs under her chair.

"Where's James Chester?" Farnsworth said.

"Father kept him in to do his homework. That's what he said, but I think he's just in a bad mood."

"Why?" said Hetty, perking up.

Erin had heard from Farnsworth that for a while Hetty was sweet on James Marlowe, until he let it be it known he didn't share her ardor. Still rankled by it, she seemed to relish any bad news about him.

"That police detective came to the store yesterday, and he seemed upset about it afterwards," said Polly.

"What did he say that upset your father?" Erin asked.

"He wouldn't say—he just looked really annoyed," Polly said, reaching for the sugar bowl. "Anyway, he told me I'm not allowed to come tonight, because it's too dangerous."

"Dangerous?" said Prudence.

"Is he afraid there'll be another poisoning?" Erin said.

Polly shrugged and helped herself to more sugar. "I don't know."

"That doesn't make any sense at all," Hetty remarked disdainfully. "Whoever did it was out to get Sylvia, not the whole society."

"But what about the car that ran us off the road?" Pru asked Erin nervously. "And you on your bike—are they related?"

"Obviously," said Farnsworth. "Clearly someone is—"

Erin caught her eye and shook her head, warning her not to alarm the others, but it was too late.

"What?" Hetty said, looking terrified. "Someone is trying to *what*?"

"Nothing," said Farnsworth.

"Farnsworth!" Prudence hissed. "The *child*!"

"Don't mind me," said Polly. "I've heard worse on Nickelodeon."

Pru went a little white and turned to Erin. "Do *you* think it's safe?"

Erin looked out over the field behind her house. A slight breeze lifted the branches of the old willow tree stooping gracefully over the old wooden footbridge. It was hard to imagine that a place of such bucolic beauty had produced a heartless poisoner. But she also knew that evil burrowed into the loveliest of landscapes.

She turned back to her friends, their faces eager with expectation.

"To be honest, I really don't know."

She wished she had more comforting words for them, but the truth was that a killer still lurked among the rolling hills of the Yorkshire moors.

Chapter Fifty-One

～

After her friends left, Erin lay down on the couch, intending to rest her eyes, but when she awoke an hour later it was time to leave for the meeting. Outside, the air was heavy with impending rain, so overcast that not a single star was visible through the cloud cover.

She entered the church meeting room to find it nearly half full. She heard the din of voices as she came down the stairs; most of her friends had already arrived. Dressed in tight jeans and a blouse that revealed a lot of coastline, Hetty Miller stood next to Prudence, who looked frumpy as ever in a brown cardigan two sizes too large. Both were flirting with Jonathan Alder, looking appealing in a black turtleneck and jeans. Winton Pettibone stood a few feet away from everyone, looking out of place as usual.

Farnsworth waved at her from across the room, just as Erin felt a hand on her shoulder. She turned to see Reverend Motley beaming at her through watery blue eyes.

"I heard about your unfortunate accident. How are you feeling?"

"Better, thanks. And it wasn't an accident."

"Goodness!" he exclaimed, but Erin thought he didn't look very surprised. "You mean—"

"Someone deliberately ran me down."

Before he could answer, Erin slipped in between the folding chairs to sit next to Farnsworth.

"We're not the only ones who had the bright idea to show up

early," Farnsworth said, pulling a thermos from a large flowered Tesco bag. "At least I came prepared—since there'll be no tea service, it's strictly BYOT."

"You're a treasure."

In the back of the room, leaning against the wall, was Detective Hemming. Arms crossed, he quietly observed the members as they arrived. Instead of his usual suit and tie, he wore a red-and-black flannel shirt over black trousers. Erin's throat contracted at the sight of him, and she felt a little light-headed. Then she remembered she hadn't eaten dinner.

"Did you bring anything to eat?" she asked Farnsworth.

Farnsworth rolled her eyes. "You *do* realize who you're talking to?"

"I'll rephrase that. *What* did you bring to eat?"

Farnsworth smiled as she extracted a baguette and a hunk of Saint-André cheese from the Tesco bag.

Erin inhaled the aroma of the soft, creamy cheese. "Did I ever tell you how much I love you?"

"And for the health conscious," Farnsworth said, producing an apple and a bunch of Concord grapes.

"Will you marry me?"

"It would break too many hearts. Speaking of heartbreakers, incoming Mr. Wickham at three o'clock."

Erin turned to see Jonathan Alder approaching rather tentatively.

"Hello there," he said. "I had the impression for a moment you were avoiding me."

"Not at all," Erin lied. Her feelings about Detective Hemming were confusing enough—she didn't need to worry about Jonathan as well. But his presence gave her a frisson of pleasure.

"Why would anyone avoid *you*?" Farnsworth said. Her tone was flirtatious, but with an ironic edge. With Farnsworth it could be hard to tell. "Would you like some cheese and fruit?"

"Thanks, but I just ate," he said, looking around at the people filing in. The room was filling up—not so many people as at the last meeting, but more than usual. "We could be in for some fireworks tonight."

"Who do you think is the most likely candidate for president?" Farnsworth asked.

"I don't even know who's in the running."

"What about you?" Hetty said, sauntering over to join them. She eyed Jonathan as if he were an expensive steak; she was practically salivating.

"Good heavens, no," he said, blushing.

"You're certainly popular enough," said Hetty, "at least with the ladies."

"And you don't have many negatives, since no one knows much about you," Farnsworth remarked.

"I don't know about that—"

"It's true," Hetty said. "A real man of mystery. No one even knows where you came from."

"Will you excuse me for a moment?" he said. "Sorry, but I have to run to the loo before we start."

"When nature calls, you have to answer," said Hetty.

"Interesting," Erin, said, looking at her watch when he had gone. "We're not due to start for another ten minutes."

"He's obviously avoiding talking about himself," said Farnsworth.

"How odd," said Hetty. "Most people love to talk about themselves."

"Definitely a Mr. Wickham type," Farnsworth remarked. "Not to be trusted. I'd watch out if I were you," she told Erin.

"I'm not—" Erin began, but her attention was diverted by the sight of Winton and Prudence Pettibone, seated at a folding table, deep in conversation. She wondered if he was at last telling her about his illness, though this seemed an odd place to do it.

"Wonder what that's all about?" Farnsworth murmured, following her gaze.

"Pru is desperate to run for president," Hetty said, helping herself to a slice of cheese.

"I can't imagine anyone wanting the job now," said Farnsworth.

"Because they might become the next victim?" Hetty said, biting into a crisp slice of apple.

"Because it's a den of vipers," Farnsworth replied.

An attractive, athletic-looking blonde slid into the seat nearest the entrance. Her wide sunglasses and broad-brimmed floppy hat effectively hid her expression, but her firm, pointed chin and taut body suggested an iron will and strong personality. She immersed herself in her mobile phone, texting so quickly with her manicured thumbs that Erin couldn't help sneaking a look at her.

She was clad in a red plastic raincoat, fastened snugly around her trim waist, and carried a tiny leather backpack, the kind that was all the rage among stylish urban women. Her heels were too high to be comfortable, her lipstick was perfectly applied, and her manicure was new. Everything about her looked expensive and pampered, carefully chosen for effect over utility.

"Who's she?" Farnsworth whispered.

"I have no idea," Erin answered.

After a few minutes, the woman rose and headed toward the lavatory, high heels clicking smartly on the polished floor. Erin wondered that the thought had not occurred to her earlier—suddenly the resemblance seemed so obvious.

She was Suzanne Becker's sister.

As she approached the little hall leading to the restrooms, Kurt Becker emerged from the men's room. Spotting her, he frowned, though he didn't look entirely surprised to see her. He tried to brush past her, but she caught his arm and pulled him aside.

"*Was hast Du getan?*" she said, shaking her perfectly groomed head.

"*Ich habe Dir gesagt, dass es nicht mein Schuld ist,*" he said in a low voice.

"*Unglaublich,*" she said, a look of disgust on her taut face as he disappeared into the stairwell. She continued on her way to the ladies' room, emerging a few minutes later with a fresh coat of lipstick. Sauntering back into the room, she stopped when she reached Erin and Farnsworth.

"I don't believe we've been introduced," she added, offering a slim hand. "I'm Katrine Auer, Suzanne's sister."

"Pleased to meet you," Erin said, shaking it. It was cool and dry, the skin powdery, as though it had been dusted with talcum. "I'm Erin Coleridge, and this is Farnsworth Appleby."

"Farnsworth—isn't that an odd name for a female?" Katrine asked with a little smirk.

"I'm an odd female," said Farnsworth. "Where's Suzanne?"

"She's indisposed," Katrine replied. "I understand there has been a lot of excitement around here lately."

"Is that what you call it in Germany?" Farnsworth said. "Here we call it murder."

A frown flashed across her taut face, replaced by a tight smile. "I'd better find a seat before they start," Katrine said. "Nice to meet you."

"She thinks she's all that and a packet of crisps," Farnsworth muttered. "You speak German. What was that all about?"

"She said 'What have you done?'" Erin said. "And he said it wasn't his fault."

"That's interesting. Think they were talking about Sylvia's death?"

"I wish I knew."

At that moment Carolyn and Owen Hardacker entered the room. Simply clad in a long black linen dress, hair loose about her shoulders, Carolyn looked fragile, with dark circles under her eyes, while Owen wore a scowl suggesting it would be a good idea to keep a distance from him.

Carolyn walked over to Erin, opened her leather shoulder bag, and pulled out *The Poisoner's Handbook*. "I'm so sorry. I was looking at this in your shop the other day and it ended up in my bag. I've been meaning to return it to you. Of course, I'd be glad to pay for it if you'd rather."

"That's not necessary," Erin said, tucking the book into her backpack. Obviously the explanation was entirely for Owen's sake, and she wasn't going to embarrass Carolyn further by saying anything.

"Right," said Owen, tipping his hat to the ladies, "now that we've got that sorted, shall we go sit down?"

"Go ahead, darling—I'll be with you in a moment," Carolyn said. Owen shrugged and obeyed. When it came to his wife, Erin thought, he was a pussycat.

Erin turned to see Jonathan approaching, but instead of talking to her, he addressed Carolyn.

"How are you feeling?"

"Rough, but I think it's working," she said.

"I'm so glad," he said, squeezing her hand.

"I can't thank you enough."

"You already have."

"It was worth every penny," she said, hugging him before returning to her seat in the back row next to her husband.

"What was that all about?" Farnsworth whispered. "What was worth every penny?"

Erin stood up and went over to talk with Jonathan. After a couple of minutes, she returned to sit next to her friend.

"What did you learn?" said Farnsworth.

"Carolyn wasn't giving him money for gambling debts. She's paying him for hypnosis."

"For her addiction!" Farnsworth said. "So *that* explains what you overheard."

"Shh! Not so loud," said Erin. "Apparently he's trained in therapeutic hypnosis."

"I wonder if he can help me lose weight?" Farnsworth said wistfully as Kurt Becker emerged from the stairwell, his lean face impassive. A couple of people leaned into each other, whispering as he passed, as he took a seat near the back. Crossing his arms, he sat stony-faced, staring straight ahead.

Constable McCrary entered the room behind him, striding with purpose toward Detective Hemming. The two policemen engaged in conversation, heads close. Erin strained to hear what they were saying, but they were too far away. The constable was blocking her line of sight, so she couldn't see the detective's reaction.

"Wonder why the coppers are here," Farnsworth said. "Maybe they know something we don't."

Owen Hardacker stepped to the front of the room and cleared his throat.

"If this meeting would come to order," he said, "we'll get started. As past president, I've been asked to run things just for tonight. As you know, the reason for this meeting is to elect a new society president, so I'd like to open the floor for nominations."

As he spoke, Erin looked up to see James Marlowe tiptoeing quietly into the room. Giving her a quick smile, he took the seat nearest the door.

"So," Owen continued, "are there any nominations?"

Hetty's hand shot into the air. "I nominate Jonathan Alder."

"I second the nomination," Farnsworth called out.

Erin looked around, but there was no sign of Jonathan.

"Right," said Owen. "Any others?"

"I nominate Prudence Pettibone," Winton said quietly.

Erin craned her neck to see Pru's reaction, but her line of sight was blocked by Constable McCrary.

"I second that," said James Marlowe.

"Very well," Owen said. "Other nominations?"

He was greeted with silence. "Very well," he said. "All in favor of—"

At that moment a deafening clap of thunder sounded. The lights flickered, then shuddered and went out. A murmur arose from the crowd, and Reverend Motley's voice rose over the general noise.

"Don't panic—there are candles upstairs!"

That was followed by a cry on the other side of the room, near the staircase—it sounded like a man's voice—and the sound of a body hitting the ground. Digging frantically through her knapsack, Erin extracted a small pocket flashlight. Turning it on, she sprang from her seat and headed in the direction of the sound. A much brighter beam shone behind her, and she turned to see Constable McCrary, flashlight in hand, heading toward her. She could just make out Detective Hemming and Sergeant Jarral close behind him.

Following the beam of his flashlight, she saw, lying on the floor at her feet, Jonathan Alder. Her first thought was that he was dead, but to her relief, he stirred and sat up.

"What happened?" she said.

"Someone attacked me," he said, rubbing his neck. "Hit me on the back of the head."

The lights flickered again and went on. Blinking from the sudden brightness, Erin looked down at Jonathan, still sitting on the ground. Next to him was a broken flowerpot, its contents spilled onto the ground. She couldn't help noticing that the bedraggled blossom lying amid dirt, roots, and broken pottery was *Phalaenopsis schilleriana*, the moth orchid, the same one she had procured the cutting from for Prudence.

Erin looked at Detective Hemming, his face grim.

He scanned the crowd of stunned onlookers before speaking.

"Nobody leaves this room."

Chapter Fifty-Two

～

Wednesday afternoon Erin stood at her kitchen window, gazing out at the soft fields behind her house. The rain, having spent itself, had given way to brilliant, misty sunlight. The landscape was bathed in soft yellow light so luminous it looked as if it had been photo-shopped. Leaves glistened, grass sparkled, lush deep greens replacing the dusty autumnal weariness of the day before. It was as if Kirkbymoorside, having found a lover, was dressing itself to go out on the town in a stunning display of afternoon splendor.

The attack on Jonathan had completely broken up the meeting, of course. Erin was among the last to leave, just before midnight—not because she was under suspicion, but because she lingered, hoping to overhear something. But she was disappointed—the interviews took place upstairs in the lounge, behind closed doors. Finally she left, having learned little except that Jonathan hadn't seen his attacker; the blackout lasted long enough that the perpetrator had plenty of time to escape to another part of the room.

She had spent the day sifting through evidence, making notes, sorting out possible theories, each of which seemed to have a fatal flaw. She was left frustrated, feeling no closer to the solution than before. Tossing the remnants of her coffee into the sink, she went to the tack room and pulled on her boots. Throwing on a jacket, she climbed into her car and fishtailed down the driveway, turning in the direction of Farnsworth's house.

"Ah," Farnsworth said when she answered the door. "You showed up a bit sooner than I expected. The kettle's not yet come to a boil."

Erin smiled. "Am I that predictable?"

"Not to everyone. I'll bet that dishy detective finds you quite alluring and mysterious."

"But you—"

"I can read you like a book," she said, warming the teapot. It had just gone four, the usual time Farnsworth made herself a cup of tea.

"So I've made a list," Erin said, digging into her backpack, "of who the most viable suspects are and why."

"Oh, listen, Pru called," Farnsworth said, spooning tea into the pot with an antique silver teaspoon. Erin wouldn't have been surprised if nothing in her farmhouse was less than fifty years old.

"What did she want? Has Winton told her yet?"

"I don't think so, but she's feeling lonely. It seems Winton's gone off to that blasted bonfire without her."

"That's not like him."

"Do you think we might pop over there? Her arm's in that bloody cast, so she can't drive."

"Absolutely—let's go."

Their downed their tea quickly, and were soon seated in front of the fire at the Pettibones' ancient stone cottage, a bottle of Cognac on the table in front of them. They'd taken both cars, as Erin did want to drop by the bonfire, partially because she was sure Detective Hemming would be there.

"I thought something more bracing was called for tonight," Prudence said, pouring them each two fingers of the tawny liquid. "Cheers," she said, lifting her snifter.

"Cheers," said Erin, feeling the delicate burn as the brandy slid down her throat.

"This is the good stuff," Farnsworth said, sniffing at it. "Winton doesn't object?"

Prudence gulped down a generous swig of brandy and wiped her mouth. "Serves him right, going to the bonfire without me."

"Did you want to go?" said Erin.

"No, but I didn't think he'd go without me."

"He's usually so attentive," said Farnsworth. "Surely you don't begrudge him?"

"I suppose I'm feeling a bit fragile at the moment." She stared deep into the flames, and Erin wondered if Winton had told her about his illness. It didn't seem likely—the first thing Pru would do after news like that was pick up the phone and tell her friends.

"Where's Hetty?" Erin said.

"She's gone to the fete as well," Prudence said, throwing a handful of kindling on the fire. "Says it's a good place to meet men."

Farnsworth chuckled. "I can picture Hetty in hospital on her deathbed, thinking it's a good place to meet men."

"What about the reverend?" asked Erin.

"She says flirting with other men will help hold his interest."

Farnsworth laughed. "Some things never change."

Except when they do, Erin thought, wondering how Pru would get on without Winton. Why hadn't he told her yet?

"What about you?" Pru asked Farnsworth. "Would you rather be at the fete?"

"Good lord, no. That sort of free-form frolicking gives me a headache."

"Erin, be a dear and bring in another bottle, will you?" Pru said. "It's out in the rack in the garage. There's a pair of Wellies by the kitchen door you can use."

"Of course," she said. Leaving the warmth of the fire reluctantly, she padded out to the kitchen in her stockinged feet.

Slipping on the Wellies sitting neatly beside the back door, she stepped into the gathering gloom. A few stray stars flickered in an otherwise opaque sky, and a mourning dove murmured softly from the laurel bushes. The evening air was crisp in the wake of last night's storm, a gentle breeze carrying the aroma of fertilizer and hay from the surrounding fields.

Covering the short distance between the house and garage, Erin opened the unlocked side door, stepped inside, and flipped on the light switch. A small white compact car took up one side of the two-car structure. The Pettibones owned two cars, and Erin supposed Winton had taken the other one to the fete. She inhaled the aroma of gasoline, hay, and motor oil, which reminded her of her father's shed.

The garage was a model of tidiness, everything in its place. A large poster board hanging on the far wall held gardening tools as well as Winton's thatching equipment. Each tool was outlined on the board, its shape traced in magic marker, making it easier to know where each one belonged. One object seemed to be missing, only the black outline remaining. It appeared to be a long stick or pole with a short, curved blade on the end—Erin recognized it as belonging to a hold stick, a thatching tool.

Why hadn't the obsessively neat Winton returned the tool to its proper place? On an impulse, she bent to inspect the front bumper of the car. Seeing a spot of red on the car's bumper, she kneeled to get a closer look. The side of the bumper was dented, a larger smear streaked across it. It was paint, fire-engine red. At first she didn't want to believe it, but as she examined it more closely, her knees began to shake.

In one blinding moment, everything fell into place: the death of Pru's mother; Sylvia's poisoning, with such similar symptoms;

the attack first on her car and then on her—actions of a desperate, dying man whose one wish was to shelter—and control—the wife he adored. Hands trembling, her throat dry as paper, Erin grabbed a bottle of wine from the rack and stumbled back into the house.

Chapter Fifty-Three

～

"But you just got here," Prudence lamented when Erin abruptly announced she was leaving.

"Sorry—I forgot—I promised to meet someone at the bonfire," Erin mumbled as she slipped on her jacket.

"And who might *that* be?" Farnsworth asked with a conspiratorial wink. "A certain police detective, perhaps?"

"Uh, yes," Erin agreed, just to end the conversation. Her head was spinning—she had to get to the bonfire. She wasn't sure what she was going to do once she got there, other than find Detective Hemming and tell him of her discovery.

"We certainly wouldn't want to stand in the way of that, would we?" Prudence said.

"I'll drop by afterward and see how you're getting on."

"Oh, don't worry about us—we'll be fine," Farnsworth said. "I'll look after Pru and make sure she doesn't swill all the brandy."

"Great," Erin said, stepping outside. "See you later," she called, closing the door behind her.

The celebration was in full swing by the time Erin slid into the public car park and walked the two blocks to the village green. Men dressed in fool's motley were putting the finishing touches on the huge pile of logs and kindling, stacked so high she could barely see the buildings behind it. As she approached, they were lighting the torches, applying the flames to four corners of the great pile of wood. The flames leapt and crackled, hungrily consuming air and wood, until the entire pile was ablaze. She looked around for any sign of the policemen. Finding none, she buried herself in the crowd.

* * *

Peter Hemming stood at the edge of the village green, surveying the merrymakers as they arrived in groups of two, three, and more. Laughing and chattering, they approached the enormous woodpile in the center of the square. The noisy conviviality reminded him of how solitary his life had become, less by choice than by neglect. As he watched the happily babbling revelers, he couldn't imagine himself one of them—he was more comfortable in the role of observer.

"It's all rather primal, isn't it, sir?"

He turned to see Sergeants Jarral and Harris standing beside him.

"Very Wicker Man, if you ask me, sir," said Sergeant Harris.

"What's that?" said Jarral.

"It's a classic horror film from the seventies," said Hemming, "involving human sacrifice."

"It was based on claims the Romans made that the Celts executed criminals by imprisoning them in gigantic wooden effigies and burning them alive," Harris said.

Jarral shook his head. "That's horrible."

"It was all Roman propaganda," Hemming said. "There's no evidence the Celts ever did that." But he still felt a shiver down his spine as the costumed men, brandishing torches, lit the four corners of the woodpile.

The drumming increased in pace and volume as the three men stood watching the red flames rise and spread, greedily devouring the timber.

"Detective Hemming!"

He turned to see Erin Coleridge running toward him, hair flying behind her.

"What is it?" he said.

"I know—who—the killer—is," she said, panting heavily.

A cheer went up from the crowd as someone tossed a handful of firecrackers onto the flames. They popped and cracked, spitting multicolored streamers into the air in a burst of rainbow sparks. He looked at Erin, breathing heavily, hair in disarray, her face pale in the firelight.

"He's here," she said. "And we have to stop him—now."

Chapter Fifty-Four

✒

Erin followed a few yards behind the policemen, even though Detective Hemming had warned her sternly to keep her distance. Fear and excitement warred in the pit of her stomach—it was all quite terrible but rather thrilling. Passing a group of merrymakers, she peered at their faces, but didn't recognize any of them. The crowd included large numbers of tourists—residents of nearby towns as well as quite a few foreigners. Ever since the festival had begun showing up in tourist sites online, attendance had swelled.

An inebriated young man dressed as a monk attempted to put his arm around her. "Hello, love," he bleated drunkenly.

She shook him off, and he stumbled backward, caught in the arms of his companions. "Oy! Where's your holiday spirit?"

"Sod off," she muttered, striding onward. Seeing the policemen were some distance ahead of her, she decided to veer off and look on her own. Circling the bonfire clockwise, she peered at the revelers, many of them wearing masks, some fully costumed. The disguises, combined with the fact that it was night, made it difficult to discern anyone's identity. The general hubbub—the roar of the flames, music from the street musicians, people laughing, talking, and singing—made it hard to make out any specific voice or conversation. It was like being in a very popular pub on a Saturday night, only worse, because of the darkness.

Erin kept to the outer edge of the crowd, walking slowly but steadily around the circle. A couple of uniformed constables stood guard on the western edge of the green, and she started toward them, but a couple of young boys playing tag rushed heedlessly toward her. One of them tripped and fell into her, knocking her down. The jolt of hitting the ground took her breath away as a sharp stab of pain shot through her injured shoulder.

Rolling onto her side, she waited until the initial wave of pain subsided. She looked up into the concerned faces of a middle-aged couple festooned in green tunics covered with leaves and branches, topped off with green pointed hats. Her first impression was that they were meant to be either leprechauns or wood nymphs.

"You all right?" the woman asked as they reached out to help her up.

"I'm okay, thanks."

"Those lads oughtta look where they're goin'," the man said as his wife helped brush grass and dirt from her clothes. "Sure you're all right?"

"Yes, thanks—very kind of you," Erin said. She looked around for the uniformed officers, but they were nowhere in sight.

"You sure you wouldn't like to stop by the first-aid tent?" the woman asked.

"No, I'll be fine—thanks again," Erin said, hurrying away as fast as she could. She was moving with difficulty now, the injuries from her bicycle accident exacerbated by this fall. Her right hip didn't seem to be working correctly, and she felt a stab of pain with every step.

"Damn," she muttered as she limped toward the periphery of the crowd. On the far side of the green, a few outbuildings stood in relative solitude—including the barn where Hetty claimed she had seen the tryst between Jonathan and Sylvia. Something drew Erin to it, and she walked as quickly as she could toward it. Hearing raised voices coming from the other side of the structure, she increased her pace, breaking into a painful lopsided jog.

Rounding the far side of the building, she saw, dimly lit by a pale gibbous moon, two men engaged in a face-off. One of them was Jonathan Alder. The other was Winton Pettibone, identifiable even in a black mask with a long curved beak. He wielded a hold stick, the long wooden crofting tool Erin had noticed missing from his garage. He held it aloft over his shoulder, the short curved blade at the other end glinting silver in the pale light. Unarmed, Jonathan was cowering against the side of the barn.

"No!" she cried. "Winton, don't!"

He turned to her. In the beaked black mask, he looked like a sinister crow. "Don't come any nearer! This is between Jonathan and me." His voice, though louder in volume, still had the same flat affect, as if he was deaf to the music of ordinary speech.

"What has he ever done to you?" Erin shouted.

"My Prudence deserves to be president!"

"Is that why you killed Sylvia?"

"Thought she were so high and mighty, so superior to us 'common folk'!"

"Is that a reason to poison her?"

"She deserved what she got! And now him," Winton said, turning back toward Jonathan, whom he had cornered between the barn and the blade of his weapon.

"Winton Pettibone! I am arresting you for the murder of Sylvia Pemberthy!"

Erin turned to see DI Hemming running toward them, followed by Sergeant Harris. As she did, her injured leg gave way and she stumbled, falling toward Winton. Quick as a flash, moving faster than his stocky body looked capable of, he seized her and held her, the blade at her neck.

"Take one step closer, and I'll cut her throat!" he cried in a shrill voice.

"Let us work with you," Hemming said as Jonathan scampered to safety. "We can help you."

"Bollocks! I know the score—you lot look down on me," Winton sputtered angrily. "You don' know the first thing about real life, with your fancy degrees and snooty attitudes! The real people are folks who work with their hands, who value history and tradition!"

"I totally agree," said Hemming.

"That's a laugh!" Winton said bitterly. "I looked you up—your parents were Uni eggheads. You've come down in the world, you have."

Detective Harris stepped forward. "You know me, Winton—I would never look down on you."

"You do, though," Pettibone said, panting. "People think I don' see what goes on behind my back, but I do. You don' appreciate me, and y'make fun of my Prudy. She's worth the whole lot a' you put together!"

Out of the corner of her eye, Erin saw Sergeant Jarral creeping around the barn, and prayed that whatever he had in mind would work. Meanwhile, Pettibone tightened his grip on her—she could feel the blade, cold and smooth, on her skin. She tried to take deep breaths, but her shoulder was cramping and her legs felt like they were made of papier-mâché. If Winton let go of her, she would surely crumple to the ground.

Suddenly she felt her legs being swept out from under her, and Winton's weight on top of her as she hit the ground, hard. Twisting around to look, she saw Sergeant Jarral had brought them both down with a rugby tackle from behind. Scrambling rapidly away on her hands and knees, she saw Winton stagger to his feet, still clutching the holding stick. He took a vicious swipe at Jarral, who managed to duck the blow, but just as Winton was regrouping for another strike, Detective Hemming launched himself at the crofter with a roar. Spinning around, Pettibone slashed widely, catching the detective in the ribs with the blade. Erin wasn't aware she was screaming until Jonathan grabbed her by the shoulders to prevent her from rushing into the fray.

She watched in horror as DI Hemming sank to the ground, clutching his side, just as two armed patrolmen in bulletproof vests arrived. Aiming their semiautomatic pistols at Pettibone, they advanced toward him.

"Drop your weapon now, before someone else gets hurt," said the taller of the two. Pettibone looked as if he was about to charge them, but then his body sagged, and he let the holding stick fall from his hand.

A crowd was gathering around them as Jarral turned and yelled, "Get the ambulance!"

But Erin had already dashed off toward the one stationed at the edge of the green, its lights flashing by the time she arrived, her leg pain forgotten in the rush of adrenaline.

"Where's the accident?" said the EMT in charge, a tall, thin young man with a tiny mustache.

"Over there!" she panted.

"Let's go!" he said to his partner, a sturdy-looking woman with short blonde hair.

The ambulance sped toward the spot, followed by the fire truck, sirens screaming, as Erin raced after them on foot, no longer aware of her own injuries. When she arrived, they were loading DI Hemming into the back of the vehicle. Sergeants Jarral and Harris were standing close by, conferring with Constable McCrary, who had just arrived, his mustache twitching expectantly.

"Can I go with him?" Erin asked.

"Are you a relative?" the female EMT said.

"Yes," she answered, surprised at how easily the lie slid from her lips.

"Sit there," the woman commanded, pointing to a spot next to the gurney.

She did, and, sirens blaring, the ambulance sped off into the night.

Chapter Fifty-Five

⁓

"How is he?" Sergeant Jarral said as he joined Erin in the small waiting room outside the A&E treatment area. Trailing behind him was Constable McCrary.

"They're treating him now," she said.

"Is he conscious?" asked McCrary.

"I think so. What about Winton Pettibone?"

"He's in custody." The Scotsman shook his head. "I've known him for years. Such a mild fellow. Never thought him capable of such a thing."

The doctor in charge entered the room. A dark-skinned, compact man of about sixty, he had kind, weary eyes behind large, black-framed glasses.

"Hello, Constable McCrary."

"Dr. Patel—good to see you in charge," said the Scotsman. "What's the news?"

"Will he be all right?" Sergeant Jarral asked. Erin was touched by the urgency in his voice.

"It's a nasty cut, but he was lucky. He should make a complete recovery, given some time."

"When can we see him?" said Erin.

"You can go in now, but don't wear him out—he needs rest."

They followed Dr. Patel into the treatment area, where his patient lay on a gurney, his chest swathed in white bandages.

"How are you feeling, sir?" said Jarral.

Hemming smiled weakly. "I've had better days."

"You'll do just about anything to avoid work, won't you?" McCrary said.

"Hello, Erin," said Hemming.

It was the first time he had called her by her first name.

"Hello."

"Pettibone?" Hemming asked the chief constable. "You got him?"

"Aye," said McCrary. "He confessed to everything—I guess he knows the gig is up."

"He even admitted to making the mysterious phone call, sir," said Jarral.

"Did he say why he did it?"

"To throw us off our game. Also, he had a wild idea about implicating Hetty Miller, of all people."

"I knew it!" Erin said. "The perfume."

McCrary looked at her, his mustache twitching. "What perfume?"

Erin explained everything she knew. Hemming listened closely from his hospital bed, though his eyes were beginning to droop by the time the nurse came in to shoo them away.

"Sergeant Harris has been holding down the fort at the station house," McCrary said as Sergeant Jarral settled into one of the green plastic armchairs lining the wall of the waiting room. "I'm going to go relieve him. Want a ride to your hotel?"

"I think I'll stay here for a bit, if you don't mind, sir."

"Good man. Mind ye keep an eye on him," he said to Erin.

"I will," she said, smiling, though she wasn't sure if he meant Hemming or Sergeant Jarral.

"I'll call your mobile in a bit to check up on things," McCrary said to him.

"Right you are, sir."

"How long have you been working with Detective Hemming?" Erin said after the constable had gone.

"This is our first case together, miss."

"Please, call me Erin."

"Yes, miss."

"How do you like working with him?"

He shifted in his chair and cleared his throat. "He's very . . ."

"Moody?"

Jarral laughed softly. "He is that. But . . . he cares, you know, Miss?"

"Erin."

"He cares, Erin."

"I know."

"I suppose that's why he's so—intense."

"Probably."

"I could use a coffee," he said, standing up and stretching. He really was quite tall—at least six foot three. "Can I get you one?"

"Sure, thanks."

"Be right back. You staying for a while?"

"Yes," she said. "I believe I will stay."

Chapter Fifty-Six

A few days later, Erin was seated at Farnsworth's kitchen table, enjoying coffee and croissants.

"Poor Prudence," Farnsworth said, stroking the orange tabby on her lap. "How's she doing?"

"Still in shock, I think."

"She had absolutely no idea what he was up to?"

"He fooled her just like everyone else."

"Poor thing," Farnsworth said, spreading butter on an almond croissant. "She never was very perceptive, I suppose. Always the last to latch on to things. I can't imagine how it must feel to know your own husband poisoned your mother."

"I think she's still in denial about that, even though Winton confessed to it."

"You just never know about people," Farnsworth said, brushing stray crumbs onto the floor. A couple of cats investigated, tails flicking, sniffing the ground hopefully before turning away in disappointment.

"Hetty is with her," said Erin. "She's being very supportive."

"No doubt she's relieved Pru can't lord her 'perfect marriage' over her anymore."

"Farnsworth!"

"I'm just saying what everyone knows, pet. Theirs is a combative friendship—always was, long before you arrived on the scene."

"But they do care for each other."

"They do."

"The Pettibones seemed to have such a happy marriage," Erin said, pouring cream into her coffee.

"I think they did, in their own way."

"But it was all based on a lie."

"Not entirely. Winton really did care for her."

"But he's a murderer."

"That doesn't change what he felt for her, or make it less real."

"But—"

"You know," Farnsworth said, stroking the orange tabby that had jumped onto her lap, "I used to think the way you do—that love can only exist as a pure thing, between two perfect beings."

"Not perfect, but—"

"Winton's deeds were horrible, but on some level they were an expression of love for his wife."

"Which is worse, Sylvia's promiscuity or his kind of fidelity?" Erin said. "At least she didn't kill anyone."

"Love exists in many forms, some of them dark and twisted."

"Winton knew he was dying, so that must have made him more desperate."

Farnsworth took a sip of coffee. "Imagine caring that much about your wife being president of the Jane Austen Society."

"That wasn't the only motivation. Winton had killed before."

"Poor Jonathan. He didn't even want to be president, but Winton still tried to kill him. Thank God he failed," Farnsworth said, pouring them both more coffee.

"The ladies of the Jane Austen Society need their fantasies."

"Speaking of fantasies, I wonder what Jonathan and Sylvia *were* doing behind the barn at the fete last summer?"

"Oh, I asked him, and he said they were talking about Carolyn's addiction."

"So Sylvia knew about it?"

"Yes—she told him it was the reason Carolyn lost her job and asked him to help. Apparently she knew of his hypnotic skills."

"In more ways than one," Farnsworth said, winking. "But weren't she and Carolyn over by then?"

"Yes, but Sylvia still cared for her."

"She was a complicated person." She sighed. "It sounds crazy but, I miss her."

"Me too," Erin said, realizing it fully for the first time. "She was so good at focusing everyone's emotions. She was like a lightning rod."

"What about Jonathan's 'secret' she was keeping? What do you suppose that was about?"

"Probably his father's crime. He's obviously worked hard to keep that hidden."

"Speaking of secrets, a little bird told me that Hetty and Mr. Collins—I mean Reverend Motley—are talking about setting a date. I must say, I never took her for a Charlotte Lucas."

"I'll grant you Reverend Motley is a good deal like Mr. Collins," Erin agreed, "but Hetty is hardly a Charlotte Lucas. She's no spinster—she's been married at least three times."

"Is there some doubt as to the exact number of her romantic entanglements?"

"I heard rumor of a fourth, but it could be just spite."

The sound of a car horn outside brought them both to the window. Parked outside was Detective Hemming's battered Citroën. They watched as he climbed slowly and painfully from the passenger side.

"Go out and meet him," Farnsworth said.

"But—"

"He's not here to see me, pet."

Erin stepped out into the glare of the midday sun streaming through the canopy of dead and dying leaves still clinging to a few trees. Shielding her eyes, she walked toward him.

"Hello," he said. "You weren't at your bookstore, so I came here."

"How are you?"

"I'll live. The docs gave me something for the pain, so I'm letting Sergeant Jarral do the driving."

"No doubt he's thrilled."

"I just wanted to say thanks. If it weren't for you, well—let's just say I appreciate your help."

"Anytime," she said, suddenly acutely aware of the insistent chirping of a sparrow on the low branch of a nearby oak tree. "Can I ask a couple of follow-up questions?"

"Sure."

"How did Winton pull off the attack on Jonathan?"

"It was spur-of-the-moment. When the storm made the lights go out, he grabbed the flowerpot and hit Jonathan with it."

"So he didn't cause the blackout?"

"No, the storm did—he just took advantage of it."

"But how could he see—"

"Jonathan happened to be standing near the flowerpot, and Winton used his little pin flashlight to locate him. In the chaos and confusion, no one noticed."

"I remember he had one of those penlights!" Erin said. "He used it at his house when I was there."

"And he confessed to the crank call to your cottage—he was trying to scare you off. I imagine he'll be sent straight to a prison hospital, since he's not well. With his confession on record, I doubt there will even be a trial."

"And he faked the attack on him, I suppose?"

"Yes—actually hit himself in the back of the head with a board to make it more realistic."

"And tried to frame poor Farnsworth by saying he smelled her perfume."

"He didn't mention that detail, but that seems right."

"Now that the case is over, maybe I can . . . see you again," she said, her ears burning.

"I thought everyone in this town was keen on Jonathan Alder," he said, squinting against the glare as the sun climbed higher in the sky.

"But you make a better Darcy."

"Do I?" he said, wincing as he shifted position. "Why is that?"

"Because you're cold and remote, just like him."

"Do you find me cold and remote?"

"Mind you, I don't buy it."

"What do you mean?"

"I think you're a softy."

He laughed—a sad, sweet sound that made her want to wrap him in her arms.

"If you're right, I wouldn't be a very good copper."

"Who says you are?"

"Ouch. That's harsh."

Sergeant Jarral climbed out of the car and waved at them. "Sir, DCI Witherspoon is on the line—he wants to know when we'll be back."

"Be right there," Hemming called back to him. "Well," he said to Erin, "I guess this is good-bye."

"Good-bye," she said, looking up at him, and her knees felt hollow. Her hands twitched, longing to reach for his, but she made no move.

"I'll call you," he said, turning to go.

She observed his retreating figure as if memorizing it—the square set of his shoulders, the well-shaped head with wavy, wheat-colored hair. He waved one final time as he climbed into the old car, wincing as he bent to climb in. Erin stood watching as the Citroën turned and rattled down the driveway, until it disappeared around the corner.

She stood a few moments listening to the noisy sparrow in the oak tree, wondering what it was chattering about. She felt light and heavy all at the same time—happy and sad, emotionally wrought yet at peace, sadness tugging at a deep sense of contentment. How glad she was to be on this little patch of earth, in this village, at this time of year. Stretching her arms out, she breathed in the sweet, melancholy smell of autumn before turning around and walking back toward the house.

Acknowledgments

Thanks to my awesome agent, Paige Wheeler, as always. Deepest gratitude to Terri Bischoff and Jenny Chen, for their superb editorial advice, patience, and unwavering support.

Thanks to Anthony Moore, for introducing me to the wonders of the Yorkshire Moors, always sharing my passion and sense of adventure; and to the staff of the Lion Inn, Blakey Ridge, for an unforgettable night, splendid meal, and wonderful gift of *A Coast to Coast Walk* by Alfred Wainwright. Deepest thanks to Alan Macquarie, scholar, musician, and historian, for being such a gracious host in his glorious Glasgow flat, and to Anne Clackson, for being such a boon (and bonny) companion. Special thanks to my dear friend Rachel Fallon for her generosity and loyal spirit. And a big shout-out to the baristas at Gatehouse Coffee in historic York, the most glorious coffeehouse I have had the pleasure of visiting.

Thanks to Hawthornden Castle for awarding me a Fellowship— my time there was unforgettable—and to Byrdcliffe Colony in Woodstock, where I enjoyed many happy years of residency, as well as to the Animal Care Sanctuary in East Smithfield, Pennsylvania, Craig Lukatch and the fabulous Lacawac Sanctuary, where so much of this was written. I can't wait to return!

Special thanks to my dear friend and colleague Marvin Kaye for his continued support, and for all the many wonderful dinners at Keens. Thanks to my assistant, Frank Goad, for his intelligence and expertise. Thanks too to my good friend Ahmad Ali, whose support and good energy has always lifted my spirits, and to the Stone Ridge Library, my upstate writing home away from home.

Finally, special thanks to my parents—raconteurs, performers, and musicians—who taught me the importance of art and the power of a good story.